MW01077376

THIS SAME EARTH

Beatrice De Novo thought she had left the supernatural world behind, but when a love from the past returns to her, she's forced to abandon her peaceful life to solve a puzzle that could change the immortal world forever. Giovanni Vecchio has returned, and this time, nothing will stop him from claiming the woman who has captured his attention and stoked the fire within his heart.

THIS SAME EARTH is the second book in the Elemental Mysteries. It is a paranormal romance and mystery by ten-time USA Today bestselling author, Elizabeth Hunter.

The Elemental
Mysteries

This Tame Earth

To Earth

Revelation, divine and mortal
We are of you, in you, upon you
Preposing ourselves in the chain of life
That came before us and will endure
Long after you have consumed us
Only to bear another from our dust.
Mother, we call you
And no other name is as whole or holy
For the one who births life must needs
Deliver death.

All men are by nature equal, made of the same earth by one workman

And however we deceive ourselves
As dear unto God is the poor peasant as the mighty prince.

— PLATO

PROLOGUE

Cochamó Valley
Chile

August 3, 2005

I'm here.

Where are you?

And do you know it takes two days to get here from Los Angeles? I had to wait an extra day in Santiago so I could catch the plane to Puerto Montt. I thought you'd be the one meeting me at the trail, not Gustavo, but it was nice to catch up. Also, ouch. My legs are going to kill me tomorrow from all that riding.

So, where are you?

August 4, 2005

Isabel says you wrote her to say that I would be coming but didn't say when you would be coming. Should I be worried?

August 5, 2005

And now everyone is doing the whole vampire clam-up-and-not-tell-me-anything thing. Screw you all. If Isabel and Gustavo aren't worried, then I'm not going to worry about you, either.

August 17, 2005

I've been here for two weeks now. Where the hell are you?

Ever since you came to my apartment (Do you know you always smell like smoke to me, by the way? I thought something was burning when I came home that night.) I've been looking forward to seeing you.

Is this you being pissed at me for leaving Houston?

You never once came to visit me in L.A. Not once. Except to break into my apartment and leave me the sonnets (which I brought by the way) and take one of my favorite pictures, of course. Would it have killed you to hang around for a while?

Haha. I just realized that was unintentionally funny.

August 20, 2005

Took a ride today.

You still aren't here.

Think I might go rock-climbing tomorrow—with the Reverte's oldest son. The really handsome one.

Why aren't you here?

I've been sleeping in your room, and I discovered that without any light to wake me up in the morning, I sleep a really long time. I'm very well rested.

Is that what this was? Just a getaway for Beatrice so she could relax? Not saying I don't appreciate it, but...

No, actually, I don't appreciate it. I love this place, but I came here to see you, not ride horses, and hike, and eat Señora Reverte's really excellent cooking.

So, where the hell are you?

I have a return ticket for the thirty-first. I'm not hanging out until you get here. If you even plan on getting here.

August 25, 2005

Why the hell am I even writing in this stupid journal? It was just lying open on the kitchen table when I got here. Did you know this whole place smells like you? It does. I kind of hate that at this point.

August 31, 2005

Go to hell. I never want to see you again.

Cochamó Valley
Chile

August 2, 2006

S o, since I'm here again (and I'm just assuming you're going to be a no-show) I want to explain a few things.

1. I wasn't going to come this year until Dez (that's Desiree, my best friend, who you would know about if you communicated with me at all) convinced me that I should just take the free ticket because I love it here and I could use a vacation. So I'm here. That's why, and that's the only reason. Not because I wanted or expected to see you again.

2. I'm more than a little pissed that you seem to be able to

communicate with everyone we know (Caspar, Carwyn, Tenzin—you even called my grandma on her birthday) but not me. Yay for you. You're traveling the world and won't tell anyone where you are. I don't even give a shit anymore, but it's just rude. I hope my grandma told you off. She probably didn't.

3. If you have any illusions about me "waiting for you" or some romantic crap like that, don't kid yourself. I'm dating. I'm dating a really nice guy, as a matter of fact. His name is Kevin, and I met him in my graduate program. He's handsome and smart and we have an amazing time together, and when I get back from this vacation, we're going to have sex. Lots of it. And that's going to be great, too.

August 15, 2006

I love this place. I really do. I mean, I love L.A. and I love school, but this place is just... magic. Do you come here when I'm not here? I bet you do. I'm betting you read this journal last year because it looked like it had been paged through, and I greatly doubt Isabel went to look under the pillows on our bed to set it out on the table for when I got here this year.

So I think you were here.

And I have no idea how to feel about that.

August 20, 2006

Does time stand still for you? Have you been living so long that a year or two is nothing? It seems so long to me, but it's probably like the blink of an eye to you. I remember you telling me once that a year was like a day when you are immortal.

So what does that mean? If I was just the blink of an eye in your life, why do you keep breaking into my apartment and giving me tickets to come here? Also, if you want pictures of me, you could call and ask for them instead of swiping the ones at my place. I really liked that picture of me at the beach. I actually had a tan.

August 23, 2006

I hate that everything in this house smells like you.

August 24, 2006

And I hate that I dream about you when I'm here.

August 29, 2006

I'm leaving tomorrow. I'm feeling very relaxed, so thanks for that.

I don't know what to think about you anymore. Were you really a part of my life? I'd say it was all a crazy dream except for the cryptic postcards that I'm assuming are from you, and the tickets, and the fact that I'm friends with all your friends now.

I'm going to finish my master's this winter. Only two and a half years. Not bad. I could have done better, but I was having a lot of fun. I learned how to rock-climb, kickbox, and I'm fairly good at a couple of martial arts, too. I'm even a pretty decent dancer now. Surprise, surprise. So I'm not going to regret the extra months.

Want to come to my graduation in December?

Yeah, didn't think so.

Cochamó Valley
Chile

August 1, 2007

I just got the best job! I'm in heaven. I think I might have finally found a library to top yours! I turned down a couple of positions because I was waiting for the right one and I got it! I'm starting at the Huntington Library next month! (I'm using a million exclamation points, but I don't care!)

I wasn't worried about money so much (thanks to my superior embezzling skills) but I wanted to find a place where I was really passionate about working. The Huntington is a private foundation, and its facilities are amazing.

Plus, they have this gorgeous botanical garden surrounding it, so it's a beautiful place to work, and it's an easy commute from my house in Silver Lake.

Oh, I bought a house. It's pretty damn cute. It's one of those Spanish bungalows built about eighty years ago and it has really nice architectural details. At least, that's what my realtor, Matt, told me. Now he's my neighbor, as a matter of fact. The house next door to his went on the market right after I met him, so I got a great deal because he found it right away and I could put in a quick offer. He's a nice neighbor. We're the only people on our block who are under eighty, I think. It's an old part of L.A. up in the hills, but I really like it.

We're not dating or anything. Actually, I'm pretty sure Dez has a crush on him, but she refuses to ask him out despite the fact that she's usually very outgoing. Oh, and I'm not dating that Kevin guy either. I mean, I did for a while, but... he was kind of boring, to be honest. And he snored a lot. Like... a lot.

August 17, 2007

You're missing it, but I'm a great rider now. Really. I even beat Gustavo in a race the other night. Still can't beat Isabel, though. Damn, she is good. And on sidesaddle, too. How does she even do that?

Oh, and I'm a pretty good rock-climber, if I do say so myself. I'm still studying tai chi and judo, but I'm taking jujitsu now, too. I'm going to be sitting a lot as a librarian (yes! I can officially call myself a librarian now!) so I want to keep active so I don't expand. You never have to worry about that, do you?

Jerk.

August 20, 2007

I have a boyfriend.

I don't know why that's weird to write. I just... I know we're not like that. I mean, I thought at one point that maybe we would be, but obviously, we're not. Don't get me wrong, I was really mad at you for a long time, but I guess I understand. I'm going to live, what? Another sixty or seventy years? And you'll still be here.

So, I get it now. I really do.

And my boyfriend is great. He's kind of your exact opposite (not that I was looking for that, it just happened) except he's tall like you. He's Hawaiian. And gorgeous. His name is Mano, which means 'shark' in Hawaiian. He surfs, and he's tan and has this amazing long, dark hair and black eyes.

He used to be a Navy diver, but now he has his own dive shop, and he and his friend run SCUBA classes and dive trips to Catalina. I met him in May when Dez forced me to take one of his classes. He has such a great smile. He's just... so open and honest and he's so... great. He's great, and he's really good to me, and everyone likes him. He wants to go to Houston and meet Grandma and Caspar this fall.

By the way, did Caspar tell you about Doyle and the Vietnamese vase in the entry way? I know you loved that vase, but please don't kill the cat when you get back from... wherever you are.

August 29, 2007

I'm trying to be really mature and well-adjusted here, but I'm crying right now, you jerk.

I miss you.

I miss you so much. Why the hell are you never here? Why? Where are you? I want to feel your arms around me and sleep next to you and talk to you and tease you and I hate you, Gio. I can't help it. I hate you.

But I don't really, even though I wish I did.

I still think about you every day. And I compare every man I meet to you. And every time I smell smoke or whiskey, I turn and expect to see you there. Do you know I studied Latin so I could impress you? How pathetic, huh? At least that one might come in handy professionally at some point.

When I bought my house, I checked how many windows were in the bedroom (just one) and imagined them with heavy drapes as if you might actually stay there at some point.

And it's pathetic. Because I will probably never see you again.

I'm leaving tomorrow. I don't know if I'm going to come back next year. I just don't know if I can keep doing this to myself no matter how much I love it here. Because when I'm in Cochamó, you're everywhere.

I should probably take this journal with me. I can't believe I just wrote that stuff.

Cochamó Valley
Chile

August 5, 2008

Ah, ha ha. Very funny. So I threaten to take the last journal, so you take it (I'm assuming) and leave me with a new one. Clever.

Also, what are all these journals in the bedroom? There's got to be a couple hundred of them and they're all in Latin. Do you expect me to work while I'm here?

News flash: I don't work for you anymore.

I do love working at the Huntington, though. Such an amazing job. I only get three weeks of vacation, so only two weeks in the valley this year. Bummer. But if I skipped out on Christmas with Cas and Grandma, they'd kill me.

August 6, 2008

Holy shit. These are your journals. These are your whole life.

Why did you leave these here? Are they safe? Don't they need to be in a temperature-controlled room? And it gets really damp here in the winter. Though I suppose the bedroom is pretty good with the way it's cut into the rock.

I feel like I can't leave the house now, even though they were probably here for weeks before I came and I'm sure they're perfectly secure.

You knew Napoleon? Really?

Was he as insecure about his height as everyone says? You must have looked like a giant next to him.

August 10, 2008

These things are incredible. There's no way I'm going to get through all of them, though. My Latin is not that good.

So you've found an ingenious way of keeping me coming back here.

Bastard.

It's irritating how intelligent you are sometimes.

August 17, 2008

I have to leave tomorrow. I hate not having more time here, but I have to go.

Yes, I'll come back. You knew I would.

And just so you know, Mano and I are still together. Grandma and Caspar love him. Carwyn met him last winter when he came for a visit. I think he likes him, too. Carwyn made noises about Mano and I sleeping together, though. I forget he's a priest sometimes. Oops. Must be the Hawaiian shirts. You should have seen this green one he bought the last time he came to L.A. It was hideous. He loved it.

I got a letter from Tenzin last month. She's so... weird. In the best way, but... yeah, she's old. Did you know she calls me every three or four months? It's the most hilarious thing. I think whoever her human is puts it on speaker phone and Tenzin just yells. I have to hold the phone away from my ear so she doesn't break my eardrums. I think I'm the closest thing she has to a female friend. Not that we talk about braiding our hair or anything. She said she's going to come for a visit one of these days. Should be... interesting.

I'm not ready to leave. I want to read more about your life. You're very hard on yourself, Jacopo. Be kinder.

And wherever you are, be safe.

Cochamó Valley
Chile

August 5, 2009

Four weeks of vacation now! Score. Well, I still only get three weeks paid, but they let me take an additional week off unpaid, so I'm using that to go see Grandma and Caspar for Christmas and I can take three weeks here.

By the way, could you surface at some point, please? I think Cas and Grandma would like to get married and they're waiting for you to be a part of our lives again in more ways than cryptic phone calls, letters, and postcards.

Just a suggestion. Going to read now.

August 11, 2009

I can't even... you have had such an amazing life, Gio. And now that I'm more used to your writing style in Latin, your journals are really hilarious at times.

And then sometimes they make me cry.

Don't worry, I'm taking good care of them.

August 14, 2009

I think Mano is starting to think about marriage and babies and all that stuff. I'm only twenty-eight, but he's older than me; he's already thirty-two. (And yes, I'm sure you're probably laughing when you read that, old man.)

I just don't know. He wanted to move in together last winter, but I like having my space. When he's there too much... well, we just get on each other's nerves, you know? I like having my alone time. We had a huge fight about it, but we worked through it. He's a good guy, and I love him a lot.

August 19, 2009

I'm so fucking mad right now, I can hardly write.

Was that you in the trees last night? It better not have been! I cannot believe you would come that close and not even—

Nevermind, I can believe it.

It was you. I could even smell the smoke. I can't believe you would do that to me.

Yes, I can.

Damn it, Gio. Damn it! Damn you. Damn this valley. Damn this house. Damn your journals. Damn everything.

I'm not doing it anymore. I refuse. What do you want from me? What? Just call me or write me or do anything! But I'm not doing this anymore. I'm done.

You know what? Don't write me. Don't contact me. I never want to see you again, or hear from you, or anything. I'm moving on with my life. I have a life! Do you realize that? And you're not in it, so leave me alone.

I'm not coming back here. I'm through.

You asshole! I've had enough of pale faces haunting me. I've done it before and I'm not going to let you get to me the way my father did. I'm leaving tomorrow and I'm not coming back.

Do you understand me?

And when Mano asks me to marry him, I'm saying yes.

ONE

Los Angeles, California
October 2009

"B?"

"Hmph."

"Baby, the alarm already went off."

She looked over her shoulder at Mano, who appeared to be wearing nothing more than a lazy grin.

"It went off already?" she croaked, shutting her eyes against the morning sun.

He nodded. "Yep. I let you sleep in a little, but I knew you'd kick me if I let you miss work."

The morning sun streamed through the small window in the bedroom. Mano must have propped it open the night before, and she could smell the Meyer lemon tree blossoming on the patio.

"Why am I so tired?"

"Apparently, it was a scotch night last night," he snickered. "I came over and let myself in, but you were already asleep."

Beatrice rolled over and blinked at her gorgeous boyfriend.

"You came over and crawled in my bed looking like that, and I missed it?"

"Your loss."

She groaned and burrowed into his warm chest. "Why did I drink the Laphroaig? It was not my friend last night. And I have to work late because Dr. Stevens asked me to help her close."

His low voice rumbled in her ear as she pressed her cheek to his chest. "How late? You want me to come over and cook dinner?"

She sighed and rubbed her eyes. "We've got that group visiting from USC right now and they've been staying as late as she'll let them, so... I don't know, probably not till eight-thirty or so."

"Leaving from work? So you won't be home till after nine."

She cuddled closer to him and reached up to brush the long, black hair out of his eyes. "Probably not. Can you come over anyway?"

"I can tonight, but not tomorrow night. We've got a group leaving early for an all-day dive, so I'll have to be at the boat by six."

She moved to lay kisses along his stubbled chin. "You know, we should be environmentally conscious this morning. There's a water shortage."

"Oh yeah?" he asked with a cocked eyebrow. He pulled her closer and hooked her leg over his hip. "Shower together, huh? You up for being environmentally responsible after last night?"

"Yes." She smiled. "Are you?"

Mano hugged her to his chest and rolled them out of bed before he stood and walked to the bathroom, his strong arms supporting her as she clung to him. "I'm always up for you, baby."

Beatrice giggled as he carried her to the bathroom, glancing at the bottle of scotch and the small book bound in red leather that lay on her desk in the corner. She hugged Mano closer and breathed in the scent of sun and ocean that clung to him.

S he waved as he stood on her front porch, still shirtless and wearing a lazy smile, while he held a cup of coffee as she sped away on her bike. She hopped onto Interstate 5 and gunned the engine, cutting lanes on her way to the 110 Freeway.

She'd bought the new Triumph Scrambler after Carwyn convinced her a motorcycle with a British pedigree was superior to an American bike. Since the Welshman had been the one to teach her to ride, and she liked the look of the matte-black bike, she'd relented and had it customized for her short frame.

Beatrice loved the freedom of being on the back of the bike, along with the ability to cut quickly through the Southern California traffic. While some moaned about their daily commute, for Beatrice, it was one of her favorite parts of the day.

By the time she arrived in San Marino—a small, wealthy enclave in the middle of South Pasadena—she'd made up for her late start that morning. She didn't know why she'd given in to the temptation to read Giuliana's sonnets the night before, but going down that road never led to a happy night.

She pulled off her helmet as she walked through the alley of jacaranda trees leading to the entrance of the library.

"Mornin', B!"

Beatrice waved at one of the guards as she climbed the white stone stairs leading to the grand entrance.

"Hey, Art. How are you today?"

The jovial man grinned and gave her a wink. "Oh, you know... just hangin'," he laughed. "Get it? Hangin'? 'Cause my name is 'Art?'"

She snorted and shook her head. "Yeah, good one."

"You closing with Dr. Stevens tonight?"

"Yup. You going to be here?"

He nodded and smiled, his brown eyes crinkling in the corners. "You betcha. I'll see you later then."

"See you."

"Hey, B?"

She turned before she reached the black glass of the library doors. "Yeah?"

"This is probably out of left field, but do you know a kid around twelve or thirteen named Ben?"

"Ben?" She frowned. "I don't think so, why?"

He shrugged. "Just a kid poking around the front of the gardens the other day. He was riding a bike and asked if I knew a librarian named Beatrice. That's your name, right?"

Beatrice's mouth dropped open. "Yeah, that's my name, but I don't know any kids that age. I don't really know any kids, period. I mean... maybe one of the school groups? That take the tours of the public exhibits? I've led a few of those."

Art nodded. "Yeah, that's probably it. Maybe he came last year with his class and remembered you or something."

"Huh." She frowned. "I guess. That's the only thing I can figure. Did he look... I don't know. What did he look like?"

"Just a kid. Hispanic, I think. Kinda skinny. He seemed smart, said his name was Ben, but didn't say anything else."

She paused, searching her memory for any hint of recognition. There wasn't one. "Well, if you see him again, let me know, okay?"

He nodded and gave her a small salute before he turned to help a guest that was signaling for attention. "You got it."

Walking into the cool of the library, Beatrice tucked her helmet under her arm, smoothed back her hair, and thought about what classes she might have led for that age last spring. She couldn't remember any that stood out.

"Weird."

The Huntington Library and Botanical Gardens was given to the city of San Marino by railroad magnate Henry Huntington when he passed away. While the gardens and house of the former estate were open to the public, the library, containing over six million rare books, manuscripts, and archived materials, was restricted and only open to special guests and Ph.D.s with recommendations. Beatrice had been more than fortunate her adviser at UCLA was willing to recommend her to Dr. Karen Stevens, a friend and colleague who happened to be the curator of the Western American archives.

The assistant's job didn't pay all that much, but it had decent benefits, and since Beatrice was independently—if quietly—wealthy, money wasn't her chief concern.

"Hey, B!"

"Morning."

"How's it going?"

She waved and smiled at the quiet morning greetings of her coworkers as she made her way to the small office where she spent her days. She was currently using her rather extensive knowledge of Spanish and Latin to translate early documents from the California missions. Many of the old papers were just storage records or letters between priests, but occasionally, she came upon something in the jumbled records that gave insight into the complicated political workings of California's early Spanish settlements.

"Good morning, Beatrice." Dr. Stevens poked her head into Beatrice's small office and smiled. An attractive blond woman in her mid-fifties, she wore a heather grey suit and a pair of stylish black glasses that framed her blue eyes. "Can you still help me close tonight?"

Beatrice nodded at her boss and grabbed her coffee cup, preparing to get a refill in the lunchroom. A headache from the night before started to gnaw at the space between her eyes.

"Morning. And yes, I can. I was wondering if I could take an extra hour at lunch today since I'm staying late. I'm supposed to meet a friend downtown, and if I had some extra time I'd appreciate it."

Dr. Stevens thought for a moment, then shrugged. "That shouldn't be a problem. I need you to finish those letters, but you'll be able to work late tonight. I really just need an extra body here to meet staff requirements. The group from USC doesn't need much help, and we've just got one other late appointment who's looking at some of the Lincoln archives."

She lifted an eyebrow as she turned on her computer. "Lincoln, huh?"

"Have you worked with those at all? The bodyguard's papers are particularly fascinating. Some of the letters—"

"Yeah, I did a whole project on some Lincoln documents as an undergrad. Not really relevant to what I'm doing now."

Dr. Stevens cocked her head. Beatrice immediately regretted her curt tone and looked up at her boss with an embarrassed smile. "Sorry. I'm feeling rotten this morning. Please excuse me. I appreciate the information."

The curator smirked. "Late night with the boyfriend?"

"I wish. No, just some... stupid stuff. And I think I might be getting sick." ...of thinking about a man I'm never going to see again and regretting words in a journal he'll probably never read.

"I hope not. You just got back from vacation."

Two months ago. Beatrice offered her a tight smile and stood, brushing her hands along her slim-cut, black slacks. She picked up her empty mug and walked toward the doorway.

"I'm going to grab some coffee, can I get you anything?"

"No," Dr. Stevens said. "I'm fine. I'm supposed to be giving a talk with a visiting lecturer at ten, so I'm going to go prepare, and I'll let you get back to work. Take the extra hour at lunch, and I'll see you this evening."

Beatrice nodded and walked down to get more coffee, glancing at the framed art along the walls.

"Hangin' around, Art," she said. "Just hangin' around."

W hen she finally broke for lunch and sped down to Colorado Street to meet Dez at their favorite Spanish restaurant, she had moved past headache and into starving. She sat at one of the sidewalk tables and ordered a small plate of oil-roasted almonds to nibble on until her friend arrived.

Desiree Riley, or Dez as her friends called her, was the quintessential California girl. She'd grown up in Santa Monica and—if not for her parents insisting she leave for a few months to tour Europe after she graduated—would have happily stayed in Southern California her entire life. She'd gone to UCLA for both undergraduate and graduate work, completing her Masters in Information Science the same year as Beatrice.

They had become unexpected friends, the blond surfer girl and the quiet Texan in black boots and even blacker eyeliner; but as the years passed, they found their own friendly equilibrium. Beatrice stopped dying her hair pitch-black in favor of her natural, dark chocolate brown, and Dez had learned how to ride a motorcycle and even had a few piercings that mom and dad didn't know about.

"B!"

She heard her name shouted from a passing car and looked up to see Dez's silver Jetta slowing as cars honked behind her.

"Dez, stop blocking the road!"

"Oh," she waved a careless hand. "I will, but parking is crazy today. Order that sangria pitcher for two, okay?"

"I'm working today, you lush."

The honking behind the Jetta only got more persistent.

"Who says I'm sharing? I'll be there as soon as I find a spot." She lifted her hand to daintily flip off the driver behind her, who was shouting out his window.

"Red wine sangria for two, please," Beatrice said to the waiter, who had been staring at the commotion. He nodded with an amused smile and walked back inside. Dez huffed up the sidewalk a few minutes later and plopped down in the chair across from her friend, blowing a kiss to the waiter who dropped off the drinks.

"Okay, I'm drinking and so are you."

"Dez—"

"No 'buts.' You have been in a mood ever since you got back from Chile, and it's irritating. This is the first chance we've had to talk without Mano around, so spill. Everything."

Beatrice sighed in defeat and poured herself a glass.

An hour later, Dez was leaning on the table and staring raptly as Beatrice finished the story. Her best friend knew a very carefully edited version of the tale of Beatrice and Giovanni, as Dez liked to call it. But she knew that Beatrice went to Chile every summer only to return weeks later, alone and usually in a bad mood.

"So you think he was there? Watching the house?"

"Yeah, I'm pretty sure I saw him." And smelled him. She didn't really feel like explaining that part.

Dez sat back and frowned as she took another bite of her tortilla española. "Don't you think that's kind of creepy?"

Beatrice had never told Dez that Giovanni broke into her house at least once a year to leave plane tickets and occasionally grab a photograph. "Um ... no, it's not really. I mean, it is his house. It's not creepy to me. I was mostly just pissed off that he didn't come to the door."

"Yeah, I can see that." Dez took another sip of the sangria and silently munched on an olive.

"What?"

"What what?" Dez asked, the picture of innocence.

"You have something to say, I can tell."

She didn't deny it but folded her hands on her lap and sighed a little as she looked across the table.

"You need to stop going there."

"I am. I told you, I'm done."

"I know you have friends there, and I know how much you love it, but it just... you've got to move on from this guy."

Beatrice rolled her eyes. "Did you not hear me? I told you, I wrote him in the journal and told him—"

"Yeah, you told him you were done. Got it. You told me that, too. Remember?"

Beatrice pursed her lips and looked away, biting her lip as Dez continued in a quiet voice.

"You told me you were done with him three years ago. And then you went back. And then two years ago, you said the same thing. And you still went back."

She bit her lip to keep the tears at bay as her friend recounted the last five years of an obsession she knew she needed to abandon.

"And then last year, even though Mano practically begged you not to go, you went again."

"I know—"

"I'm not sure you do, B. Because he and I are the ones who have to put up with your moody-ass, depressed behavior for a month afterward every time you go down there and get your heart broken again."

"My heart is not broken. You're being melodramatic," Beatrice muttered and took another sip of her water.

"Fine," she rolled her eyes. "Whatever you want to tell yourself. But stop, okay? For real. When you get the ticket in the mail next time, toss it. Donate it. Change it to a flight to the Bahamas and take your boyfriend, but do not go chasing that ghost again."

Beatrice swallowed the lump in her throat and clenched her jaw as she contained her tears. "I know," she whispered.

"Do you? Really?"

"Yes, I'm done. I'm... moving past it."

"You know I love you," Dez whispered. Beatrice could see the concerned tears in her eyes.

"I know."

"And I'm only saying this—"

"It's fine." She nodded. "I get it. Really, I do."

"You have an amazing man in your life, one who wants a

future with you. That wants to move forward. Not everyone gets that, you know?"

Beatrice sniffed and brushed at her eyes. "And some people never know because they won't ask the person who's perfect for them out on a single date."

Dez straightened up and a flush rose in her cheeks. "I have no idea what you're talking about, Beatrice De Novo."

"Oh," she said with a smile, happy that the conversation had turned. "I can't imagine. Did I mention I saw my lovely neighbor, Matt, yesterday? Yeah, he was sitting on his front porch working on his mountain bike. It must have been hot, because Ken—I mean Matt—wasn't wearing a stitch more than a pair of little biking shorts. It was quite the view, I'll say that."

"He is not a Ken-doll," Dez muttered and threw an olive at Beatrice. She caught it and popped it into her mouth.

"You do some investigation about whether he's anatomically accurate, and I'll consider changing my opinion of him. Until then? Ken-doll."

Dez huffed, "Why do you even—"

"And you're a total Barbie. Librarian Barbie. Do you know how many naughty fantasies poor Ken—I mean Matt—has probably had about you already? You'd be putting him out of his misery. Besides, Ken and Barbie belong together," she said with a wicked grin.

"I hate you," Dez said in a prim voice, "and I hope someone scratches your ugly black motorcycle in the parking lot."

Beatrice reached down and threw an olive at Dez, but this time, her friend caught it and threw it back, hitting Beatrice right between the eyes. She snorted and then belly laughed at Beatrice's shocked expression.

"Forget Librarian Barbie," Beatrice muttered. "I'm going to go with Big League Barbie instead."

The two friends finished lunch and made plans to meet the following weekend for brunch at one of their favorite hangouts near the beach. Beatrice hopped on her bike and returned to the Huntington to finish the translation of the mission letter she'd been working on before lunch.

As the hours passed, she fell into a steady rhythm, speeding through not one, but two complete letters before Dr. Stevens called her to the reading room.

She packed up the document she'd been working on and moved it to one of the library tables in the quietest corner of the room. Dr. Stevens had asked her to be available if the group needed help, but she didn't really expect to be interrupted.

She was looking up a Latin noun she thought might have been misspelled when she heard the quiet footsteps. The smell of smoke reached her nose before she could look up into the green eyes that had haunted her for five years. An enigmatic smile flickered across his face before he spoke.

"I'm looking for Miss De Novo."

Two

"Hello, tesoro," he whispered.

Giovanni had expected her anger, but he hadn't expected the sheen of tears that touched her eyes when they finally met his own.

She stood, her fury palpable when she responded. "You don't get to call me that anymore." She looked around the room.

"I've introduced myself to everyone," he murmured, "shaken everyone's hand. You don't need to worry about anyone paying us any attention."

"So you used your mind voodoo on my boss and colleagues. Thanks."

He smiled a little. "I didn't want to be interrupted. Librarians can be such sticklers for rules."

"Why are you here?"

"For you."

Her mouth fell open before she finally sputtered back, "Well, you're about five years too late."

She bent over her desk and began to gather the letters she had been working on. He stood, watching her, taking in her appearance, and drinking in her welcome scent. He couldn't stop the smile. "You have no idea how much I've missed you."

She glared at him and glanced around the room.

"They won't remember us talking?"

He waved a careless hand. "No, they're barely registering my presence right now."

"Good." She walked around the table, drew back her hand, and slapped him across the face. "You missed me?" she spit out. "You don't get to say that."

She turned and picked up her materials to take back to her office, leaving Dr. Stevens in the reading room with the oblivious scholars from USC. Giovanni enjoyed the view of her walking away from him for a few moments before he followed.

"Beatrice?"

"Go to hell," she called over her shoulder as she made her way through the halls of the institution. She had changed in subtle ways he hadn't been able to detect in photographs. Her figure was fuller, and she carried herself with a grace and confidence she hadn't known five years before. Her walk was more assured, and the almost imperceptible lines that touched her face only added to the depth of her dramatic features.

She was absolutely stunning. And really, really pissed-off.

Her scent was the same, a sweet melange of honeysuckle and lemon that made his fangs descend when he thought of the single taste of her blood he'd enjoyed years before.

"Beatrice," he called again. "I've already told Dr. Stevens you'll be helping me on my project while I'm doing my research here."

She whirled around at her office door. "Well, you can just use that voodoo to change her mind then, can't you?"

He came to stand in front of her and took a deep breath, staring at her mouth, which was pursed in displeasure. "I could." He shrugged. "But I won't."

Beatrice looked like she wanted to slap him again, but her

hands were full of documents and books, so he reached behind her and opened her door, scenting her as he leaned over her shoulder.

"You still smell like honeysuckle," he murmured before she shoved him aside so she could enter the office.

"Go away," she said. "I don't want to see you."

He closed the door and leaned against it. "Well, that's certainly understandable."

"Why?" she asked again as she put her work away. "Why are you here? Why now?"

Giovanni couldn't help but smile at her, despite her anger. He had to resist the urge to walk across the room and kiss her senseless; he had a feeling bodily injury would result. "I already told you. I'm here for you."

She paused in her work, and he could hear her heart begin to race, but her angry expression did not waver.

"Well, you can't have me. So what else are you here for?"

He let her entertain the notion she was unavailable for the time being. "I'm doing some work for a client who's looking for a journal that was carried to the new world in one of Father Junipero Serra's first missionary journeys in California." He smiled innocently when she looked up in shock. "I was told there was a very bright librarian here who could help me translate some of the Spanish and Latin correspondence from the era."

Her eyes narrowed. "Is that so?"

"She came very highly recommended by a mutual friend," he said with a wink.

"Remind me to call Carwyn and bitch at him later."

"Do I hear you're riding a motorcycle now?" He looked her up and down as she grabbed her backpack and helmet, staring at her legs in an obvious manner. "That, I really need to see. Very sexy."

He smiled when he realized he had rendered her speechless again.

"I'm leaving now," she finally said.

He glanced at the clock above her desk. "Look at the time. I should finish up my meeting with Dr. Stevens before I go. After all, I'll see you tomorrow night."

Beatrice shook her head. "You bastard," she muttered through a clenched jaw.

He held open the door, but his arm shot out when she tried to walk past him. His hand curled around her waist, and he felt the familiar frisson of electricity run between them when they touched for the first time in five years. His temperature rose when he leaned over and murmured in her ear.

"I'm back, Beatrice. I'm back for you, and I'm not going anywhere. You're not a girl anymore, so run home for now but know that I'll see you again tomorrow. And I'm not leaving you again."

She turned her head to meet his green eyes and her mouth was only a breath away.

"What if I ask you to go?" she whispered. "Are you just going to hang around and be a nuisance forever?"

He paused, the words almost catching in his throat. "If you ever had any feelings for me, give me a chance. Please."

She didn't respond, pushing his arm away from her body before she rushed down the hall. He heard her pass through the reading room to say goodnight to her boss before she exited out the glass doors. When she left the building, the energy fled with her, and he slumped against her office wall.

"This is going to be harder than I thought."

He finalized plans with Dr. Stevens before he left the Huntington that night, strolling the four blocks to the large Tudor-style home he'd purchased the month before. He was still getting used to the layout of the house but had been charmed by the dense trees that surrounded the property and the tiered gardens and ponds that filled the yard.

As he walked through the front doors, he looked around and listened for the activity that should have been going on in the library on the first floor. He heard nothing except the bouncing of a basketball behind the garage. Laughing under his breath, he turned and walked silently through the kitchen and out the back doors.

The boy was bouncing the ball in a pool of light that shone from the back of the garage. He was bent over, dribbling through his scrawny legs, his attention focused on the rhythmic bouncing of the orange ball in his hands. Just then, he crouched down and shot up, tossing a precise shot toward the basket mounted over the garage door.

"He shoots... he scores!" the boy shouted when the ball sailed through the hoop. "And the crowd goes wild for Ben Vecchio, lead scorer of the—" He turned then and spotted Giovanni, leaning against the wall.

"Scorer of the what?" Giovanni asked with a raised eyebrow.

"Um... of the top college in the country, which I will be getting into with no problem because I already finished my math and my Latin translation?"

"Reading?"

"Done before you woke up tonight."

"History?"

"Well, not quite... "

"Composition?"

"You know, you're back a lot sooner than I thought you'd be."

"How about piano?"

Ben's mouth gaped open and his shoulders slumped. "It hasn't even been delivered yet!"

Giovanni frowned. "I forgot that part. Did you call the movers today?"

Ben nodded. "Yep, they said that it'd be here next Thursday at the latest and to make sure that we had room for the truck."

"Excellent. Toss me the ball then."

"Pass, Gio. Pass the ball."

"Fine, whatever," he muttered as Ben passed the ball to him. He dribbled it, then tossed it toward the backboard, where it bounced off the rim before Ben ran over to catch it. He bounced it back to Giovanni.

"Okay, you need to square up your shoulders with the basket before you shoot. Try again."

Giovanni dribbled the ball a few more times before he tried again, squaring his shoulders like Ben had directed. "You know, if you put half the concentration into your composition that you do into this game—"

"Game, Gio. Remember? We're supposed to talk about non-school stuff when we play."

He rolled his eyes and shot again, this time getting slightly closer to the square behind the hoop.

"There," Ben encouraged. "That's better." The boy rebounded the shot and took some time dribbling it before he tossed it toward the hoop, where it sailed in. "So, did you talk to her?"

Giovanni watched as the boy ran around the small court, shooting baskets and chasing rebounds. His lanky limbs and awkward gait seemed to disappear on the basketball court, as he exhibited the natural confidence that had brought him to Giovanni's attention when he'd seen the boy in New York over a year ago.

"I did."

"Is she really mad at you?"

He nodded as Ben passed him the ball. "Yes, she's... fairly angry."

"Did you tell her about me yet?" he asked in a small voice.

"Not yet," he smiled. "I told you, Beatrice is far more apt to like you than me at the moment. Don't worry about that."

Ben gave a nonchalant shrug. "Girls always like me more, G.

It's 'cause I'm so good-looking."

Giovanni laughed and passed the ball back to him. "I worry about your self-esteem, Benjamin. Really, I do. Have you eaten dinner yet?"

"Just a few more minutes?" His eyes pleaded. "Then I'll go in."

"Fine. But after that, you're finishing your homework."

"Sweet!" Ben shot a few rapid baskets. "So how long do you think it's going to be before she's not mad at you anymore?"

"How long was it before you started liking me after I took you off the streets and made you start bathing regularly?"

Ben snickered and passed the ball back to Giovanni. "Not as long as I acted. The food was a lot better at your house."

"Better than the randomly purloined hot dog? I should hope even my cooking beat that."

"Well, it was close, but—hey!" Ben dodged the ball that Giovanni threw at him. It hit the wall of the garage and bounced back toward Ben. Giovanni grinned at the boy's sharp reflexes, which had been part of the reason he'd been such a successful pick-pocket until a little over a year before.

"I'll go start dinner. Come to the kitchen in a few minutes."

Giovanni walked back in the house and went to start a pot of water to boil. He had little interest in food that night, but because he was determined to civilize Benjamin as much as possible for a twelve-year-old boy, he had made nightly dinner at the table a priority.

When he'd found the boy in New York, Giovanni had spotted his wasted potential almost immediately. The urchin had stolen his wallet, and if Giovanni hadn't had preternatural senses, he would have easily gotten away with it. As it was, he'd let the boy have the wallet, followed him, and done some investigating.

Ben was the illegitimate son of a con woman and a cabbie. After looking into both parents and talking to the boy, Giovanni decided that neither one of them was deserving of his help—or their own child. One physically abusive and the other a manipulator, they had passed on to Ben little more than the ability to fend for himself and lie convincingly to authorities.

Giovanni, however, had seen the sharp intelligence and survival instinct the boy exhibited and decided he deserved more than to be chewed up on the streets of the city. On paper, Ben had become Giovanni's nephew, the son of his deceased brother and his wife, who had died in a tragic car accident the year before. They had spent the previous year resolving the details of the adoption and catching Ben up on the realities of his new world.

The boy barreled into the kitchen just as Giovanni finished putting the jar of sauce on the spaghetti. He set it on the table along with a salad he'd put together from a bag and a bowl of olives.

"Spaghetti again?"

He cocked an eyebrow at the boy. "Tomorrow night you can cook. Besides," he said as he flicked the back of the boy's ear as he sat at the table, "you're an Italian now, you need to eat lots of pasta."

Ben snorted and dug into the food. Giovanni watched him scarf down his food with gusto; it reminded him of how much Caspar had eaten at that age. It had been harder to find food for Caspar in postwar Britain, but with the proliferation of American all-night markets and Ben's natural independence, the two of them managed just fine.

"I'm not Italian, really," Ben said between bites. "I'm Leba-Rican."

Giovanni smiled at the boy's quick wit. Ben was half Lebanese and half Puerto Rican, but their coloring was close enough that no one questioned their relation. The only difference was Ben's dark brown eyes, which had always reminded Giovanni of Beatrice.

"You might have to be the one to convince her," he mused.

"Convince who? Beatrice?"

"Mmmhmm. You'll have to convince her I'm not a complete bastard."

"Well, technically," Ben said between bites, "we both are."

Giovanni flicked the boy's ear again. "You know what I mean."

Ben paused and set down his fork. "You know, if we were friends and then you went away and I didn't see you for five years, I'd be pretty mad, too."

"You don't have to worry about me leaving you, Ben."

"I know, but she—"

"It was important for her to have time on her own. Without all the vampire stuff, as you like to call it. That's part of why she came here." He paused. "It's complicated, Benjamin."

Ben smirked before he began eating again. "That's always what grown-ups say when they're not sure they're right. So did she decide all that? Or did you? 'Cause you're pretty bossy, you know."

He decided to change the subject. "It's a good thing I am, or you'd never finish school. Finish up your dinner, then go upstairs and do the rest of your work. Do you need help with anything?"

Ben shook his head. "I don't think so."

"If you do, I'll be on the patio talking to Carwyn."

"Okay."

"No video games until after your work is finished. None."

The boy rolled his eyes. "I got it, I got it."

Taking the bowl of olives and a glass of wine with him, he went outside to the large covered patio that spread across the back of the house. He'd set up a rotary phone connection there, which he used to dial his friend in Northern Wales.

"Uncle Gio!" Carwyn answered. "How's the boy doing?"

"Well," Giovanni sipped his wine. "Very well. His studies are coming along, and he hasn't run away since the last time I called you."

"That's progress. I knew he'd come around."

"He still runs off on his bike during the day, though. He had to talk himself out of a truancy ticket last week."

"I doubt that was a problem for him. He's got quite the smart mouth."

"He's conniving in the best way."

They both chuckled a little but quickly fell silent.

Giovanni took a deep breath. "I saw her today."

Carwyn made no response for a few moments. "How did it go?"

"About as well as I deserve, I suppose."

Carwyn was quiet as Giovanni sipped his wine.

"How did she look?"

"Beautiful," he murmured. "Stunning. Angry."

"I told you—"

"I know what you told me." He rubbed a hand across his face. "And you know I had my reasons for staying away."

Carwyn said, "You wanted her to have her own life? She does. She's got a damn good one, as a matter of fact."

"Tell me about the boyfriend."

"I realize you'd like Mano to be some kind of miscreant, but he's not. He's a very good man, and he absolutely adores her."

Giovanni sighed and pinched the bridge of his nose. "Tell me about the boyfriend."

Carwyn took a deep breath. "Ex-navy diver. Has his own business with one of his military mates. Does fairly well for himself. He's a hard worker and very well-respected. Not much family of his own, but talks about wanting one with our girl."

Giovanni had the sudden vision of Beatrice swollen with child, her face full and glowing as she smiled. His breath caught, knowing that if she chose him, it would never be his child she would carry, and for the first time in five hundred years, he regretted that. Then, thinking of the boy upstairs and a small boy hiding in an attic many years before, he reminded himself that family came in many forms.

"She's too smart to be with anyone for that long if he wasn't a good man," he muttered. "How does she feel about him? Really. Does she love him?"

"I can't answer that," the priest said. "I'm sure she does, but she's been half in love with your memory for more than five years now. I doubt she knows how to feel about either of you at this point."

He pulled the picture of her riding the horse in Cochamó out of his pocket and looked at it. The sun glinted off her hair and a huge smile spread across her face. "I'll just have to convince her then."

He heard Carwyn clear his throat and Giovanni could almost sense the lecture from his old friend approaching. "Gio, you have been my friend for over three hundred years, and I love you dearly, but that girl is precious to me."

"I know."

"Her father isn't here to ask you, so I will. What are your intentions toward her? She has a good life now. She has friends, and a career, and a good man who loves her, so—"

"He can't—" Giovanni cleared his throat and closed his eyes. "He can't love her like I do, Carwyn. He can't. Because I promise you, he doesn't know her like I do."

There was a long pause on the other end of the line. "That doesn't mean she'll agree with you, my friend. What you're asking of her... it's not a small thing. She may not want to give up her life, even if it means forever with you."

He shrugged, though no one could see in the dark yard. "She may not. It's her decision, but I wouldn't bet against me." His thumb brushed over her cheek as he stared at the photograph. "I've given her time. Time to grow however she needed, free from the complications of our world. You may not have agreed with me, but I did what I felt like I needed to. For her."

"And now?"

He lifted the picture to stare into her dark, smiling eyes, wishing she was next to him, as he had for the past five years. He took a deep breath.

"Now I plan to convince her she wants eternity with me."

THREE

"I know, but Dr. Stevens didn't really give me a choice, Mano."

She heard her boyfriend sigh over the phone. "Well, I suppose I'll just tell Dan that I can't handle the morning dives for a while. On my schedule right now, we're never going to see each other."

"I know."

"How long is this guy going to be doing research? And why does he have to do it in the evenings? Are you going to miss judo and kickboxing, too?"

She curled her lip; she'd forgotten about her martial arts classes that met twice a week. Damn vampire.

"I think he has to do nights because of his other job or something. It's probably only going to be a couple of weeks."

It better only be that long. Giovanni had two weeks to convince her of... she wasn't sure what, but two weeks was her limit. She clenched her eyes in frustration. She felt as if the careful wall she'd constructed between her past and her present, between the supernatural world and the normal one, was starting to crumble, and she didn't know where to draw the lines.

Mano was still talking. "I know it's not your choice. And it's great that this guy requested you specifically. I'm really proud of you, B."

Her heart twisted, and she couldn't help feeling like she was deceiving him by not telling her boyfriend that Giovanni was the scholar she was helping with translation. Mano knew an even more abbreviated version of the Giovanni and Beatrice story than she had told Dez, and she had never told him she'd been romantically involved with her former employer.

Or whatever they had been.

She felt the hum of energy when Giovanni entered the room and looked up to see the vampire approach the table where she was sitting. Beatrice cursed mentally when she felt her heart begin to race, knowing he could hear it. She met his intense stare as he crossed the room, but she didn't hang up her phone. Mano was still talking.

"—so I'll see you tomorrow afternoon. Hey, baby, I gotta go. Dan's waiting for me to close up the shop. Love you."

She stared back at Giovanni when she responded. "I love you, too. Have a great night! Miss you, and I'll see you tomorrow."

He sat down next to her and leaned his elbow on the table, propping his chin on his hand to watch her. He was wearing a charcoal grey button-down shirt, a pair of black slacks she knew would show off his incredible ass, and a small, satisfied smile.

"How's your friend, Beatrice?" he asked when she hung up the phone.

She gave him a tight smile. "My boyfriend's great. I'll have to apologize," she said as she yawned. "I'm so tired today; he kept me up pretty late last night."

"Is that so?" He leaned toward her, smiling when her heart picked up. "I'll remember that. I'm sure I can think of inventive ways to stimulate you."

She rolled her eyes and opened the document files he had requested through Dr. Stevens. "Fine. Whatever. Now, what do you actually want? Since I know you don't need my help with the translations."

"I really am looking for provenance on an old journal. I found it for my client, but he wants documentation on the origins," he said in a more professional voice.

Beatrice felt her heart sink. "Oh, you mean, you really only came for—"

"Asking for your help with the translation was a pure ploy for your attention, of course." His eyes swept from her boots to her face, which she could feel heat up, much to her own annoyance. "I could have just requested the documents and not your help, but where's the fun in that?"

She fought the smile that wanted to surface. "Well, here they are. Do you want me to go through them with you? I'm familiar with this set."

"I'd appreciate your eyes. There are a lot to go through, and I know you're far more familiar with them than I am."

"Well, it's nice to be appreciated."

"Let me know what else you'd like me to appreciate," he whispered. "I'll be happy to oblige."

Beatrice bit her lip and ignored him as she began to sort through the letters on the table. She'd walked right into that one. She was having problems not reacting to the playful version of Giovanni she only had faint memories of from Houston. He could be very flirtatious when he let himself, but it was usually only when he hadn't fed for a while and let his guard down.

"Need to go grab a bite to eat?" she muttered. "You're in quite the mood."

He leaned closer and she could hear him inhale, even though she refused to look at him. "Are you offering? Because I could have feasted last night, and I still wouldn't turn that down."

The blood rushed to her face. "Stop."

"Stop what? Telling you how good you smell? How good you

look? You look amazing, by the way. How about how good you taste?"

She could feel his breath on her neck.

You're not supposed to be here! Beatrice wanted to scream. Where have you been?

His voice only dropped. "Should I not tell you how many times I've replayed in my memory the one time I tasted you in my bed? How I've dreamed about your skin? Is that what I should stop, tesoro mio?"

She could feel the heat radiating off him, and Beatrice knew he was as affected as she was. The smell of smoke and whiskey was even stronger than the night before, and she clenched her eyes, trying to keep herself from breaking down and throwing herself into his arms. Nothing about their attraction to each other had dissipated in the five years they'd been apart. She forced her mind into the present.

"Don't. Just... don't. Let's get to work, all right?"

Please, she almost begged.

His green eyes raked over her face, and she saw the edge of his fangs peek out from behind his lips.

"Fine," he murmured. "I'll stop... for now."

She let out a ragged breath and started sorting through the letters again.

Since he'd shown up the night before, Beatrice hadn't been able to think of anything else. And she was furious with herself for not being able to give him the cold shoulder the way she'd imagined for so many years. She could lie to him, but he would know.

He'd always known.

She'd attacked Mano the night before, clinging to him as if he was a life raft. He'd been amused by her sudden rush of desire, but he was an enthusiastic participant, nonetheless. Afterward, Beatrice had lain awake for hours, shaking and confused. She felt herself slipping into the tangled maze of emotion that gripped her on rare occasions when she allowed herself to remember her last year in Houston, her abduction to Greece, and her time with Giovanni at his house in the Cochamó Valley. The persistent questions about her father's whereabouts and what Lorenzo wanted from him had surfaced along with Giovanni, and she was already having trouble sleeping.

In the years she had lived in Los Angeles, Beatrice had carefully constructed a "normal life," distancing herself from most of the more supernatural elements unless Carwyn or Tenzin happened to visit. She'd even been able to distance herself when she visited Cochamó, fooling herself that her visits could be part of her "normal" life since Giovanni was never there. Now sitting next to him, smelling him, sensing the familiar energy that always seemed to radiate from him like her own personal magnetic field, made her want to throw herself into his arms, wrap herself around him, and forget the past five years.

She took deep breaths, finally calming the beat of her heart and the rush of her blood. She focused her mind and tried to see him as just another visiting Ph.D.

"Well, Dr. Vecchio, let's get started."

They worked silently for another hour, quickly falling back into the unspoken communication they'd always shared. But then, Giovanni had always had an uncanny knack for understanding the way her brain worked, and she'd had the same understanding of him.

"Did you find that one letter from Governor Portolá to—"

"Yes, I did. Thank you, that mention of the young friar—"

"Yeah, I thought that might be what you were looking for there."

They skimmed through the first stack of documents from Mission San Diego and moved on to a stack of letters from Monterey. They continued to whisper back and forth throughout the evening.

"Have you seen any further correspondence from the priest in San Diego that—"

"You mean the young Catalán? I think there's something in this stack here... "

"Ah, exactly. That's what I'm looking for. Thank you, tesoro. Look at the year. That's promising."

As they worked, the years seemed to slip away. Strangely, Beatrice felt even more at ease than she had when she'd first worked with Giovanni. She supposed the years she'd spent at school and working with visiting scholars had given her much-needed confidence. She was no longer intimidated by his intellect or his experience, and she realized he no longer treated her as a bright student but more like a colleague.

When it was time to leave, she felt reluctant to go back to her empty house, even though she knew she should. He hadn't made any more suggestive overtures, but five years of questions tugged at her mind. Luckily—or unluckily, she couldn't decide—he was waiting on the steps outside the library when she exited holding her helmet and the black backpack she wore riding.

"So... a motorcycle?"

She sat down on the steps, keeping a careful distance from him. "It's easy on gas and good for traffic."

"And sexy. Beautiful woman on a fast bike? Very sexy." He winked.

Well, that hadn't taken long.

"Gio, you need to—"

"Don't shush me. I'm allowed to express an opinion."

"What—" Beatrice paused, waiting for Dr. Stevens to pass. "Where have you been? Since you have appeared out of nowhere and apparently want back in my life, I think I have a right to know."

He leaned toward her and tucked a piece of hair behind her ear. "I definitely want back in your life. And I like the hair, by the way. It suits you, though I do miss the length. I had dreams about that long hair—"

"Damn it!" She slapped his hand away. "Stop saying shit like that, all right? I have a boyfriend, and I'm trying to have an actual conversation with you."

Giovanni smiled but leaned back, placing his elbows on the steps above and stretching his long legs in front of him. She rolled her eyes, wishing she didn't notice the way his shirt stretched across his defined chest.

"Fine. And of course you have a right to know where I've been. I've been traveling mostly—"

"Yeah, got the postcards, thanks a bunch."

He smiled. "Did you keep them? Those are all the places your father left me a clue, then disappeared before I could get there."

Her heart almost stopped. "You—you've been looking for my father?" she whispered. "All this time?"

He looked away. "On and off, yes. I told you I'd find him. I have a great desire to meet your father. He is both impressively and irritatingly good at hiding himself."

When Beatrice had moved to L.A.—and the threat of Lorenzo seemed to disappear—she had hoped her father would find her. She'd waited, keeping a faint hope alive he could be part of her life again. But as the years passed, Stephen De Novo, and whatever mystery he carried with him, remained stubbornly out of reach. So, she tucked him away into a dark corner of her heart and tried to forget.

She was still trying to process the idea of Giovanni spending the previous five years looking for her missing father. "How did you know where to look?"

"Oh," Giovanni murmured, "I would get word through certain channels that he'd been asking questions of this associate or that acquaintance. Looking for records at a certain library or auction house. All little clues he must have known I would pick up on, if I was looking for him."

"Did he know you were looking for him?"

"Yes." His expression darkened. "I let it be known I wanted to meet with him. De Novo kept leaving traces, but by the time I would get to any location, he would be gone."

Beatrice frowned, twisting her hands together. "Does he think you want to hurt him? Is that why he's hiding?"

"I don't know, though it's fairly well-known that his daughter is... "

"What? His daughter is what?"

Giovanni cleared his throat. "To put it bluntly, his daughter is my human and—

Her eyes popped wide. "What?"

"—I wanted to speak to him—"

"*Your* human?" she hissed.

"Beatrice."

"Was there some sort of memo I should have gotten about this?"

"Beatrice?"

"Because it's been five years, and I sure don't remember—"

"Beatrice!"

She fell silent, glaring at him, but he only leaned closer.

"You stole an almost unspeakable amount of money from an immortal. One who still has many friends. You've been living here in peace for five years now. Do you think that was some sort of accident or luck?"

"I don't know! I thought you said I'd be safe."

"You are safe, but did you think everyone in my world... " Giovanni glanced over at the trees and lowered his voice. "Did you think they had forgotten? You've been under my protection since I kissed you at The Night Hawk pub six years ago. That has never changed."

She felt like she'd been punched in the chest. "But—"

"It doesn't matter whether you have a boyfriend," he bit out, "or whether we see each other or not. You'll be under my aegis for as long as you live." He paused, but there was no amusement or victory in his eyes. "Or you're fair game, Beatrice. And that is not acceptable to me."

Beatrice whispered, "I wish you'd told me."

She'd been fooling herself. The graduate degree. The very respectable job. The little house in Silver Lake. Mano... All pieces of a life that was still under someone else's control.

Giovanni took a deep breath. When he continued his voice was hoarse, "Why would I tell you all that? So you could worry? So you could have nightmares again and spend your days looking over your shoulder? I didn't want that for you."

She shook her head and glared at him. "What the hell did you want for me? Why didn't you ever come to Cochamó when you knew I'd be there? Did you want me to miss you? To wonder every night if you were alive or—" She broke off when he held up a hand.

"You should be quiet unless you want an audience," he muttered, looking at the trees again.

"What? What are you talking about?" She craned her neck, trying to see in the darkness.

Giovanni sighed. "Benjamin, stop hiding in the trees and come introduce yourself."

"Benjamin?" Her eyes narrowed. "Ben?"

"Are you going to be mad at me?" She heard a child's voice call from the shadows and looked back at Giovanni, who was sitting with an expression both sulking and amused.

"No." He stood and reached for her hand. "Just come out." He muttered something else in Italian she didn't understand.

"Will you please tell me what is going on?" Beatrice walked down the steps, clutching her helmet in front of her. At the edge of the trees, she saw a boy emerge holding onto a bicycle and looking at Giovanni with a crooked smile. He was thin and a bit clumsy as he emerged from the brush, but his sharp brown eyes looked her over, and a smile grew on his face.

"Are you Beatrice?"

"Are you the Ben who was asking for me last week?"

He grinned and nodded. "Yep. That guard actually told you? I didn't think he would."

Giovanni frowned. "What do you mean, you were asking after her?"

Ben looked at Giovanni innocently. "Well, you were so nervous about talking to her—"

"Tell me why you're out on your bike at nine-thirty, Benjamin." Giovanni interrupted.

Oh really? So Giovanni wasn't quite as confident as he seemed. She looked over to Ben, who grinned at her.

"I was wondering whether my uncle was going to provide a delicious and nutritious meal for me. Family time is so important and all."

Giovanni cocked an eyebrow in the boy's direction. "And I suppose you missed the note about the leftovers in the fridge?"

"Wait," Beatrice held up a hand. "Uncle? Am I missing something here?"

"Only me," Ben said with a mischievous smile. "But I'm here now, so no need to worry."

Giovanni reached over and pinched the boy's ear. "Don't be rude. Introduce yourself."

Ben propped his bike on the kickstand and held out his hand. "Benjamin Vecchio. Former pickpocket, con man, runaway, and fake nephew of the vampire to your right. You must be the beautiful Beatrice."

She held out her hand and Ben took it, bending down to kiss the back in a gallant gesture. She laughed and looked at Giovanni. "And you think *you're* charming?"

Giovanni rolled his eyes as Ben continued kissing up her arm. He reached over and tugged Ben's collar, pulling him away from Beatrice, who was still laughing.

"Stop it, she's too old for you."

"Well, technically," Ben said with a smile, "she's way too young for you, old man."

"Do you like that Xbox I bought you? How about the daily meals?"

"Shutting up now," Ben quipped. "But really, Beatrice, it's nice to finally meet you."

"Um... " She frowned. "Likewise. And please call me B, only the professor here calls me Beatrice. So you're his fake nephew, huh?"

Giovanni put an arm around Ben's shoulders. "My poor, departed brother's child. Tragic accident."

"Very tragic," Ben nodded solemnly. "I still cry sometimes. Not really. My real parents were assholes."

She nodded along, trying to integrate this new, paternal side of the vampire. She knew it shouldn't surprise her—after all, he had raised Caspar—but it was still difficult to think about the man that made her blood boil with anger and desire in equal measure being, for all practical purposes, a father.

Despite the fact he was over five hundred years old.

"Okay then, well, on that very interesting note—"

"Do you ride a motorcycle?" Ben pointed at her helmet. "Cool! Can I see it?"

"Um, sure. I guess. I mean if it's okay with Gio. "

Giovanni nodded, probably glad he had managed to trap her into further conversation. They walked toward the parking lot and she looked over at Ben. "How did you get all the way here? Where do you guys live?"

"Well," Giovanni started, "I happened to find an appropriate house—"

"We just live a couple blocks from here! Gio thought it would be great 'cause he could walk to where you work instead of worrying about the driving thing. I keep telling him he should teach me to drive, and then he wouldn't have to worry about breaking cars, but he tells me I have to wait till I'm fourteen, or at least until my feet touch the pedals."

"So you could walk to where I work, huh?" she muttered under her breath, knowing he could hear her, even if Ben could not. He simply cocked an eyebrow at her and shrugged.

"I told you I was here for you. And the house next to yours was too small."

"You wouldn't—"

"Is that your bike? It's awesome! I've never seen one like that. Gio, can I have—"

"No," he said quickly and looked at her with a smile. Leaning down, he whispered in her ear. "Very sexy. I can just imagine your legs wrapping around—"

"So, Ben," Beatrice cleared her throat as she interrupted the thought she really didn't want him to finish. "Want to sit on it?"

"Cool!" Ben threw his bike on the ground and scrambled over to Beatrice's Triumph. As she helped the boy onto the back and explained some of the features of the bike, she could feel Giovanni's gaze as if it was a physical touch. She tried to concentrate on Ben's enthusiasm and ignore what the vampire's eyes were doing to her heart rate.

"So," Ben said, "are you going to take the job? He asked you already, right?"

"Wha—what job?" She looked over her shoulder at Giovanni, who was frowning and glaring at Ben in frustration. He closed his eyes and she thought she saw his lips move like he was counting.

"Oh." Ben grinned meekly. "I guess not. Oops."

She walked over and stood in front of Giovanni with her hands on her hips.

"What job?"

FOUR

"Tell me more about my dad."

"Is this really the time, Beatrice?"

Giovanni looked up from the letter he was examining and around the reading room at the Huntington. They were finishing up the letters in the collection and, so far, he was relieved they hadn't found what he was expecting.

Beatrice whispered as she paged through a journal from a Franciscan friar in San Francisco. "Since you're not going to convince me to work for you, I think now would be an excellent time."

"I really wish you'd reconsider."

"I'm sure you would."

He slipped his hand over to trace along the skin of her forearm. She batted him away, but he could still feel her heart race.

"Stop it."

"I can almost promise my benefits package is better than the Huntington."

He saw her trying to suppress the smile. "Did you just say 'package?'" she snickered.

Giovanni cleared his throat and glanced at Dr. Stevens, who

was looking at them. He smiled politely and nodded in the librarian's direction.

"You are never allowed to call me juvenile again, Gio."

"I never called you juvenile in the first place."

She cut her eyes toward him. "You thought it, though."

He let his eyes roam over her. "Not in a long time."

"Nice way to distract me, by the way. Tell me about my dad."

Giovanni rolled his eyes. "Your father is very good at hiding."

"He never contacted me. Do you think he even knows that I want to see him?"

She had cocked her shoulders in his direction and he wished he could reach over and smooth the frown that had gathered between her eyes. "Yes, I'm quite sure he does."

"So why wouldn't he—"

"He's avoiding me."

That only caused the frown to grow. "But why would he avoid you?"

"Oh... " He cleared his throat and glanced up to see Dr. Stevens watching them again. "You forget that he spent his formative vampire years with Lorenzo. I very much doubt my son has any nice things to say about me."

"But you said he would hate Lorenzo."

"And I'm sure he hates Lorenzo's sire, as well."

He saw her face fall a little. "But, you've protected me. You've... you said I was seen as 'yours' so wouldn't he know you were protecting me?"

Giovanni scanned one letter and began on another. "I'm sure he doesn't know what to think. And he's been quite elusive, so I'm sure he doesn't trust me."

Beatrice fell silent. They both worked quietly as the minutes passed. He was running out of time. He knew they would find the provenance on the journal eventually, or he would run out of research material, and then he would have no regular excuse to see her since she refused to quit her job and come work for him.

"I was in Shanghai a few years ago meeting with some old contacts. I was able to see some amazing martial arts demonstrations. You would have loved them." He knew Beatrice had developed an interest in self-defense and martial arts in the years they had been apart. Considering her kidnapping, it was not a surprise.

He saw her smile. "Are you trying to tempt me with exotic travel and intrigue if I come work for you?"

"Yes. Is it working?"

She looked around the reading room and over at Dr. Stevens, who was still watching her like a hawk, no doubt wondering why Giovanni had requested her specifically. He'd have to alter the woman's memories again before he left for the night.

"I like Southern California."

"Good, we'll make our base here and come back between research trips." He continued before she had time to interrupt. "Have I told you how nice it is to be working with you again? Or in a library at all, for that matter? I've been doing irritating political things in the past few years. Very annoying. I have to talk with all sorts of unpleasant people who like to hear themselves speak. Whining and simpering. They all remind me of my time with my father."

"What kind of political things?"

"Oh, visiting people who owe me favors. Trying to determine what my son is up to. A kind of intelligence gathering, I suppose. All those things I tried to avoid for the past three hundred years."

She said, "I'd apologize, but you're the one who made him."

"No apologies necessary. I put the matter of dealing with him off for too long."

"And your books? Andros's library?" She put down the journal she'd been working on and picked up another. "Any clues about that?"

"A bit. The majority of it remains a mystery, but he's sold off some of the more easily moveable pieces of the collection, so I've reacquired a few things. You really must have wiped him out when you took his accounts, tesoro."

"That's always nice to hear."

"And you appear to be doing quite well financially."

Giovanni saw her smirk. "I don't have to worry about paying the bills, no."

He gave a quiet laugh. "So I've collected a few more of my father's books. I've tried to track your father. I've reestablished myself among some allies. Then I found Benjamin, and that's been quite the project."

"Sounds like you were busy," she said in a small voice.

"And I missed you every day."

She was silent for a few long minutes. He wondered if she would respond at all.

"You knew where to find me," she finally said.

Giovanni had no answer for her. He had known where to find her, but he had also known that she needed time to grow and mature. He only hoped he could convince her that it was worth giving him another chance.

"Beatrice—"

"So have you heard anything more about Lorenzo? He still staying under the radar?"

He sighed and picked up another letter. "He has been. I'll hear something every now and then about him or one of his children, but for the most part he's been quiet."

"Why do I find that disturbing?"

"Probably because it's easier to kill the snake on the path than the one in the rocks."

She looked at him. "That's an excellent description of him."

"A snake?" He cocked an eyebrow. "It's an accurate one."

She murmured under her breath, "He's like this ghost in the back of my mind. I try to forget him, but... "

He reached over and squeezed her hand quickly. "Don't forget about him until he's dead."

Beatrice shook her head. "Why did I ever fool myself?"

He frowned. "What? What are you talking about?"

She looked at him for a long moment before she turned back to the journal she'd been studying. "Nothing."

Giovanni knew it wasn't nothing, but he also knew she wouldn't tell him. They worked silently together for another half an hour. Finally, he saw her studying a page in the journal intently and her heart began to race.

"Here," she said quietly, but there was no victorious smile on her face. He took the journal from her and studied the page she had pointed to. "Found a mention in the Catalan's notes."

"Let me see," he said as he read the pages from the old book, reading about the young priest the father had met and how they compared journal notes on the journey up the California coast. It was consistent with the diary his client had acquired. It gave him a name and a year. It was as much as he could hope for from the Huntington collection.

"Guess I found your provenance," Beatrice said.

His eyes raked over her face. "I always knew you would."

Beatrice thrust her hip back, tossing her sparring partner over her shoulder. The large man hit the floor with a loud slap, and she straightened with a grunt as her sensei smiled from across the mat. She held a hand out to her partner to help him up. They bowed to each other and shook hands as they finished the freestyle judo practice.

Pete called out, "B, you are on a roll today! What's gotten into you? Very nice randori, both of you. Very nice." The wiry, grey-haired man strode across the mat and shook both Beatrice and her partner's hands before all three walked to the lockers near the free weights. "B, you still have one of the strongest harai goshi I've seen.

I know you were dissatisfied with your last teacher, but your forms are really strong."

She nodded and wiped the sweat from her eyes. "Thanks. He was great, I just felt like he'd taken me as far as I could go in my training. I felt like I was in a rut, you know?"

Pete nodded and slapped her shoulder. "No worries, I understand. Sometimes a relationship just runs its course. I hope you parted on good terms."

Beatrice nodded and untied her belt, taking off her heavy judogi and stripping down to a tank top to hit the punching bags on the side of the studio.

"How long have you been studying?"

"Judo?"

Pete nodded.

"Well, when I first moved out to L.A., I started studying martial arts. First, it was just some tai chi at the university. A friend suggested it. Then I decided to take a self-defense class—"

"Always a good idea for anyone."

"Yeah, I can agree with that. Anyway, the place I went to taught judo and jujitsu, too, so I got interested that way. I've been studying almost five years now."

She slipped on her gloves and Pete joined her at the bags. They both began hitting the teardrop shaped speed bags that hung from platforms in the low ceiling. Soon, Beatrice was zoning out to the sound and the rhythm of the quick punches as she tried to release the stress of the day and her last meeting with Giovanni.

Focus, focus, focus, she thought as she tried to wipe the image of his deep green eyes from her mind.

"Your focus is really impressive," Pete said as he worked the bag to her right. "You should be proud of yourself. You look like you've been studying twice as long."

"That's nice to hear." Even though I'm completely distracted at the moment.

Suddenly, he grinned. "What did you like about judo at first? I can almost guess."

Beatrice laughed. "I saw this little girl toss a guy about a foot taller and seventy pounds heavier than her."

Pete chuckled as he continued hitting the bag. "Yeah, that'll do it. It's pretty great when you realize you can take down someone way stronger than you if you know what you're doing and use their own strengths against them, right?"

She shook her head. "Pete, you have no idea."

"Why am I so upset?" Beatrice asked as she drank another glass of wine at Dez's apartment.

Dez only raised an eyebrow. "Because you now have no handy excuse to see the man you've been in love with for five years?"

"I'm not in love with him."

"Yeah." Her best friend snorted. "Whatever."

"I'm not."

"Okay, then you're upset because... you're going to miss the challenge of the project? That is way cooler than most of the stuff we do." Dez couldn't contain the grin. "I mean, what a cool job! When you worked for him before, did you ever have a kind of treasure hunt like that? Or was it mostly research and catalogue work?"

Dez sat on the edge of her seat while Beatrice stared at her. "Uh... there may have been a mystery or two that we worked on, yeah."

"And did you solve it? I mean, how does that work? That's got to pay pretty well, right? It's like hiring a private detective to find something. Only it's someone who knows rare books! Do you think he's looking for an assistant? I would totally dig something like—"

"He's kind of a loner, to be honest." Kinda. "I doubt he'd hire... someone to do that stuff when he could just do it himself." She did wonder who he had doing his computer work for him. Did he just use amnis to get random people to search online? That wasn't very ethical. Maybe he did need—

"Yeah," Dez sighed. "I totally get why you're so hung up on him though. A good-looking Italian book collector who solves historical mysteries? That's just... "

"What?" Implausible?

"Hot. I can't believe Mano's not insanely jealous of all the time you're spending with him."

Beatrice felt her face heat up, and she caught Dez's wide-eyed look.

"He doesn't know, does he?"

She shrugged. There was no way on God's green earth Beatrice was telling Mano that she was working alongside a five-hundred-year-old vampire who was linked to her missing father and was the sire of the monster who had kidnapped her. There was no way she was telling anyone any of that. They'd think she was insane.

"He's going to be pissed!"

"Why? The research is done." And her heart still ached over it. "Why would I see him anymore?" She shook her head and continued quietly. "He'll probably leave town again now that he has it."

Dez frowned. "I thought you said he bought a house?"

So he had, and she'd been asked over for dinner more than once by the persistent Ben. It was both despicable and adorable that Giovanni seemed to have Ben on his team in his attempts to win her back. She had to admit, the boy was charming.

As was his fake uncle.

"So he's probably going to use Southern California as a base for work if he did that," Dez reasoned. "It would be a good one. Easy airport access and lots of international flights to both Europe and Asia. Big research libraries and plenty of resources."

"That's true."

"And a cute librarian he's obviously still got the hots for."

"Shut up, Dez."

"Not on your life."

Beatrice was still thinking about what Dez had said when her best friend dropped her off at her empty house. Would Giovanni leave? What if he really was serious about staying in her life? What did that mean for her? For him? For her relationship with her incredibly loving but clueless boyfriend? Mano had a dive in the morning, so she was alone when she picked up the shoebox she had brought from Houston five years before.

Beatrice opened the lid and pulled out a picture of her and her father. Stephen De Novo's dark brown eyes stared at her. She still missed him so much. It was worse knowing he was out there somewhere, and she just couldn't find him. What did it all mean? Why had he never come? Maybe her father didn't trust Giovanni, but couldn't he trust her? What was the secret he was still running from after fifteen years?

Was Giovanni her best chance at finding him?

Had Lorenzo already found him?

Would Giovanni's son find her again?

She shook her head and replaced the lid on the old box, shoving it back on the bottom of the bookshelf in the living room. She didn't have room in her life for another mystery. She had built a good life. A safe life. She didn't want to be pulled into the chaos of the past.

But when she closed her eyes that night, a dulcet laugh haunted her dreams, and her father's eyes pleaded with her to find him. Beatrice woke with a start to see the moon shining through the narrow window of her bedroom. In her drowsy state, she looked for Giovanni beside her.

Just as it had been for the past five years, he was nowhere to be found.

FIVE

wo weeks.

Giovanni's immortal life was measured in two-week intervals.

After her find at the library, Beatrice had given him two weeks to prove they could be friends again. While he knew he wouldn't be satisfied with only that, he realized she still had doubts about his intentions, so he tried to back off and give her some space. They had been friends first, and he could be a friend again.

For a while.

So they met for coffee and conversation. She came to dinner at the house with Ben acting as an enthusiastic chaperone. Giovanni waited outside the library when she worked late just to walk her to her motorcycle.

And at the end of two weeks, she told him he was allowed to be in her life... as a friend. So he gamely ignored her racing heart every time she saw him and the loaded looks she cast his direction when she thought he wasn't looking and pretended to be Beatrice's friend for a while.

Two weeks turned into four, and they met for coffee a few

times each week after her judo class. She had recently begun practice with a new teacher.

"Pete's so good. I mean, he kind of beats me up—"

Giovanni couldn't contain the low growl, and she shot him a look.

"—but in a good way. Since I've changed to this studio, I've made a lot more progress. And I'm a lot stronger. They focus on conditioning more than my old place."

"You look stronger. And your balance has improved."

She smiled. "I love judo. It's so much fun. Have you ever studied martial arts?" She laughed. "Do you even need to?"

"My physical conditioning with my father was based on the Spartan agoge, so I learned about most military and fighting techniques that way, but Tenzin trained me more on hand-to-hand fighting styles. I picked up whatever she taught me, which was a strange mix of 'do whatever will kill your opponent the fastest,' and her sire's form of wushu, or kung fu, as humans refer to it."

"Cool. Tenzin's the one who recommended I take tai chi when I first moved to California. That's kind of what started me out. I still practice."

"Tai chi?"

"Yeah."

He nodded, letting a smirk cross his lips when he thought about his old friend.

"And Mano studied martial arts in the military. He still does some kick boxing. Sometimes we practice together."

He made no response, choosing to ignore the existence of the boyfriend whenever she brought him up.

Beatrice had told Mano that Giovanni was an old friend from Houston who had recently moved to town and a mutual friend of Carwyn's whom she had worked for in the past. He had a feeling that the boyfriend was clueless about more than his and Beatrice's past relationship.

He leaned toward her in the crowded café. "So you really

haven't told anyone? Not even Dez? About your father or Carwyn or... anything?" He blew on the fragrant coffee he held, heating his breath to heighten the scent since it had cooled.

"No, I didn't tell anyone. What would I say?" She lowered her voice. "Oh, hey, Dez, you know my friend, Carwyn? He's a thousand-year-old Welsh priest who hunts deer and drinks their blood. Oh, and my father is a vampire, too, but I haven't seen him for almost fifteen years so I don't know what he eats. And I was kidnapped by a vampire once, but don't worry, my boss—who I was kind of involved with, but not really—rescued me with his two best friends, one of whom can fly and the other who can tunnel underground like a giant gopher."

He shrugged. "Seems totally believable to me. And we were most definitely involved."

Beatrice rolled her eyes and took a sip of coffee. "Right, and were you going to swoop in and rescue me when they carted me off to the looney bin?"

"I will always swoop in and rescue you, whether from psychotic vampires or the men in white coats."

He caught the small smile she tried to hide and held up his cup of coffee, inhaling deeply.

"Why do you even order it, Gio?"

"I told you, I like the way it smells."

Beatrice shook her head and leaned back in the plush chair. She closed her eyes and he allowed his gaze to caress her face while she was unaware. He'd been dancing around his feelings for well over a month, and it was becoming increasingly harder to keep silent.

He forced himself to remain casual, more interested in regaining her trust than in satisfying himself. Tenzin's admonition to be patient seemed more and more apt every day.

"So," he cleared his throat. "I have a favor to ask, which you are in no way obligated to grant, but I thought I'd ask anyway."

She kept her eyes closed but mumbled, "Does it involve blood donation?"

"Are you offering?"

Beatrice cracked one eye open and grimaced. "No."

"Then how about taking Ben to the doctor?"

Her head shot up. "Why? Is he okay?"

"Nothing to worry about that I know of. He just needs a regular doctor. And you wouldn't even have to go in with him— I'm sure he'd be mortified if you did—just drive him. He needs a checkup and none of the pediatricians in the area have evening hours. I can write a note as his guardian, of course."

She thought for a moment before she nodded. "I can do that. Let me get my schedule for next week and I'll see what days would be best."

"Thank you. I appreciate it."

"Oh! Next week is Thanksgiving. That might not be the best week to go."

He nodded. "You are the one doing the favor, so you let me know what day will work for you. I'll make the appointment from there. And thank you again."

She shrugged. "I'm refusing to work for you, so it's the least I can do."

"I really wish you'd reconsider your—"

"I'm sure you would," she interrupted, "but I'm very happy at the Huntington."

He cocked an eyebrow. "Translating and researching for scholars with less intelligence than you? Taking orders from someone you could run circles around intellectually? It must be so stimulating."

"Don't start, or I'll leave."

He exhaled and let his head fall back into the armchair. "Fine, I'll refrain from stating the obvious."

"Just... " she sighed. "It's only been a month. Give me time to have you back in my life like this. Give me some time to make room for you on my terms."

Why don't you get rid of the excess boyfriend? That should leave exactly the right amount of room. He thought it but bit his tongue and smiled. "Of course."

"So what are you and Ben doing for Thanksgiving? Going back to Houston?"

"No, no, we're going back to Texas for Christmas, but I thought we'd stay around here for a quiet meal."

Her mouth dropped open exactly how he had imagined the granddaughter of Isadora De Novo's would. "What? You're going to feed the child spaghetti for Thanksgiving dinner?"

Giovanni shrugged. "Well, he's never celebrated it properly anyway. And I thought I'd try to make that macaroni and cheese he likes. I think I'd be able to manage that. We didn't do much last year, either." He frowned. "Of course, I think we were still fighting about stealing from my wallet last year."

"You're bringing him over to my place," she stated. "The boy's never even had a turkey dinner? What are you thinking, Gio?"

I'm thinking I wrangled exactly the invitation to your house I've been looking for. "Beatrice, you really don't—"

"Are you kidding me? Mac and cheese? You can barely manage spaghetti from a jar. And my grandmother would die if she heard I let you feed that kid junk food on Thanksgiving. Come over to my house. Sunset's around five now, I'll make dinner for six-thirty. Bring some wine."

He smothered his satisfied smile. "Thank you. I'm sure Benjamin will appreciate the decent meal. As will I."

She shook her head and muttered under her breath. "Macaroni and cheese... "

T he following Thursday, he was trying to convince Ben that a collared shirt would not inflict bodily injury.

"She wears Docs! She'd like my CBGB's shirt way better. It's vintage. Vintage is better than a tux to a Doc Marten girl."

"It most certainly is not, Benjamin. And be grateful I'm not making you wear a tie."

"Oh man, I'm not wearing a tie. No way!"

Giovanni tucked in a dark green button down shirt and fastened the buttons at his wrists. "Trust me, women always appreciate a well-dressed man."

The boy looked at him suspiciously as he pulled on his hated dress shoes. "I don't know. She's not your girlfriend yet."

"Well, there's another lesson. Things and people of value are worth waiting for."

"If you say so."

"I know so."

"Hey, Gio?"

"Yes?"

Ben's face was free of its usual sarcasm when Giovanni looked at him. "I get why you love her so much. She's pretty great."

He smiled at the perceptive boy. "I have only the finest taste in people."

Ben looked embarrassed but quickly shot back, "Dude, I don't want to know about your blood-drinking habits."

Giovanni snorted and looked in the mirror before he walked over to the boy and mussed his hair. "Comb this mess. It's almost time to go."

They drove to Beatrice's small house, Ben carrying on a constant chatter in the old Mustang that had finally arrived from Houston, and Giovanni trying to prepare himself to curb his natural instincts so he could meet Beatrice's boyfriend without killing or maiming him.

They were met at the door by a blond woman Giovanni assumed was Beatrice's best friend, Desiree Riley.

"You must be Desiree." He held out his hand politely and nudged Ben to do the same. "It's a pleasure to meet you. I've heard a lot about you."

She smiled. "It's Dez. You must be Gio. I can almost promise I've heard more about you." She cocked her head and looked at Ben. "Or is this Gio? You're not that tall yet, but you've got the dark and handsome part down."

Ben grinned, winking at Dez and holding his arm out for her to take. She giggled and took it as they walked inside. "Well, Dez, my name's Ben, I'm the smarter and more charming of the Vecchio men..."

Giovanni shook his head as he followed them into the small 1920s era Spanish bungalow. He crossed the small living room and paused when he saw a large man bending over Beatrice's shoulder as she stood in front of the stove.

There were few times in his five hundred years that Giovanni had truly been grateful for the vicious training of his sire, Niccolo Andros. The fifteen years he'd spent under the vampire's thumb had been brutal and draining, both mentally and physically.

But as he watched former Navy diver, Mano Akana, put his hands on Beatrice's waist and pull her close, he knew he'd relive every one of those torturous training sessions if it allowed him to not kill the oblivious man holding onto his woman.

That level of violence would, no doubt, put most of the guests off their dinner.

He quieted the growl that wanted to escape his throat and cut his eyes toward Matt Kirby, his associate who had been living next to Beatrice on his orders for more than three years. Matt gave him a small nod and returned his attention to Dez and Ben. Ben was busy introducing himself.

"Gio!" Beatrice called, as she extricated herself from the grasp of the over-muscled behemoth who held her. She walked into the living room and gave Ben a quick hug before she walked to Giovanni.

She hesitated a moment but leaned forward and embraced him. He pushed his amnis toward her and felt the shiver travel down her back. Glancing past her, he noticed the boyfriend watching them intently and knew, without a doubt, that Beatrice was the only one fooling herself that they were nothing more than friends.

"Happy Thanksgiving, tesoro," he said quietly before he approached Mano in the kitchen. He held out his hand and tried not to imagine how many ways he could kill the man.

"Giovanni Vecchio. You must be Mano."

The man's hair may have fallen to his shoulders, but the eyes that examined him revealed his military background more than any uniform.

"Nice to meet you. You're a friend of Carwyn's, right? And B's old boss?"

"I'm both. And a friend as well. She's a remarkable woman. You're very lucky." To not be dead right now.

"Oh, I know I am," Mano murmured, a look of challenge in his eyes. "And this is your nephew?"

"Benjamin, yes. Ben, come introduce yourself to Beatrice's friend."

Mano cut his eyes toward Giovanni and smirked. Both men nodded toward the other, as if a challenge had been accepted, before Ben came over to introduce himself and the tension was cut.

The dinner was far better than anything he could have produced, and Giovanni ate more than he usually did. He'd been buying donated blood in Los Angeles and feeding on that unless the opportunity to feed from a criminal presented itself—which it did with fair regularity. In the past five years, he'd lost his appetite for random women and the blood they could offer him, so he'd been making do. He knew he was not at full strength, and it bothered him.

Giovanni wished that he hated the boyfriend but realized under other circumstances, he would probably like the man. No matter. After observing Beatrice and Mano throughout the evening, he had no qualms about doing everything in his power to separate them.

She was trying to convince herself she was in love with him. She most likely did love the human in some fashion, but she did not look at Mano the way she had once looked at him. Nor did she react to the man with the same physical intensity she did to Giovanni.

Mano, however, was very obviously in love with Beatrice. He could hardly blame the man, but his determination to make Beatrice his own suffered no setback at the thought of the human's impending disappointment.

"Giovanni? What are you working on right now? Are you settling in L.A. permanently?" Dez asked from across the table. He smiled at the blond woman, noticing the longing look Matt Kirby threw toward her every time she opened her mouth.

"I am for now," he answered. "It's a good place for research, and I like my house in Pasadena."

"It's totally awesome, and I have my own basketball court," Ben added.

"You should have a party!" Dez said.

Matt chuckled. "Gio's not really one for entertaining." His eyes widened and he added, "At least, you don't seem like the type to me."

Giovanni clenched his jaw and glanced at Matt's apologetic face before he looked toward Beatrice, who was glaring at him.

"Hey, Gio," she asked, "can you help me with something in the kitchen?"

He excused himself from the table, glancing at Mano's

perturbed face as he left. He walked into the kitchen and leaned against the counter.

"Matt?" she whispered.

He shrugged. "I've worked with him on and off for a number of years. He's very trustworthy."

"But he's been watching me? This whole time?"

"He's not a stalker, Beatrice. He's security, and he's very good. He likes you, as well, if you're curious. And I'm fairly certain he's romantically interested in your friend."

"This whole time?"

"I did what I needed to keep you safe. I'm not going to apologize for it."

She crossed her arms and glanced toward the dining room. "Well, did he 'save' me from anything? In all these years?"

He crossed his arms and mirrored her. "As a matter of fact, no."

"Then I think I deserve an apology."

"No. Absolutely not."

"Why not?" She was fuming. "Apparently he was unnecessary."

Giovanni stepped close to her, towering over her as she glared at him. "An apology would imply that I am regretful or sorry in some way, and I make no apologies for doing everything in my power to protect you."

He didn't expect the flash of tears in her eyes. "You wanted me protected? It was that important? Then why wasn't it you?" she hissed before she stormed toward the hall bathroom. Mano entered the kitchen a few minutes later wearing a smug look. Giovanni felt a small burst of flame rise near his hand, so he crossed his arms again and pulled his temper back.

"You managed to piss her off pretty well, Giovanni."

"Oh," he muttered. "That's nothing new. I've been doing that for years."

"Not for the past five, you haven't," Mano muttered. "That's how long it's been, right? That's how long she's been following your ghost to some old house in Chile?"

Giovanni smiled. "Did she tell you that?" He saw Mano deflate a bit. "No, I didn't think so. She's very good at keeping secrets, isn't she?"

"She's private."

"Call it what you will." Giovanni leaned back against the counter.

"Well, you don't know her anymore. Not like I do."

Giovanni laughed. "Oh really? And why do you say that?"

"Because you weren't here, asshole. Were you at her party when she bought this house? We'd only been dating a few weeks, but I made being there a priority. How about when she got her job at the Huntington? She was so proud of herself. Or maybe when her grandmother had the scare with her heart a couple years ago? Miss out on that, too?"

He just stared in silence when Mano stepped closer in the small room.

"How about when her scum bag of a mother showed up last year and tried to get money from her? Did you know about that?" he asked. "Of course not, because you weren't here. Know who was? Me. I was here. And I'm not going anywhere."

He smiled at the tall man who knew so little. "You think you know her fairly well, don't you?"

"I do know her. And I love her."

"I'm sure you do. But you don't know her like I do." Giovanni shrugged. "It's not your fault. She hasn't allowed you to know her that well, has she?"

"You're so damn arrogant."

"I am, but am I wrong?" he asked and glanced toward the dining room, noting that Ben seemed to be entertaining Matt and Dez with some amusing story. "I know a lot about you, Mano. Can you say the same about me?"

"What does that even—"

"She's very protective of the ones she loves. So who is she protecting with her secrets? You?" Giovanni stepped closer and let his swirling green eyes bore into Mano's. "Or is she protecting me?"

Mano glared at him before he retreated, turning to walk down the hall in search of Beatrice. Giovanni could hear him knocking on the bathroom door when he walked back into the dining room.

"Benjamin, it's time for us to go."

T wo weeks.

She refused his calls for two weeks, until finally, Giovanni sat outside the library, waiting for her on the steps. When she walked through the glass doors and spotted him, she didn't stop, so he followed her.

"Beatrice."

She kept walking past the walkway to the parking lot and toward a small grove of isolated oak trees. She did not look back. For the first time since he'd come back into her life, Giovanni felt a hint of panic.

"I want to talk to you," he called as she paced through the trees.

She whirled around and he almost ran into her. "Yeah, I think that's a good idea, Gio. Let's talk."

"Fine. I think you need to tell Dez and Mano the truth about me. About everything."

She backed away from him and her mouth gaped open. "What?"

"You need to tell them." He cocked an eyebrow at her. "You say you love them and you want them to be a part of your life, so why don't you trust them?"

She might tell Dez... but he was betting she wouldn't tell Mano.

Beatrice only blinked at him. "I don't—you want me to tell them?"

"Do you love them?" She didn't answer, so he shrugged. "It's up to you, but you can't continue to live with these secrets. It's going to make you sick. It's already making you angry."

"No." She strode toward him, pointing a finger at his chest. "You made me angry. When you told Mano about us. It's none of his business."

"Why were you hiding it?"

"To protect you!"

"I didn't ask you to do that. I didn't ask you to protect me." He stepped closer and they circled each other under the oak trees.

"And I didn't ask you to protect me, but you did. Why the hell did you hire someone to live next to me all these years?" Her face was red and furious, but he could see the tears filling her eyes. "What was the point? Did he tell you when guys stayed over? Did he tell you when I flirted with him myself?"

His fists clenched, but he forced himself to remain calm. "It didn't matter, I don't care about that. I care about you." He approached cautiously, as if walking too quickly might scare her off. "You deserved a life. A normal life without me, so you knew—"

"I didn't want a life without you!" she exploded, tears finally falling down her face. "Don't you get that? Are you that dense? Don't you realize I was in love with you?"

His heart ached. "Beatrice—"

"Five hundred years and you couldn't tell?"

He walked toward her, desperate to take her in his arms, but she stepped back, dashing the tears from her eyes. "Tesoro—"

"Why didn't you come?" she sobbed. "Why? I waited for years! I never loved a man the way I loved you. I've never loved anyone that way. I never wanted anyone that way."

For the first time in his immortal life, he felt as if his heart could bleed from another's pain. Giovanni could only whisper, "I know."

He stepped within arm's distance and put a single hand on her cheek, which was flushed and wet with tears. In that moment, Beatrice didn't look like a confident woman of twenty-eight; she looked like the girl he had forced himself to leave.

"So why, Gio? If you knew, why? Don't you realize I would have done anything for you? I would have run away with you."

"Beatrice—"

"Didn't you know?" She slapped his hand away, and her voice rose. "I would have left my family behind. I would have begged Carwyn to turn me so I could stay with you forever! Why?"

"That's why!" he yelled, grabbing onto her shoulders. "Don't you see, Beatrice? That's why I couldn't come to you!"

Giovanni dragged her to his chest, and their mouths crashed together. He wrapped his arms around her, his fingers gripping her back. He breathed her in, desperate to get closer, to take away the ache of her loss.

After a few moments, he backed away so she could draw breath, but his hands reached up to frame her face.

"Don't you see?" he pleaded. "I couldn't have denied you anything. I would have given you anything you wanted! You might have hated me in a hundred years, but if you had asked me, I would have done it." He leaned down and kissed along her eyelids, threading his hands through her hair as he pulled her into a more gentle kiss.

"Don't you realize how I adore you?" he whispered against her mouth. "But I couldn't steal the life of a girl when I wanted a woman's love. I wanted you to have a choice, not an infatuation."

"So damn arrogant," she whispered, clutching the collar of his shirt.

"I know," he said, as his mouth brushed over her skin, touching the face that had haunted his waking dreams.

"I loved you. It wasn't an infatuation."

He pressed his cheek to hers and whispered in her ear. "Then I will earn the woman's love, if I have lost the girl's."

Giovanni drew her into another kiss, and her arms reached around his waist as she kissed him back. He didn't know how long they embraced in the darkness, but he groaned when he felt Beatrice reach up to his chest and slowly push him back.

"I can't do this. It's not right."

"Yes, it is right. You know it is."

She shook her head. "What do you want from me, Gio?"

He blinked in surprise. "Isn't it obvious?"

"Five years ago, I would have said yes. Not now."

He closed his eyes and sighed. "Fine, let me make it clear." He reached up to hold her face between his hands and look into her eyes. "I love you, Beatrice De Novo. I fell in love with the girl I met six years ago, and I love the woman in front of me even more."

"Gio—"

"So you make the decision, tesoro mio." He murmured and his thumbs stroked the soft swell of her cheeks. "It's your choice. I want eternity with you, and I'm not leaving again." He gave her a sad smile. "You can't make me."

A storm raged in her eyes. Giovanni wanted to kiss her again, but he knew it wasn't welcome. Her tentative hand reached up and stroked his cheek; he leaned into it, a low hum of satisfaction rumbling from his chest, until they were interrupted by the ringing of her mobile phone.

"Who... " She pulled away and reached into her backpack. Giovanni tensed when he heard the panicked voice on the other end, even before she put it to her ear.

"Danny? What—" she frowned. "Slow down, what's going on? A what?" The color drained from her face. "What kind of accident?"

SIX

Beatrice didn't remember much about the ride to the hospital in Long Beach except for the familiar smell of leather and smoke that filled Giovanni's old Mustang. She remembered the first night she'd ridden in it, the night she had learned about vampires and blue fire and men who lived forever.

Men who wouldn't be in the hospital after a freak diving accident.

"It was the weirdest thing," Danny said after he'd calmed down. "I've never seen anything like it. It looked like he was being attacked down there, but there was nothing around him. Then, it was like his mask was just sucked off of his face like the water was pulling on it."

"I'm heading over there right now. What did the doctors say?"

"I got him to the surface and got him resuscitated. Thank God we weren't that far from the marina. They're going to keep him overnight and release him in the morning if everything looks okay."

Giovanni wouldn't let her ride her bike to the hospital, much as he had refused to let her drive home the night six years before. She had never felt more confused in her life.

"Danny said it looked like the water was pulling on him."

"Pulling on him?"

She nodded. "Like he was being attacked, but there was nothing around."

She glanced over, and his face was grim. They drove in silence for a few more minutes.

"It's him, isn't it? It's Lorenzo. He's back."

He frowned. "The last time I had information on Lorenzo was a year ago; he was lurking around Northern Africa. None of my contacts have reported any movement from him." He shook his head. "He's very recognizable. It's more likely an associate of some sort, or someone he hired."

Someone Lorenzo hired to kill a man she loved. A combination of guilt and fury began to churn in her gut.

"Did I ever tell you Mano was a diver in the Navy?" she said. "He's really good. Danny says Mano's the best diver he's ever worked with, and Danny was a Master Diver before he retired."

"Beatrice—"

"Two and a half years we've been together," she whispered, "and he's never had an accident. I used to worry so much about him, especially at night, I worried… but nothing ever happened. Everything was fine. Mano was always so careful."

I did this, her mind kept repeating. This is my fault. She suddenly had more sympathy for her missing father and the complicated mess he'd inadvertently drawn her into years before.

Giovanni started to say something but paused and reached over to squeeze her limp hand. "I'll find out who it was."

"Who controls L.A.?" she asked in a whisper.

She could see his face harden in the passing streetlights.

"Are you sure you want to know? Sure you want back into this world? Into my world?"

"Do I have a choice?"

"Yes," he hissed. "You have a choice! That's what all of this was about, giving you a choice."

Beatrice shrugged, fighting back the tears in her eyes. She didn't feel like there was a choice. She felt like she'd been hiding her head in the sand and others would be the ones to pay the price. She didn't know what to do, and all she could think about was seeing Mano.

She forced Giovanni to go home to Ben after he dropped her off at the emergency room. Beatrice walked in and found Danny in the lobby, waiting to take her upstairs.

When she walked in, Mano was sleeping, and the quiet words of his doctor assured her that a week of rest and a break from diving were the only things needed for him to make a full recovery. Danny finally left them, and she curled up in the bed, squeezing herself into his side and laying her head on his chest as she listened to the steady beat of his heart.

Beatrice spent hours watching Mano sleep, seeing his steady chest rise and fall and listening to the faint murmurs as he dreamed. He had always looked so peaceful when he slept, his huge body relaxed and still in marked contrast to his waking vitality.

She called in to work and took some of her vacation time to be with him, though she knew he didn't really need her there the whole time.

"Hey, Mano, what do you want for lunch?"

"How about a break from hovering?"

She snickered and looked over at him. "I'm serious. There's some soup left, or I could make you a—"

"I'm serious, too." He gave her a slight frown. "Why are you being like this? You're not a hoverer."

"You scared me." She frowned. "That's all. You've never had an accident and—"

"Accidents happen, baby. It was a weird one, but... "

"What?"

He tried to smile but could only shrug. "You don't seem like yourself lately."

"Don't be silly. I'm fine. You're the one who needs—"

"What's going on?"

Beatrice walked over and straddled his lap, pulling his arms around her. She put her ear to his chest, listening to his heartbeat as his strong arms held her. What could she say?

You know my friends Carwyn and Gio? They're vampires who drink blood and manipulate elements. Oh, and your accident was probably caused by a bad vampire who once kidnapped me because he's trying to get to my father... who's a vampire, too. But don't worry, the good vampires rescued me. Then I stole a whole bunch of money from the bad guy, which is why he's now trying to kill you.

And Gio says he's in love with me.

"Nothing's going on. I told you, you just gave me a scare. It's fine. We're fine. Nothing is going on."

She sat up and saw a bitter smile curling his lips. "You're a bad liar, you know that?"

Beatrice wanted to protest, to defend herself, but she couldn't think of anything that wouldn't be another lie, so she simply leaned forward, holding him closer and listening to the steady beat of his heart. Mano gently stroked her dark hair, and she felt his chest rise as he sighed.

"Lately, baby, I feel like being with you is like watching the tide go out."

"What?" She cleared her throat. "What are you talking about?"

"You don't notice the ebb at first, you're still listening to those waves go back and forth. They keep coming in, but... never quite as high as the last one."

"Mano—"

"And you know there's nothing you can do." He kept running his hands through her hair in long, soothing strokes. "You could try to hold on, to chase the waves, but the water's still going to slip away."

Beatrice bit her lip and felt tears come to her eyes as a portion of her heart began to crumble. "I don't... I don't—"

"I'd say it was this guy, but I think the tide started going out months ago. Otherwise, we'd be living together now, you know?" She heard him choke a little. "And I wouldn't be worried about your answer when I asked you to marry me."

She shook her head, still wishing she could deny the words coming out of his mouth as she turned her face and stained his shirt with her tears. Mano placed a warm hand on her cheek.

"I feel like you're on this wave. And you're slipping away from me a little more every day. Slipping away somewhere you don't want me to go. Someplace I just—I can't quite see." He leaned down and whispered in her ear. "I want to catch you, but I don't think you want to be caught."

Beatrice cried, and her mind screamed, 'No,' but she couldn't form the words.

"And I've been chasing the waves, thinking if I could just catch you, I could hold you back, and maybe you'd finally love me the way I love you."

She curled her fingers in his shirt. "I do love you, Mano," she whispered, wishing desperately that it was enough.

"But not—not the way you love him." He cleared his throat. "I wish it wasn't the truth, but it is."

He tilted her chin up and wiped her cheeks with the sleeve of his shirt, but Beatrice couldn't stop crying.

"Mano," she choked out, reaching up to touch his face with shaking hands. He stared at her with sad eyes.

"There's this huge thing you two hold between each other. I don't think you even realize how much I can see it. It's like all the dark places in you, the ones you never let me into, are open to him. And I'd chase away the dark for you—I've been trying for years— but I don't think you want me to."

He cupped her cheeks with his warm, callused hands and pulled her tear stained face to his so he could lay a soft kiss on her mouth.

"I love you so much," Beatrice said as her tears rolled into his hands.

"But it's not enough, is it?"

She met his dark eyes and whispered in surrender, "No."

His face fell in pain, and his grip tightened on her jaw for only a second before his hands went lax and his arms fell to the side.

"You need to go now, B."

She choked on her tears but managed to nod as she climbed off his lap. Beatrice silently gathered the few things she kept at Mano's apartment and walked back to him. She leaned down to kiss his cheek but he turned away from her.

"Please don't."

"Okay," she whispered. "Okay."

She was shaking by the time she made it to the door, and she heard his low voice for the last time. "Don't disappear completely. I want to know you're okay."

"Bye, Mano," Beatrice whispered before she opened the door, stumbling down the stairs as the tears ran down her face and the sun blinded her. She walked to the shade of the small carport and pulled out her phone to dial with trembling hands.

"Dez? Can you come get me?" She paused to wipe her eyes with her sleeve. "I think I need to stay with you for a while."

Beatrice stayed in Dez's guest room for three nights, ignoring the calls Giovanni made to her mobile phone and crying more than she had since her father died. Giovanni came to Dez's door every night, but she always sent him away.

She cried for days.

She cried for the guilt of not being able to love Mano the way he deserved. She cried for the lies she had told him and herself for so many years. And she cried because she already missed him.

She didn't allow herself to think about her argument with Giovanni the night of the "accident" or the stunning emotional revelations he had made. It was too much, and her heart, along with her head, felt like it would burst.

By the end of the week, she was utterly and completely spent by tears and the weight of decisions that hung over her. Dez couldn't comfort her, and she refused to call her grandmother while she was such a mess.

The one thing that kept echoing in her mind was the admonition Giovanni had given her the night they'd kissed.

"You need to tell them. You say you love them and you want them to be a part of your life, so why don't you trust them?"

She'd already killed her relationship with Mano with the weight of her secrets and the walls she had built, so she called Dez into the pale blue room where she was lying on the bed, determined not to lose another person she loved.

"Dez, I need to talk to you."

B eatrice told her everything.

She told her about murdered fathers and missing books. About mysterious men with blue fire and secrets. About blood and betrayal. Sacrifice and rescue. She told her best friend everything except Giovanni's secrets. Beatrice even called Matt to confirm the story, so Dez didn't feel like she had to call the men in white coats. Her friend was sitting on the bed with a dazed expression, looking like she'd just fallen down a very long rabbit hole.

"Was I wrong to tell you?"

Dez frowned. "I'm not quite sure at this point."

She nodded. "If you want, he can erase it all. Gio can, I mean. If you don't want to know. If it's too much."

"Did he offer that?" Dez looked worried. "Does he know you told me?"

"He told me I should tell the people I love."

Dez thought for a moment.

"Did you tell Mano? Is that why you broke up?"

"No." She shook her head. "I didn't tell Mano."

"Oh... okay," Dez stuttered. "Just give me a few minutes here."

"Okay."

They sat in silence for a few more minutes.

"B?"

"Yeah?"

"Why did Giovanni come back? Is it this Lorenzo guy? Is he back now?"

She took a deep breath. "He says he came back for me. He said... "

"What?"

"That he loves me. That he wants me to be with him."

"You mean like... "

"Yeah, I think so."

Dez paused again. "So, he wants you to... "

"It sounds like it."

"Because he loves you?"

Beatrice shrugged. "I guess so."

"But you don't believe him."

She shook her head. "I don't know what to believe anymore. I'm really... "

"What?"

"Confused," Beatrice sighed.

"Yeah, there's a lot of that going around."

"I'm so sorry."

Dez frowned at her. "Why?"

"I should have told you before. I shouldn't have lied about so much of my past."

"Oh, sweetie," Dez pulled her into a hug. "I totally understand why."

"And now that I told you, I feel like I'm putting you in danger."

Dez pulled away and a familiar, stubborn expression settled over her face. "That is not something that you should be worried about. If that's the cost of being your friend… "

"What?"

Dez reached over and enveloped her in another hug.

"Totally worth it."

She sniffed as the tears started again. "Thanks, Dezi. I love you. I don't know what I'd do if I lost you."

"I know. I'm pretty awesome."

Beatrice snorted, then they both laughed. Beatrice began to slump as the days of emotional exhaustion started to catch up with her. Dez, however, was looking surprisingly perky.

"So, Matt knows about all this stuff?"

Beatrice called her next-door neighbor and asked him to drive her to the Huntington to get her motorcycle so she could go home for the first time in a week.

"Do you think she'll be okay?" she asked Matt as he drove her back to Pasadena.

"She'll be fine," he said with a smile. "Dez is tougher than she looks. And really smart. Don't you remember that crazy feeling you had when you first found out?" He shrugged. "She'll manage."

"How long have you known Gio?"

"About ten years. About vampires, longer. My father did some work for him back in the day, and Gio... well, he trusts our family, I guess."

"What do you actually do?" she asked with a frown. "You can't be a realtor."

He chuckled and reached a hand across the front seat. "Matt Kirby, private investigator. Nice to meet you, Beatrice De Novo."

She shook her head and slapped at his hand. He laughed and faced forward again, watching for the exit as they neared South Pasadena. Beatrice noticed that he was unusually chipper.

"You're going to ask Dez out, aren't you?"

"Yep," he said with a grin.

"Good. Why did you wait so long?"

He shrugged. "Too many secrets. You think I could keep all that from her and have a chance?"

She sighed and shook her head. "Probably not, Matt. Good luck."

"You too," he said with a smile.

Beatrice saw the Mustang parked at the curb and Giovanni sitting in the dim light of the porch when she arrived. He looked at her, no doubt noticing the exhaustion that lined her face and her eyes, which felt like they had been swollen with tears for days on end.

She was irritated he was there, and she didn't know any of the answers he was probably looking for. She just wanted to be alone.

"Hi," he said.

"Hi."

"Kirby called me."

"Good for him." She attempted to walk past him as she dug out her keys. He shot up and tried to block her path to the front door.

"Beatrice—"

"Nothing you say," she bit out, "is going to make me feel better right now. Nothing." She took a deep breath. "I don't want to talk to you or see you for a while, so please leave me alone."

"I have information about who attacked Mano."

She closed her eyes and pressed the heel of her hand into her forehead to try to still the headache that began pounding.

"Just... give me a few days," she whispered. "I need a few days, Gio."

He tried to touch her shoulder, but she pushed him away.

"I understand," he murmured.

"No, you really, really don't."

He paused before speaking. "I'll put them off for a few days. Call me when you're ready to talk."

Beatrice still had her eyes closed when she heard him walk past her, down the porch, and toward his car. She didn't open them until she heard the Mustang pull away. Then she opened the door and retreated to her silent house.

SEVEN

"Anything else?"

"I got a call from Ernesto's assistant today wondering whether you were going to bring B by this week."

Giovanni frowned and tugged on his hair. It still wasn't as long as when he first met Beatrice, but it had grown around four inches from the time he'd singed it off when Lorenzo had taken her.

"When does he need to know?"

"Kelli said he was going down to Mexico for some business next week so he was hoping to meet with you both tomorrow evening, if possible."

He nodded. "Let me ask her tonight. She and Benjamin are due back soon."

Matt smiled. "Spending time with the kid, huh?"

Giovanni grumbled, "He's been her preferred company for the last couple of weeks."

"Well... " The private detective shifted in his seat, looking slightly nervous. "Mano... he was a good guy. I mean, I know it's none of my business and all—"

"Do you consider yourself her friend, Kirby?"

Matt nodded. "I do."

"Then it's your business," Giovanni said, giving the tacit approval the man seemed to need. "And I'm not going to kill you for liking Beatrice's ex."

"Good to know," he said with a tight smile.

"How is the lovely Desiree? Beatrice said you two are seeing each other."

Matt chuckled. "Well, after the initial shock, she's fairly fascinated by all of it, to be honest. I think being part of the supernatural world gave me a leg up dating her."

Giovanni smiled before he burst into laughter. "Well, you've certainly taken enough risks over the years, I'm glad it finally paid off for you. Thank God for curious women."

Matt's head cocked when he heard the hum of the Mustang coming up the drive. "I should go."

"I'll call you about the meeting with Alvarez later tonight."

"Let me know. I'm sure he won't mind putting it off for the girl, with their connection, but it's getting close to Christmas and I know you're leaving for Texas... "

"No, I understand the urgency."

"And I'm not sure how long you want that guy to sit in the dry room, either."

"Oh," Giovanni murmured. "The longer the better as far as that goes. As long as he's conscious, he'll suit my purposes."

Matt nodded. "Just give me a call when you have a date. If it's not office hours for you, I'll take care of arranging the appointment."

"Thank you, Kirby. Your assistance, as always, has been excellent."

"No problem at all." He nodded toward the vampire, who showed him to the door.

"And give your father and mother my best."

"Of course. Have a nice night."

Giovanni closed the door and walked back to the kitchen,

curious why he hadn't heard the stomping and shouting that normally followed Ben's return to the house. When the basketball began to bounce, he had his answer. He heated a glass of bagged blood and sat down at the counter to drink. Soon, Ben and Beatrice's quiet conversation drifted to his ears.

"—doesn't matter if you want to go. It's part of life. Just get it over with."

"But I hear really bad stuff about going to the dentist, and I've never been. My teeth are probably super bad, and he'll have to pull them all or something."

He could hear Beatrice laugh. "You're not going to get all your teeth pulled. I'll make the appointment with my dentist. She's really cool, and I'm sure she can fit you in next week."

"Hey, did you ask Gio if we could go to the blue alien movie?"

"Not yet." He could barely hear her mutter.

"Oh, come on, B! Will you guys stop fighting already? You could at least start talking to each other again."

He was tempted to go out and yank Ben's ear for talking to Beatrice that way, but he was too curious what she would say in response.

"Gee, Ben, I'm so sorry my disagreement with your uncle is cutting into your precious movie attendance. I'll see what I can do."

"It's not that, and you know it." Giovanni heard the basketball bounce a few more times and someone threw it toward the basket. "You guys are both just... "

"What?" she asked the question on the tip of his own tongue as he listened in.

"You're sad. Both of you. It sucks."

"Well," he heard her start, "sometimes shitty things just happen, Ben, and it takes time to work through them. It's not like I like being mad at him. Besides—" Her voice dropped. "—I'm mostly mad at myself."

His heart ached for her, and he had to fight the urge to rush out and embrace her. Giovanni knew his comfort was still unwelcome.

"Well, figure it out by Christmas, okay? This is my first huge Christmas with lots of grown-ups giving me stuff, and I don't want you two spoiling it."

Giovanni almost snorted blood through his nose, and he grabbed a napkin from the holder on the counter. Luckily, he heard the welcome sound of Beatrice's laughter, as well.

"I'll keep that in mind."

"You know he's listening to us in the kitchen right now, don't you? You should go say hi and stay for dinner. Actually, you should cook because you're way better at it than Gio is. Or we could order pizza! I know where he keeps his wallet."

Giovanni rolled his eyes and sent a small prayer toward heaven. Carwyn would be pleased, he thought, he hadn't prayed this much since Caspar started driving. Just as his eyes opened, he heard the kitchen door open and Beatrice walked into the house. He took a deep breath, enjoying the scent of her, fresh from the brisk air outside.

"Hi," she said.

"Hello."

"Apparently I'm a better cook than you are."

"I have a hard time imagining that's a surprise," he said with a smile.

He saw her glance at his glass. "Bagged blood?"

Giovanni shrugged. "Unless you're offering... "

Her eyes darted around the kitchen and she walked to the refrigerator to open it. "Uh, no. Not tonight. And there are tons of clubs in Los Angeles, why don't you just—"

"No thanks," he said. "Haven't gone that route in years."

Beatrice turned to look at him. "What? Years?"

He glanced meaningfully at her neck and sipped his glass. "Yes, years."

She turned back to the refrigerator and paused before she

started pulling out what looked like the ingredients for a salad, or maybe tacos, which he knew Ben loved.

She worked quietly as Ben continued playing outside and Giovanni pretended to read a book. He heard her start to say something a number of times, but she stopped herself and continued working.

"Ben's doctor said he's healthy as a horse, by the way."

He nodded. "I assumed he was. I had him checked out in New York and his scent hasn't changed significantly."

"So if a person is sick or something, they smell different?"

He nodded. "Yes, human scent changes quite significantly for all sorts of reasons. Health, hormones, even age ... "

She laughed. "I just had the realization that you have to smell adolescent boy on a daily basis."

Giovanni winced before he grinned. "You have no idea."

She shook her head, still laughing, and he suddenly realized they were smiling at each other for the first time in weeks. She must have realized it at the same time, and a sad smile replaced her laugh.

"So, your sense of smell is a little scary, to be honest. I always wonder if I'm wearing enough deodorant around you and Carwyn."

"I wouldn't worry. You usually smell lovely. Especially when you first wake up," he added quietly.

He smiled when he saw her pause, but she didn't get angry.

"You always smell the same to me," she said.

He cocked his head. "How? What do I smell like to you?"

She didn't look at him but turned on the burner to heat a pan on the stove. "Kind of like smoke. Wood smoke and whiskey."

"I remember you wrote that in the journal. About the smoke."

She looked up at him. "Did you read that? All of it?"

"Of course."

"Even the parts when I cussed at you? I wasn't very nice."

He shrugged. "Did you read my journals? Most of them are far harsher than yours."

"I haven't read all of them yet," she said as she put the ground beef on to cook. "You live in a rough world, you know?"

He folded his hands under his chin and put down the book he was pretending to read. "I don't want you to have any illusions, Beatrice. My world, and the world your father lives in, can be very brutal."

"I'm getting that impression."

"Good."

She glared at him. "Don't use the professor-voice with me, Gio. I'm not a kid anymore."

He allowed his eyes to run over her slim cut black jeans and the tight black t-shirt that hugged her breasts. It was her normal uniform on her days off and suited her to the ground. "No, you most certainly are not," he muttered. "I don't want to lie about anything to you, Beatrice. It doesn't do either of us any favors in the long run."

"The long run, huh?"

"That's what I'm talking about."

She paused to look at him, and he didn't flinch from her steady gaze.

"Yeah, we'll see."

Giovanni was annoyed by her dismissal, but he forced himself to remain calm. "Speaking of immortal matters, there is a certain vampire in town that you should meet."

The meat sizzled in the pan as she added the onions and chiles. "Who?"

"You asked who ran Los Angeles, but the answer is somewhat complicated. As a matter of fact, the reason I never worried much about you living here—"

"Hiring someone to move next door to me isn't worrying much?"

"—is because of who controls the city." He ignored her question and continued. "Tell me about your grandmother's family."

"What?" she frowned. "The Alvarezes? Why? They're from Mexico. Guadalajara. I've never even been there, but I hear it's pretty. I think Grandma has one cousin she keeps in contact with."

"Your grandmother is descended from a very old and very wealthy Spanish family that was once large land owners in Alta California."

"Okay," she said slowly as she alternated between stirring the meat for the tacos and chopping tomatoes.

"He won't eat those," he said, looking at the cutting board.

"He will if he wants me to feed him."

Giovanni grinned and continued talking. "Don Ernesto Alvarez was a very wealthy man, and he had a very large family. A tradition he continued even after he was turned into a vampire in the late 1700s."

She had looked up as soon as he said the name 'Alvarez.'

"Gio, are you telling me I'm related to another vampire?"

He smiled. "Well, if it makes you feel any better, probably ten percent of California and Northern Mexico is related to him in some way. It was a very large family."

She shook her head and continued preparing dinner. "So what? This Don Ernesto is my great-great-a whole bunch of times-great-grandfather?"

"Yes, he is. And you're a direct descendant, which is rare and brings out his sentimental side."

"And he runs the city of Los Angeles?"

"And most of the surrounding areas, yes. Most of the area between here and the Mexican border is under his and his clan's control."

"Is he an earth vampire? You told me once they tend to stay in clans."

"Ah, but they don't like politics much, and where there are cities and large populations, there are usually politics. No, most larger cities are controlled by water vampires. London, Athens, Rome, Beijing, Buenos Aires. Water vamps tend to be quite tricky. Very smart and they like manipulation."

"The perfect politician," she said.

"Exactly."

"What about Houston? Was there a lot of that there?"

He smiled. "Houston is a bit of an anomaly, to be honest. That's one of the reasons I like it. Because of the proximity of New Orleans, it has an extremely low vampire population. It's an easy place to lie low, if that's what you're looking for."

She gave him a rueful smile. "Kind of spoiled the lying low thing for you, didn't I?"

He winked. "You were worth every singed hair."

"It's growing back," she said quietly, reaching over to run her fingers through his short locks. He leaned into her hand and she let it rest on his cheek briefly. Their eyes met again, and he saw hers soften.

"So," she said after a few quiet moments of contact, "this Don Ernesto knows about me? Does he know about my dad?"

He nodded and she continued fixing dinner. "He knows the basics, but not the specifics. I met with him the night I left the sonnets at your home. He was pleased to learn of the connection and more than happy to offer additional protection. An umbrella, of sorts."

She shrugged. "What's the big deal? You said he was related to a bunch of humans."

"But not any under my aegis, tesoro. He did me a favor by helping me protect you. And now I am in his debt."

She looked worried. "Is that a bad thing?"

"No," he shook his head. "He's a very decent sort, and if you're going to be related to a vampire, it's good that it's him. He's very protective of his people. Very old-fashioned. And he's pleased to have the connection to me, as well."

She smiled a little. "You really are kind of a bad-ass, aren't you?

I read your journals. You and Tenzin made quite the reputation for yourselves for a couple hundred years."

Giovanni shrugged. "I did what I needed to survive and build a reputation that no one would question. The more you are feared, the more you are respected and left alone. It's the way of the world."

"The vampire world, anyway."

"It's the way of any world, Beatrice," he said grimly. "Don't let the politicians fool you."

Giovanni watched her grate the cheese for the tacos. He could hear Ben outside, still bouncing the basketball by the garage.

"So why did I need all the super-secret vampire info? Besides being well-informed."

"Don Ernesto has the vampire who attacked Mano in his custody. I will be interrogating him tomorrow evening, and he's asked that you accompany me so he can meet you. You will not go to the interrogation."

He could see the blood drain from her face. "What does he want from me?"

"I suspect Ernesto only wants to know you. As I said, he's very fond of his family and has been wanting to meet you for some time. It's only been out of courtesy to me that he has maintained his distance. He knew I wanted you left alone."

"And the guy who attacked Mano?" she asked quietly.

"He was apprehended after I spoke to Ernesto's enforcer, Baojia. The vampire is Greek, unknown, and not particularly valuable. He hadn't caused any trouble in the area but was spotted near the port the night Mano was attacked. They picked him up the next night."

Her mouth fell open. "So they've had him for two and a half weeks? What are they doing to him?"

"Do you care?"

She hesitated, frowning a little. "Not really, I'm just curious."

Giovanni smirked. "They have him in a very ingenious little

place called a dry room. Quite torturous for water vampires. Saps them of their power. It's a bit like a giant dehumidifying chamber."

"I don't want to picture that after two and a half weeks."

He shook his head. "It won't be pretty, but he should be miserable enough to give up any information about Lorenzo if he has it."

"Do you have any doubt about it being Lorenzo?"

He paused. "No."

Beatrice nodded. "So that must mean he still hasn't found my dad, right?"

"If you are still a target for him, then probably not. You did steal most of his money, though. That had to be irritating."

"And lucrative," she muttered. His only response was a snort. "And then what? After you interrogate this guy, what then?"

Giovanni watched her carefully. "I will kill him."

Her dark eyes seemed to lighten, her mouth a thin line. "Good."

"So, will you meet with Don Ernesto Alvarez tomorrow after work?"

"Sure. I'll come here and we can take your car. What about Ben?"

"The fewer people who know about Ben, the better. I'll see if Kirby and Dez can watch him. He seems to be fond of blondes."

Beatrice shook her head. "That kid is fond of females. Doesn't seem to matter what kind."

"He'll learn to be choosy in time. It only took me five hundred years to find the one I really want."

She blushed and tried to hide her smile. Giovanni was trying to keep the innuendo to a minimum, but he wasn't a saint. He knew she was grieving her relationship with Mano and blamed herself for the human's pain, but he also knew she would eventually see the wisdom of not dwelling in the past.

He'd had enough of the past; he wanted her future.

"Okay, I'll call Dez in the morning and then head over here after work. I'm sure she'll be happy to help. Then we can go over and talk to this Ernesto."

"He'll expect you to treat him like family, just so you know. He already knows all about you and considers you a granddaughter. He's quite proud of you."

Beatrice made a face and Giovanni started to laugh. "I'm not going to lie," she said, laughing along. "That's kind of weird."

"And he'll probably try to persuade you to let him sire you."

She fumbled the knife. "What?"

"He won't force the issue, far from it, he fears me too much, but he can be very persuasive. He loves having a large family and he particularly likes having human descendants in it. It's a peculiarity of his, but not an obsessive one."

Beatrice took a deep breath. "Okay, as long as he's not going to try to force me or anything."

"No, I'll be in his home with you. No one would dare."

"It's a date then."

He propped his elbows on the counter and watched her warm the tortillas, one by one, in the flame from the stove. "Maybe we should try the theater next time. Might be less stressful."

Beatrice looked over at him, glanced at his hands and held up another tortilla with a pair of tongs. "Little help here?"

He grinned, snapped his fingers, and let the warm flames fill his hands as he helped her finish preparing the meal.

"Ben wants to know if I can take him to that movie with the blue aliens."

"That movie looks horrible."

She shrugged and folded the tortillas in a clean dishtowel to keep them warm. "He's twelve."

"Remind me to make him read some Jules Verne."

She grinned and nodded toward the door. "You're such a snob. Can you call him in to set the table?"

Giovanni turned his head toward the door and yelled, "Benjamin! Come inside and set the table!"

She gave him a disgusted look.

"What? He heard me."

Beatrice rolled her eyes. "Boys. Five hundred or twelve. Mortal or immortal. Still kind of the same... "

He grinned, pleased beyond measure to have her in his kitchen, in his home, in his life. Giovanni couldn't help but imagine what it would be like to have her living with him, working with him, and helping him raise Ben.

Loving him.

His feelings must have spilled out of his eyes as he watched her take the food to the table, because she glanced over at him and quickly looked away. He stood, walked into the kitchen, and took the plate of food from her.

He leaned down and brushed a kiss over her cheek before he whispered in her ear, "Grazie, tesoro. For dinner. For being here."

She swallowed and opened her mouth as if she was about to speak, but just then, Ben barreled into the kitchen.

"Awesome, tacos—" And then. "— Ew, are those tomatoes?"

EIGHT

The lights of the three-tiered yacht glowed in the harbor as Giovanni and Beatrice were ferried out in the small white boat. Don Ernesto Alvarez had spent his mortal and immortal life in the accumulation of wealth, power, and influence and had no qualms about enjoying and sharing that wealth with those he favored.

"So, the water vampire lives on a yacht, huh?" she leaned toward Giovanni and whispered.

"No need to be intimidated, but do be careful."

"See, those two statements seem like they contradict each other to me, Gio."

He chuckled and slipped an arm around her, warming her when she shivered. She relaxed into his side and allowed herself to enjoy the simple comfort of his touch.

He'd been careful with her the past weeks, respecting the fact that she still grieved the loss of her relationship with Mano. No matter his own feelings, he had respected hers and was showing an extraordinary amount of patience.

And that, more than anything, softened the brittle wall she'd put up to protect herself.

It would have been as easy as breathing to fall into his arms. She knew he loved her and wanted her, but Beatrice also knew she was past the point in her life where she would jump head first into a situation she knew little about. She had been cautious six years ago; she was even more wary now.

Giovanni claimed he wanted her. Not just for this life, but for eternity. She was still trying to wrap her mind around the idea; what he was asking wasn't a decision she could make lightly.

"Señorita De Novo, Señor Vecchio, welcome aboard," the dark haired steward called down in greeting when they came alongside the anchored cruiser. They climbed up the large angled ladder that dipped toward the water, and she felt Giovanni's hand on the small of her back as she climbed. She was slightly unsteady on her feet, but she felt him behind her, steadying her legs as she climbed.

"I feel like I'm underdressed," she muttered, eyeing the formally dressed steward.

He chuckled and pinched her leg. "I told you to wear your boots."

"Haha. All the same, with this ladder I'm sure glad I didn't wear a skirt."

"I'm not," she heard him grumble.

"Oh really? Want me to share the view with all the boys in the boat below?"

She looked down to see one of the crewmen on the small boat wink at her. Beatrice snickered and Giovanni glanced over his shoulder to see the man quickly busy himself coiling rope.

"Fair point. Skirts for my eyes only, if you please."

Beatrice rolled her eyes and continued climbing. Normally, she would consider his possessive behavior annoying, but in the unknown situation she was putting herself into, it was more comforting than anything else.

"Tesoro mio," Giovanni called from below, "can we hurry up a bit?"

"Why? You getting grey down there, professor?"

She squeaked when she felt him grab her by the waist and pull her into an embrace as he scooted up next to her. She clung to his neck and he shimmied up the ladder to the teak deck above. He held onto her a bit longer than necessary and bent down to murmur in her ear.

"It was getting hard to resist the temptation to sink my teeth in your thigh when I was staring at it for so long."

Her breath caught, her temperature shot up, and her heart raced at the rough sound of his voice. She made an effort to calm down so she didn't meet her great-great-however many great-grandfather completely turned on by her... whatever Giovanni was.

Beatrice saw two scantily clad women strolling along the deck; both of them shot Giovanni a look as they passed. He was dressed in surprisingly casual clothes that evening, though his dark jeans and black button-down shirt did nothing to detract from his good looks. The women swayed their hips as they walked past, but he didn't even glance at them. Instead, he held his hand out, searching for her own.

Whatever Giovanni was, she was beginning to realize he was most certainly hers.

She flushed when she realized she was more than a little possessive herself. The steward, who had been chatting with Giovanni in soft Italian, escorted them from the boat landing and up the stairs toward the decks above.

"Wow, how big is this thing?" she asked.

"The Esmeralda is over four hundred feet long, Señorita De Novo. It has forty cabins, twenty of which are interior and secured for our immortal guests."

"Does Don Ernesto live here full time?"

The man smiled enigmatically, and she sensed she wouldn't be getting a straight answer. "He stays here when it suits him."

"Okay then," she murmured as Giovanni slipped an arm

around her waist. They left the stairwell and walked across a broad deck leading to what sounded like a party. In the distance, the lights of the Long Beach Pike glistened and she could see the giant Ferris wheel turn as families enjoyed Friday night at the pier.

There was a sudden gust of wind, and she pulled her leather riding jacket close to her body, tucking herself under Giovanni's shoulder. She felt the heat begin to radiate off him when he sensed her shiver.

"If you'll continue this way, Don Ernesto and his family will meet you on the veranda."

"Thank you for your help, Enzo," Giovanni said.

"Yeah, thanks." She followed Giovanni, taking tentative steps toward the sound of glasses clinking and quiet murmuring voices that drifted in the breeze. She was ambushed by a sudden memory of the wild parties Lorenzo had thrown on the island, and she tensed when she remembered the drained human guests who had been casually flung into the sea when the vampires were done with them. She froze and her heart began to race. Giovanni pulled her closer and whispered in her ear.

"It's not what you're thinking. If you feel uncomfortable, we'll go, but it's to your benefit if you meet him, Beatrice."

"No," she said, nodding, "no, it's fine."

He squeezed her waist and they continued walking. When they turned the corner, she saw what could only be described as a very elegant dinner party. Though she saw more than one glass filled with what she thought might be blood and more than one human sitting among the vampires, no one was being bitten, and everyone talked and laughed together.

"Ah, Giovanni!" A short, barrel-chested man rose from the far end of the table. He was small and stocky, but his pale skin was set off by dark hair, a thick mustache, and a pair of startling emerald eyes that made Beatrice catch her breath. She had only seen the unusual shade in one other person in her life, and she smiled automatically to see her grandmother's eyes wink at her from the face of her ancestor.

He reached over and took her hand in his. Unlike Giovanni's hands, which were always warm, Don Ernesto's were cool as they enveloped hers. They weren't clammy the way she remembered Lorenzo's when he had touched her, so she was able to relax.

"You have finally brought my granddaughter to me," he said with a delighted smile, shaking Giovanni's hand after he released her own. "And what a beautiful young woman she is, and so very accomplished. You are a credit to our family, Beatriz."

"Well... " She laughed a little nervously. "Thank you. I'm very... pleased to meet you."

"Giovanni has been hiding you in my own city, my dear." He nodded toward Giovanni, who maintained a position behind Beatrice's right shoulder. "His prerogative, of course, and I understand you've been very successful in your studies and in your career."

"I have, thank you."

"Please call me abuelo, or Ernesto, since you are family, mi nieta. Come, sit beside me so we may acquaint ourselves." He showed them to the long table where he had been holding court and Giovanni pulled out the chair to the left of Ernesto's for her while he took the seat on her other side.

As soon as she sat, a server brought her a glass of water with no ice, asking her in a quiet voice what else he might bring. She asked for a glass of red wine and waited for Giovanni to speak to the man before she turned back to her grandfather.

"O positive, if it's available," she heard him murmur to the waiter.

"And would you prefer a donor or a glass, Señor?"

"A glass, please."

She flushed, wondering what the correct reaction would have been if he'd ordered a donor. As she glanced around the table, she realized more than one donor sitting next to a guest was feeding them from their wrist. It had none of the darkly erotic feel of the biting she had seen at Lorenzo's, nor the passionate connection she had felt the one time she had fed Giovanni.

Thinking about that night in his bed made the flush rise on her cheeks, and she was thankful that no one seemed to be paying attention to her. Except for Giovanni, who had placed a hand on her thigh under the table, holding it palm up. She placed her hand in his and felt the slight hum of energy that always buzzed when their bodies touched.

"Giovanni," Ernesto finally called. "I know you are acquainted with my son, Baojia, but have you met my daughter, Paula, and her husband, Rory?" Ernesto nodded toward the beautiful female vampire sitting at the far end of the table. She was tall and regal, no doubt towering over Ernesto, but her dark eyes were friendly, as was her smile.

The man sitting next to her looked exactly how Beatrice expected a cowboy from the old west would look. He was tan, even with the natural paleness of his kind, and had the lean, wiry look of a man who had been used to working outside. His grey, handlebar mustache drooped on either side of his thin mouth, but his eyes twinkled with a silver light.

"I know Paula by reputation, of course," Giovanni nodded toward the end where the two vampires observed them. "And I had the fortune of meeting Rory many years ago."

From the smiled that touched the cowboy's face, Beatrice had the feeling that their meeting may have been of the violent kind. Nonetheless, they nodded toward each other like old comrades before Paula began to speak.

"Giovanni, your companion looks like a delightful young woman. It's so lovely to meet another member of the family. You are from Texas, are you not, Beatrice?"

"I am," she said. "From Houston. My grandmother, who is an Alvarez, was from Guadalajara, though."

That statement sent the vampires at the table into raptures about the beauty of Colonial era Guadalajara and the music and art it produced. The tone of the conversation had the same nostalgic bent as the dinners Beatrice remembered attending with her grandmother's friends, and she chuckled in amusement.

"And what has made you laugh, my dear?"

She turned to Ernesto with a smile. "Oh… I was just reminded of my grandmother. All the talk about Guadalajara." She felt Giovanni squeeze her hand under the table as he took a sip of his blood.

"Tell me about your grandmother. She is in good health?"

"Yes, very good. She has your eyes."

His green eyes lit up. "She has Esmeralda's eyes? How wonderful!"

"Esmeralda?"

"My mother had the same brilliant green eyes that I do, my dear. That is why she was called Esmeralda, for her emerald eyes. I named the boat after her. The green eyes are quite rare in the family now, but perhaps if you have children, you will pass them on."

Her mouth gaped in shock. "Uh… well—"

"But of course… so clumsy of me," he said with a sly smile. "You are with Giovanni, so children are, perhaps, not something you wish for."

"I… I mean—"

"We have much time to think about things like that, Ernesto," Giovanni said smoothly. "Beatrice is a young woman. Tell me more about the new casino I hear you are opening next month. Is one of your children running it for you?"

Their conversation drifted into business, and Beatrice took the opportunity to sit back in her chair, sip her wine, and observe the humans and vampires who filled the room.

What appeared at first glance to be a dinner party was, upon closer observation, a very well-orchestrated meeting. In each corner and each group, there were quiet words and bent heads as canny eyes darted around the room with measuring glances. The vampires obviously had the upper hand, sending humans to fetch and carry this or that across the decks.

It all seemed to be a quiet and persistent negotiation. She heard murmurs about business deals and quarrels. New children and old relationships. There was the odd mention of acquaintances who were passing through the area. With each quiet conversation, Beatrice played a mental game trying to determine who had the upper hand, and who was trying to attract attention. It was all a kind of dance, and she smiled to herself as she observed them.

"What a mysterious smile," she heard Ernesto say. She swung her eyes back in his direction to catch him watching her with a grin. "It's all quite fascinating, isn't it?"

She glanced at Giovanni, but he only cocked an amused eyebrow at her.

"It's interesting," she said to Ernesto. "Very... dynamic."

Ernest broke into a satisfied smile. "A politician already, nieta! What an interesting young woman you are. You have very perceptive eyes, Beatrice."

"She always has," she heard Giovanni say as he tucked a piece of her hair behind her ear and leaned over to kiss her cheek. "Tesoro, I believe the man I need to meet is here for me." She glanced around and saw an Asian vampire of medium build standing in the doorway, staring at Giovanni with a blank expression.

Ernesto turned to the man and nodded in respect. "My son, Baojia, is head of our security. He has helped to capture the stranger who assaulted your friend."

She looked at the mysterious vampire, who radiated a quiet menace. His eyes were dark when she met his gaze, and she found herself nodding at him out of respect, though she could not smile.

"Beatrice? Would you like to find a peaceful spot inside?" Giovanni asked. "Or would you like to stay with Ernesto? It is up to you if you would prefer the quiet."

She could tell from the slight narrowing of Ernesto's eyes that he wasn't pleased Giovanni had given her the option, but she could also tell from the way he looked at her companion, Ernesto would not cross him.

She lifted a hand and swept it across Giovanni's cheek, which was dusted with a hint of stubble. "I'm fine, Gio. I'd like to visit a bit more with Ernesto." And observe the rather intriguing dance of influence that seemed to swirl around the room.

"Very well, I'll be back when I can." He bent down and breathed into her ear. "Be careful what you agree to."

"No hurry," she said as she studied Ernesto, who was watching their every move.

The two men left the room, quietly chatting in what she assumed was Mandarin as they disappeared down the hall.

"Tell me, my dear." Ernesto leaned toward her with a glint in his eyes. "What are your plans for the future?"

Beatrice spent the next hour in a complicated conversational game she found both stimulating and exhausting. Ernesto was completely open in his desire to turn her and make her one of his children.

"Just think of the benefits. You would have independence! If you wanted to continue in your relationship with the Italian, you certainly could or you could pursue others that might suit you more. But you would not be obligated to him or his protection any longer."

"No." She smiled. "I'd be obligated to you, right?"

He shrugged, smiling impishly. "But we are already family, nieta. I have only your best interests at heart. You could wait to turn and bear children with a human, if you like. Or if not, perhaps one of my own children might be more to your liking for a partner."

Skipping over the part about 'bearing children,' she frowned. "Wouldn't that be... I don't know, like dating your brother or something?"

Ernesto chortled at the question. "No! But of course you might think that. The attachment to your sire does not extend to all of his or her children, fortunately. There are bonds of friendship and loyalty between those of the same clan, but it is not like a human sibling relationship."

"Oh, that makes more sense, I guess."

"For instance, Paula and her husband are both my children, and I care for them both, but they are married. They have no greater bond than that."

"Ah," she nodded. "Got it. That's kind of a relief, to be honest."

She had been thinking more about the fact that her father had been turned by Lorenzo, who was technically Giovanni's son. If you were to extend the logic... well, it took Beatrice to an obviously uncomfortable place, so she was relieved that the connection only seemed to be between sire and child.

Anything more could get quite confusing.

"And if you were to remain in Los Angeles under my aegis," Ernesto continued, "what opportunities for study there would be. The academic institutions, the museums. Your skills would certainly face a challenge."

Beatrice looked around the table at the immortal beings surrounding her. Most were young, frozen in the prime of their life. Their eyes scanned the room with the kind of canny intelligence that could only come from years of experience. All carried themselves with a preternatural grace and confidence.

What would it be like to be frozen in time? Giovanni wanted her to join him in his life. She would never grow old or sick, never feel the sting of early death. She would be powerful, she thought, as she remembered the sick, helpless feeling of being held against her will in Lorenzo's mansion.

That kind of power was more than attractive.

"And perhaps, in time, even your father could come work with you."

A light shines in the darkness. She had been wondering at the dogged persistence of the water vampire, and suddenly his pursuit made sense. It seemed that Stephen De Novo held the interest of more than just Lorenzo and Giovanni.

"It seems like a lot of people want to find my father." She raised her eyebrow at her ancestor.

"Such a bright man. One does hear things... " Ernesto smirked. "I think he would be an asset to any family. As would his daughter."

Beatrice shook her head at his scheming. "Ernesto, you are an original."

"But of course," he said as he winked.

She felt no threat from the barrel-chested man with her grandmother's eyes. He seemed to enjoy their verbal dance as much as she did, though she had to admit his mental stamina outshone hers. Beatrice was beginning to droop by the time Giovanni found her an hour later.

The party was still going on, but she had retired to a bench near the edge of the deck, enjoying the quiet as she watched the human families on the pier.

Giovanni strode toward her on the open veranda and swept her into his arms, clutching her as he looked around the room. He glared at the party with heated eyes before he looked down at her.

His face held an inscrutable expression as he ran a hand down her arm, lifting her wrist before he opened his mouth and his fangs descended. Beatrice gasped as his tongue traced the blue vein that ran down the middle of her wrist, and she could feel the slight buzz under her skin where she anticipated his bite.

"Gio—" She could only utter his name before his fangs pierced her wrist. They didn't pierce deeply, it was more of a prick, but a few drops of blood leaked out and Giovanni caught them with his tongue, sucking them into his mouth as he looked around the room. She was lightheaded as his amnis flooded over her skin and she forced herself to hold back a moan.

Beatrice was more shocked than angry and confused by the uncharacteristic behavior. He bent down to kiss her, and she tasted the metallic hint of her blood as it lingered on his tongue. His mouth trailed to her ear and he whispered. "I'm sorry. Trust me, I'll explain in the car."

"Yes, you will," she murmured against his cheek.

He clutched her to his chest and raised his voice. "Beatrice is exhausted, Ernesto. We will visit more another time."

Ernesto frowned, glancing between Giovanni and Baojia, who stood in the corner of the veranda near the stairs. Beatrice watched him over her shoulder and saw the mysterious vampire give her a respectful nod. Ernesto caught it as well and cocked his head.

"Of course," Ernesto said with a cheerful smile. "You are both welcome anytime. Tend to my granddaughter, Giovanni."

In no time, he had lifted her and carried her down the stairs at vampire speed. Beatrice hardly registered anything until they were on the small boat racing back to the dock.

"Gio, what's—"

He pulled her into another breathtaking kiss as he smothered her question. She finally sighed into his mouth and relaxed, assuming he didn't want to tell her anything with an audience.

At least she could enjoy kissing an expert.

And kissing Giovanni was better than any memory she'd allowed herself. His tongue stroked hers, and he sucked her bottom lip into his mouth allowing his teeth to scrape it. She reached out with the tip of her tongue to stroke the fangs sharp in his mouth, and she could hear him quietly groan as he kissed her more deeply.

The boat sped toward shore, and within minutes they were back on the dock. Giovanni picked her up again and rushed toward the car, only to set her on the hood of the Mustang so he could stand between her legs and continue devouring her.

"Tesoro," he murmured against her neck. Then his lips travelled along her collarbone. "Beatrice... " he breathed out. Giovanni pressed closer, but she was too conscious of their place and the questions swirling in her mind, so she held back.

"Gio," she whispered as she placed her hands firmly on his shoulders and pushed him back. She heard him growl quietly as he tried to pull her back, but she grabbed his chin and forced him to look into her face. "Giovanni, what was that on the boat?"

He blinked, shaking his head to clear it. His eyes continued to fall toward her neck so she pinched his chin.

"I'm serious. I'm exhausted, and I just had a verbal fencing match for the last two and a half hours. So calm your fangs, and tell me what the heck is going on."

"Sorry," he muttered as he stepped back and cleared his throat. "My apologies, Beatrice. Let's get in the car and I'll fill you in on the interrogation and the... biting."

Beatrice nodded, sliding down the side of the car, taking care not to scratch it. She paused before she got in when she noticed the side of his head.

"You singed some hair off again," she said. "What happened?"

He frowned and felt the bare spot behind his ear. "In the car. Let's get on the road and I'll tell you."

Giovanni drove back to the house since she was exhausted. If there hadn't have been news to hear, she probably would have fallen asleep.

"One of Ernesto's people is working for Lorenzo," he said. "Baojia discovered it last week, but he wanted to tell me in person because he's still not sure who it is."

"One of Ernesto's children is working for Lorenzo?"

He shook his head. "That's highly unlikely, since your connection to him is well known. It would be almost unheard of for a child to defy their sire like that."

She couldn't help but remember Giovanni had plotted his own sire's murder, but she didn't bring that up.

"But only a small portion of the vampires you saw tonight are his children," he continued. "Many are business associates, employees, or others who have connection to him and claim his protection."

"So Bao—whatever his name is—doesn't know who it is?"

"He'll be able to find out fairly quickly with the information I gleaned from the Greek. He was most talkative after a short time with me," Giovanni smiled grimly. "I wouldn't worry about it.

"So what was up with the biting thing? Just feeling possessive?" she asked him with a curled lip. "You could have at least warned me."

"The bite on the veranda was a public display. I'm sorry I couldn't warn you, but for me to feed from Ernesto's granddaughter in front of him, and on his own ship, made a very strong statement, and since we don't know who it is yet—"

"I get it, I get it. You did the caveman dance, and we've covered our bases. Everyone knows who I 'belong' to." She rolled her eyes.

"Exactly," he said with a smile. "And, I'll confess, my blood was running after the interrogation. If I was human, you could say it was an adrenaline rush."

"Okay then," she cleared her throat. "Next time go punch something instead of biting me."

"I just had," he said in a hoarse voice.

"Oh."

"Yes, 'oh.'"

"So... " she hesitated. "Is the guy who attacked Mano dead?"

He paused before she heard his satisfied voice. "Ashes in the Pacific."

They exchanged a look Beatrice didn't want to think about too closely before he changed the subject. "So... how was your conversation with Ernesto?"

Her head fell back against the seat and her eyes drooped. "That was exhausting."

Giovanni smiled. "You did extremely well for your first small taste of vampire politics, Beatrice."

"That was a small taste?"

He smiled and reached for her hand, stroking the back of her palm with his thumb. "A small and rather friendly dip in the shark pool."

"Okay, well, it was interesting, but I could go on a vamp politics diet for a while, if you know what I mean."

"Fair enough. There's no reason I can think of for us to go back in the near future."

Beatrice must have dozed in the car, because when she woke Giovanni was lifting her from the passenger's seat and carrying her into the kitchen.

"What time is it?" she asked with a yawn.

"Around four in the morning."

"Good thing I don't have to work tomorrow."

He walked through the kitchen, still carrying her in his arms. Beatrice curled into his chest and thought of the first ride she'd made into Cochamó when he'd held her for hours in front of him on the rocking horse.

"Gio?"

"Yes?" He turned down a long hall she knew contained the guest bedrooms.

"If I stayed with you tonight... could we just sleep?"

His steps faltered, and she heard his heart give a quiet thump.

"If that's what you want."

"I miss you," she whispered as her eyes closed again. She burrowed toward the comforting smell of his skin. "I miss how warm your arms always are."

He paused in the hallway before he turned and walked up the stairs.

Beatrice didn't remember much except for his hands as they

removed her shoes, the low buzz of his skin brushing against hers, and the comfort of being enveloped in his scent as he pulled the sheets around her. She heard him moving around the room before his long arms enfolded her and he nestled behind her in the bed. He whispered in her ear as she faded to dreams.

"I love you, Beatrice."

NINE

En route to Houston

"If you're really from Texas—"

"Is that something people lie about? Being from Texas?"

"—then why don't you have an accent?"

Beatrice turned to Giovanni. "Is he serious?"

He shrugged. "I suppose so," he said, looking at Ben's curious face. "We've never been, he only met Caspar and your grandmother when they came to New York to stay with him."

They were sitting in the belly of Lorenzo's old plane, which now was stripped of its more ostentatious details. It sported a decent library, two twin beds, and the same couches, though Giovanni had made sure they'd been recovered. When he had inherited Lorenzo's converted cargo plane with the reinforced compartment that allowed him to fly, he had no idea it would be put to so much use.

Though he had spent much of the past year in New York and Los Angeles settling legal matters with Ben and preparing to reenter Beatrice's life, he had spent the four years previous flying across Europe, Asia, Africa, and South America, rebuilding old alliances and searching unsuccessfully for her father.

"I didn't know my grandmother and Caspar went to New York!"

He nodded. "They came in August when I... " When he had flown down to Cochamó, unable to resist seeing her. The farther he had pushed her to the back of his mind in their years apart, the more he had been able to successfully concentrate on preparing himself for the conflict he knew was coming.

But as the prospect of seeing her neared, he became almost desperate. Though Isabel had verbally lashed him, he hadn't been able to resist lurking around the house to try to catch a glimpse of her or a hint of her scent.

As soon as he mentioned August, her eyes hardened, Giovanni knew she realized what he was talking about. Luckily, Ben was still chattering, so she wasn't allowed to shut herself off like she so often did.

"Will there be cowboy hats? Do I get one? No, that would probably look stupid. But maybe... Gio, have you ever worn a cowboy hat?"

"I never wore a cowboy hat when I lived in Texas," he said.

Ben and Beatrice looked between each other, their eyes glinting. "That wasn't a 'no,'" she said with a sly smile.

He shrugged, thinking back to the time he had spent in Argentina with Gustavo and Isabel in the late 1800s. "It wasn't, strictly speaking, a cowboy hat."

They both started laughing and Ben finally choked out. "You —a cowboy—Gio wore a cowboy hat!"

"I'm trying to imagine it, Ben, but I just can't," Beatrice snorted.

"It wasn't a western hat—it was a gaucho-style hat. Everyone wore them."

Her eyes lit up. "But they wore them to keep the sun out of their eyes, and unless I'm missing something, sun burns you to a crispy critter, so you wouldn't need one because you wouldn't be out during the day. Admit it, you liked the cowboy hat."

"It wasn't a cowboy hat."

"I bet it was a black one," Ben said.

Beatrice nodded. "Definitely black."

He rolled his eyes and opened a book, attempting to ignore them, but in reality, his heart lightened to see them laughing together. Though he never said it, Ben had been dreading the idea of Beatrice disrupting the tentative family ties the two of them had formed.

"And you know, the sun thing isn't totally true. He once chased me out of the house about twenty feet during the day when I was trying to run away in New York. He didn't burst into flames, he just got really sunburned and a little smoky around the ears."

She cocked an eyebrow at Giovanni. "Smoky ears, huh? I'll have to remember that."

"And then he fell asleep really hard after he had two bags of blood, and he kept saying your name over and—"

Like lightning, Giovanni reached across the small compartment and grabbed Ben's hand. The boy slumped over, instantly asleep, and Giovanni sat back in his chair as Beatrice gaped at him.

"Did you just use mind voodoo to shut him up?"

"Yes."

"That's... "

She just kept gaping, seemingly unable to comprehend Ben's slumbering form. He was now snoring, just a little.

"I gave him a very nice dream about flying," he said with a shrug.

"That cannot be ethical, Gio."

"Well, call me an unorthodox parent then, but do you really think we would both be here a year later, still un-maimed, if I couldn't do that on occasion? He's a twelve-year-old boy. Trust me, it's for the best. He'll wake up when we're in Houston."

She shook her head, then stood, crouched down over the

sleeping boy and pulled him over her shoulder as she trundled him to one of the small beds.

He watched her in amusement; she was far stronger than he'd realized. When he pulled her in to kiss him on the boat the week before, he'd noticed the firmness of the muscles on her body. It felt foreign on her but not at all unpleasant.

"The judo has paid off. You're far stronger than you look," he said when she came back and sat on the couch across from him.

Beatrice nodded. "I told you, that new sensei has really been great. Between judo, jujitsu, and the tai chi I feel pretty well-rounded. I need to find a shooting class, though."

He smiled. "Gustavo mentioned that you were quite proficient with a rifle. He enjoyed shooting with you last summer. And the judo and jujitsu are good self-defense choices for you with your size."

"That was the idea. I didn't like feeling helpless."

His heart clenched at the thought of his own failure to protect her five years before. "I understand."

"I very much doubt that," she muttered.

"Do you?" he asked with a flash of irritation. "Do you forget that I was held against my will for over ten years as a human? That, even as a vampire, I was subject to a far more powerful sire. One who could easily overcome me, no matter how strong I was?"

Her mouth fell open as she stared at him in the low light of the plane. "I forgot. Sorry."

He looked back down at his book. "I have... a well of regret over what I have put you through that I doubt you'll ever understand, Beatrice." He swallowed the lump in his throat. "I am grateful you are now better able to protect yourself. It has given you confidence you lacked."

"Professor voice," she muttered under her breath.

He smirked at her and looked until she met his gaze. Then he allowed his eyes to travel suggestively down her body and back up until he met her eyes, which were heated with desire.

"You are no longer a girl," he murmured. "And I was never your professor."

"You just had the arrogance of one. Still do."

With lightning speed, he came to kneel between her knees. He could hear her sharp inhalation and the sudden rush of her pulse. Looking up, he met her dark eyes.

"You think I'm arrogant?"

"I know you are," she said breathlessly.

"Then what would you have me do, tesoro?"

She blinked and he saw her gaze drop to his mouth. "Wh—what?"

"Should I forget five hundred years of experience killing my enemies and protecting those who belong to me so that your modern sensibilities are not harmed?"

She was still looking at his mouth, and he forced himself not to smile.

"Would you have me confer with you before every move as if I was a mere boy looking for approval?"

"No, I mean—"

"You called all the shots in your relationship with that human, didn't you?"

He knew he had made a mistake bringing up Mano as soon as she twisted her mouth into a sneer.

"Yeah, I did. And he knew just how to make me happy."

He darted back to his side of the plane and draped his arm over the back of the couch. "Did he? Did he *really*?"

She paled and looked away from him, staring at the dark window over his shoulder and the stars that winked out.

"Fine," he conceded. "I shall do my utmost to consult with you on future matters of strategy and defense when it pertains to you."

"Good."

"But I reserve the right to overrule you based on my experience and superior knowledge of the immortal world."

"Bossy."

"Mortal."

They glared at each other in silent struggle for a few minutes before she walked to the other bed in the cabin and lay down, turning her back to him as she fell asleep. Giovanni watched for hours, memorizing the sound of her soft breath, steady heartbeat, and the small unintelligible murmurs that comforted him. He glanced at Ben and felt his dormant heart beat once as he remembered the interrogation of Lorenzo's man in Los Angeles.

"He knows about your boy, di Spada, and your human woman. He still has many friends," the shriveled vampire had gloated as his limbs slowly charred under Giovanni's grip. "You'll never find all of them before he kills your people."

"Is that so? Tell me more, Pirro. How did you escape the massacre on Lorenzo's island? Were you hiding in a corner? Did you run away from the fight?"

The small dark vampire grinned before another burst of flame from Giovanni's hands caused him to arch his back in agony.

"How—how does it—" He hissed, overcome with agony.

"The fire?" Giovanni leaned closer to the assassin, almost embracing the vampire as his lips murmured in his ear. "I've sent my fire through your dry veins, you fool. It's a slow burn. One that will eat you from the inside out." He gripped Pirro's arms more tightly, and he could see Baojia's approving nod from over the assassin's shoulder. "I'll stop it if you tell me who the traitor is on this boat."

"I don't know," he choked. "It burns. He didn't tell me how—"

"—badly I could hurt you? No, he likes to leave that part out because it makes him look weak, Pirro." Giovanni stepped away, keeping a hand on the vampire's shoulder and forcing the fire a little further into his veins. The gashes Giovanni had opened on the vampire's arms, face and abdomen continued to leak the sludge that was the last of his dehydrated blood. Still, he pushed his amnis onto the assassin and forced the silent fire deep into the dry body in front of him.

"Tell me," he said again. "Who is working for Lorenzo? Who gave you the information about the human diver?"

"Does it bother you that your woman keeps a lover, di Spada? Does it—" The vampire let loose a bloodcurdling scream as the fire reached his heart, which only tried to pump feverishly as the vampire curled in pain. Giovanni could hear the slow churning as it tried to move the bloody sludge through Pirro's body, which only pushed the burning further.

"Tell me," he murmured in the man's ear, "and I will kill you quickly."

"I don't know," Pirro finally croaked out of his dusty throat. Giovanni thought he could see a faint puff of smoke as the vampire spoke.

"I don't believe you." He hit him with another wave of fire, and the smoke poured out of the assassin's scream.

"I don't know!" he shrieked. "He was in Tripoli three months ago. We all knew he was meeting with the master, but none of us saw him."

Giovanni released the vampire's shoulder and allowed him to slump to the ground, where he curled into a small, smoking ball of pain.

"Tripoli?" he mused to Baojia.

The stoic vampire nodded. "I'll be able to find out who was traveling then. It's enough."

"Are you sure? I'm happy to take the time for further questioning."

Pirro whimpered on the floor, delirious from pain.

"We've been busy for quite some time. Do you know how much my father wants your human?" Baojia shook his head. "He knows you're going to take her soon. How hard do you think he's trying to persuade her to join us right now."

Giovanni's eyes darted up, as if he could see through the steel layers of the ship to the top deck where he had left Beatrice. He looked back to Ernesto's enforcer. "Why do you want her? Why is he so set on having her in his family?"

Baojia shrugged. "I have watched her these years—" The vampire was cut off by Giovanni's snarl. "—and I understand her appeal. She has a certain type of perception that is rare. Her eyes see through the layers of things, don't they? That is a very valuable trait."

Giovanni's lips curled. "She is mine."

The enforcer's eyes locked with his. "Is she? Really? I think Beatrice De Novo belongs to no one but herself, di Spada, no matter who may taste her blood."

A feral sound crawled up from his throat and he reached down to pick up Lorenzo's assassin, pummeling him until he was a lump of smoking flesh.

"Do you have any more use for him?" he asked Baojia.

The vampire frowned and shook his head, so Giovanni threw the lump to the floor, where it was quickly engulfed in blue flames that turned the body to ash. Baojia opened the doors leading to the small balcony and turned on a fan that slowly sucked the remains of Lorenzo's assassin into the wet night air.

Houston, Texas
Christmas Eve

"Da nobis quæsumus Dómine Deus noster: ut qui Navitátem Dómini nostri Jesu Christi mystériis nos frequentáre gaudémus; dignis conversatiónibus ad ejus mereámur perveníre consórtium. Qui tecum vivit et regnat in unitáte Spíritus Sancti, Deus, per ómnia sæcula sæculórum. Amen."

The familiar Latin of the priest poured over him like a balm as he sat next to Ben and Beatrice late on Christmas Eve. Isadora had insisted that the five of them celebrate midnight mass together, and Giovanni surprised himself by asking if there was one being celebrated anywhere in the old language.

He sat with his arm around Ben, who had slumped to the side in exhaustion, and his gaze rested on Beatrice's profile as she watched the priest deliver the last of the liturgy. Giovanni flashed back to the many human days he'd spent with his uncle listening to the same words spoken by ancient men who had taken the same vows as the young Irish priest standing in front of him.

It was good to remember that even some things in the human world did not change.

He may not have practiced regularly, but he had been Catholic in his human life, and in the deepest part of himself, Giovanni still considered it a part of his identity. There was little doubt in his mind that in two hundred years, he could sit in another church, thousands of miles away from this one, and listen to the same words spoken in a slightly different accent.

He heard the last of the ancient mass ring through in the stone church, and he gently shook Ben awake.

"Is it over?" he whispered.

"Yes, time to go home."

"It feels like home, even without a basketball hoop," he muttered. "That's kind of weird, huh?"

He smiled and mussed Ben's hair as the boy stood. "No. I don't think so. Home is about people." He saw Beatrice glance at him and knew she had heard him.

Caspar, Isadora, Beatrice, Ben, and Giovanni all drove back to the house in River Oaks where the humans quickly retired for the night. He went to the library and started a fire, content to sit on the couch and enjoy the quiet with Doyle, who was curled onto a chair. If he concentrated, he could still smell Beatrice's scent that seemed to linger everywhere.

The longer he concentrated, the stronger it grew until he realized he was ignoring the sound of quiet steps coming down the hall.

Beatrice entered the room, barefaced and beautiful, looking very young as she stood in the doorway. She was wearing an old Houston University t-shirt and what he thought might have been a pair of his boxers he'd left at the house years ago. He couldn't stop the smile that came to his face when he saw her.

"Couldn't sleep," she murmured before she walked over to the couch and lay down next to him, resting her head on his thigh as she stared into the fire with sleepy eyes. "I still miss you, even though I'm mad at you."

"I'll wear you down eventually."

"You do have forever, don't you?"

But you don't, he thought. "I can be patient. I told you to take as long as you need."

She continued to speak, unguarded in her exhaustion. "What if it takes a long time? What if I'm old and wrinkled before I love you again?"

A soft smile crossed his face. "I sincerely hope it doesn't take that long... " His hand lifted to stroke her hair and he could feel her begin to drift again. "But your beauty is not the reason I love you, Beatrice, even though it takes my breath away at times," he whispered as he watched the firelight dance across her skin.

"You don't breathe. Not that hard to take your breath away," she said, slowly blinking longer and longer as she stared at the fire.

"Harder than you might think. Sleep, tesoro."

And she did.

E arly the next morning, he could hear Ben's shrieks as the boy woke for his first real Christmas. He smiled in satisfaction before the day pulled him under.

When he woke and left the small room he slept in, he could still hear Ben's incessant chatter. He dressed in a pair of grey slacks and a red shirt he remembered Beatrice complimenting before he made his way downstairs.

The changes to the Houston house were subtle but perfectly reflected Isadora's tastes. She and Caspar had lived at the house since Beatrice had moved to Los Angeles, and both of them seemed exceedingly happy. Though it was late in life, Caspar finally seemed to have found the right woman for him.

"Merry Christmas," he said to Beatrice's grandmother when he saw her on the second floor landing. She was arranging a vase of flowers, and she turned to smile at him.

"Merry Christmas, Gio! We've missed you today. Especially Ben; he's so excited." She stood on her tiptoes, and he leaned down to kiss her cheek.

"Where is everyone?" he asked politely, though he could already hear the television in the living room. Isadora had never quite accustomed herself to his preternatural senses the way Beatrice had.

"Oh, they're doing their awful Christmas horror movie marathon again. Only this time, Ben is an enthusiastic participant. It's quieter than normal without Carwyn this year."

He smiled at the reminder that their lives had moved forward without him. "He's dealing with some complications at home, I believe. He apologized for not making it for the holidays."

"I know he has a large family. Is everything all right?"

That was an excellent question, he thought. The priest had

been uncharacteristically close-mouthed for the past couple of months, and Giovanni was beginning to worry.

"I'll ask him tonight. We've scheduled a call later."

He left Isadora humming as he walked downstairs and rushed into the living room at vampire speed, scooping Beatrice up and setting her on his lap before she could take a breath.

"Oh!" she gasped before she laughed. "I'll never get used to that."

Her mood was lighter; he could tell by the ease around her eyes and the quick tilt of her smile. "Merry Christmas, Beatrice."

"Gio," Ben bounced up and down next to him. "Cas and Isadora got me an iPod, and B got me an electric scooter, and there's a whole bunch more presents under the tree, too. And a lot of them are for you!"

Ben may have been a very streetwise twelve, but this morning, Giovanni thought he looked every bit the child he should have been for so many years. Then his words registered, and he turned to Beatrice, tugging her hair as she sat on his lap.

"An electric scooter?"

She grinned and leaned over to kiss his cheek. "He'll be fine, old man. I'll teach him to ride it. Just be glad it's not a dirt bike."

"A dirt bike?" Ben shouted in excitement. "I want a dirt bike!"

"If I could get headaches, I would have one right now. Thank you. I'll never hear the end of this."

"So stuffy," she muttered, but she leaned back into his chest and let him wrap his arms around her waist. They sat in silence for a few minutes, watching the old movie on the screen.

"Is this... "

"Horror of Dracula, 1958. I thought it was appropriate. Ben hadn't seen it."

"You have a sick sense of humor."

"But the vampires in this one have British accents. It's practically highbrow." She stared raptly at the screen and only wiggled in his lap when he pinched her waist. He bit back a groan before he leaned slightly closer to her neck, realizing he needed to feed if he was going to be this close to her. His fang pierced his lip, and he tried to shift in his seat.

"Tesoro," he said quietly. "I need to go."

"Why?" she asked absently.

He cleared his throat and waited for her to look at him. When she did, he let his fangs peek out from behind his lips and felt her pulse pick up.

"I need to feed." He leaned close. "Unless you're offering, in which case I'd be happy to go upstairs," he said with a soft growl.

She hesitated. "Do you have bagged blood here?"

He was tempted to lie but didn't. Instead, he nodded and tried to discern whether it was wishful thinking that he saw a hint of disappointment in her eyes. She moved off his lap, and he quickly retreated from her presence to feed himself from the bagged blood in the refrigerator.

A n hour later, and despite his meal, he was still eyeing her neck as they opened presents around the Christmas tree.

"Sweet! Another video game!"

True to Ben's fantasies, the adults in the room had showered the boy with gifts. Beatrice gave him his first computer, and she assured Giovanni she would teach him to use it responsibly. Caspar supplied the boy with a wealth of comic books, video games, and movies; while Isadora gave him enough dress clothes to make Ben shudder.

None of it seemed to fascinate Ben like the computer, and Giovanni stared in pleasure as the boy and Beatrice huddled over it while she unlocked the mysteries Giovanni couldn't.

"I'd say you look like you want to eat her alive, my friend, but I think it's much more serious than that," Caspar said quietly, his eyes following Giovanni's as he sat next to him on the couch.

"Look at them. Look how beautiful they are," he murmured as he watched their dark heads lean toward each other.

He saw Caspar smile.

"She's so good for you. I can't remember the last time I've seen you this happy."

"I'd be happier if she returned my affections."

Caspar said, "Don't be blind. She's unsure, not indifferent."

He shrugged. "Aren't I being patient?"

"Mostly. What did you get her for Christmas? I didn't see a present from you."

"None of your business, you brat."

Caspar chuckled and nodded toward Ben. "It's so odd, to see you with another child. Was I anything like that?"

Giovanni frowned. "Yes and no. Some things are the same, but he's much more independent than you were."

"That makes sense."

"And much more canny, which is both good and bad."

"Yes, I can see that, as well. The two of you are much easier around each other than you were last summer. Has B helped?"

He looked at her, and her eyes lifted to his. She offered him a small wink and a smile before she turned back to Ben.

"Yes, Beatrice has helped." Everything.

After the rest of the house had gone to bed, they kept each other company in the library, waiting for Carwyn's expected phone call.

"I never gave you your present, tesoro. Do you want it now?"

She smiled. "I wondered. I have one for you, too."

Giovanni pulled out a large box wrapped in burgundy paper

from under the side table and handed it to her. She opened it and pulled out a carefully packed book box with two small volumes inside. She looked at the spine in delight.

"PERSUASION?"

"First American edition, 1832. I found it in Paris a few years ago and thought you might enjoy it. I remember you eyeing my Austen the first time you were here."

She carefully pulled the first volume from its original book box and opened it carefully. "It's wonderful, Gio. Thank you." She smiled again. "*Persuasion*, huh?"

He shrugged and smirked. "It seemed appropriate. There's another small item in there, as well."

She closed the book, carefully packing it away before she looked into the box again and pulled out a small leather bag. She opened it, and a familiar brass key fell into her hand.

She blinked. "Is this what I think it is?"

"Well, you like that house as much as I do, so there's your key."

"You're giving me the... the Cochamó house?"

He smiled. "You still have to share it with me. That's my favorite home, but your name is on the deed, so to speak. And Gustavo and Isabel know if anything ever happens to me—"

"Nothing better happen to you."

"—the house is yours, Beatrice. It's your house, too. You can go whenever you want to now."

He couldn't read the expression on her face until she looked up and there were tears in her eyes. "Thank you," she whispered. "I love both my presents, but this one especially."

"You're welcome."

She leaned over to him and kissed his cheek. He left his arms lying across the back of the couch so he didn't grab her and cart her off to his room.

"So," he asked, clearing his throat. "Where's my present?"

"You know, you're not really bouncing around like Ben was."

He grinned and bounced in his seat just a little, making her laugh uproariously before she stood.

"Hold on; it's in my room. I'll be right back."

"I'll be here."

Giovanni stared into the fire and tried to imagine her lying in their bed at Cochamó, her smooth skin lit by candlelight. He wondered when he'd be able to persuade her to go with him again. He wanted to go in the summer with her, so she could see the waterfalls running and the meadows filled with wildflowers. They were beautiful at night, though she would be able to enjoy them during the day, as well.

"Okay," she called from the hall. "I don't have it wrapped, so close your eyes."

He smiled and closed his eyes, hoping that when he opened them, she would be modeling lingerie... or just skin, but he had a feeling that was wishful thinking. Instead, he heard her fumbling with something that sounded rather large.

"Okay, open."

He opened his eyes to see a large framed color photograph. It was his favorite waterfall in Cochamó, the midday sun reflecting off the mist and scattering rainbows. He smiled when he recognized it and looked up to see her waiting expectantly.

"I thought you could put it in your room here to go with your picture of Florence." She set it down and propped it against the chair nearest to the door. "And I got you a case of your favorite scotch, too. I called Gavin last week—"

She was cut off when he pulled her into his lap and kissed her. Beatrice tensed for a moment before she relaxed and sank into his arms. She gave a small sigh as he caressed her mouth, and she finally melted in his arms. His hands grasped her waist as she straddled him and met each surge with corresponding need. Her arms twined around his neck to pull him closer, and his hands reached up her shoulders, pressing their bodies together.

"Thank you," he murmured against her mouth before his lips

left hers to travel down her neck, nibbling in strategic places. "I love the picture."

"You sure it's not the scotch?" she asked breathlessly as she ran her hands through his hair and pulled his head into the crook of her neck.

"Positive. It's perfect. You're perfect," he said against her skin.

"I'm so far from perfect it's laughable."

"I love that you make me laugh."

"And I'm still kind of mad at you."

"I'm calling a Christmas truce. If soldiers in battle can do it, it shouldn't be that much of a stretch for us." His fingers lifted the back of her shirt and she shuddered as his hands caressed the skin at the small of her back.

He felt the normal buzz of electricity grow as his blood began to move through his veins and his fangs descended. He ignored his reaction and continued to explore the soft skin around her collarbone as her hands stroked his neck.

"Gio... "

"Let's not fight," he whispered. "Just for a little while."

"But, Gio—"

He cut her off with a deeper kiss. Giovanni felt her moan and move over him, and he became almost lightheaded with desire.

She finally grasped his shoulders and pushed back.

"Oh, tesoro," he groaned as his head fell to her shoulder. "Why are you—"

"The phone," she said breathlessly, "is ringing."

"Why?"

She smiled at him. "Carwyn, remember?"

"Damn that priest," he muttered. "I'm going to burn his Hawaiian shirts the next time I see him."

She grinned and stood. "Well, I'm going to answer the phone."

He slouched in the sofa, closing his eyes while she went to answer the phone.

"Carwyn." He heard her laugh. "You better lock up your Hawaiian—what? What are you—"

She gasped as he rushed to the phone and grabbed it out of her hand.

"—need to talk to Gio immediately. I can't—"

"I'm here," he said to his friend.

He'd heard the panic in his old friend's voice from across the room. His heartbeat sped in anticipation of danger. Carwyn hadn't panicked in two hundred years.

"I need you here, Giovanni di Spada. I need you in Ireland. It's Ioan... my son is missing."

TEN

En route to Dublin

Giovanni pulled Beatrice close as the plane took off, both of them glancing out the window to see Ben waving at the plane with a frightened look on his face. Her grandmother had one hand on the boy's shoulder and Caspar stood behind them. The three were leaving directly for the safe house in the Hill Country as soon as the plane was off the ground.

She huddled into Giovanni's side and buried her face in his collar. They had fought horribly about her going with him, but he finally relented when she threatened to fly to Dublin on her own if he left her behind.

Giovanni gripped her arm as the plane took off, and she was almost afraid he would leave bruises. She was beginning to realize he hated flying. He never said anything, but every time they flew together, he looked distinctly uncomfortable at takeoff.

"Tell me about Ioan," she said to distract him. She wondered whether he would break his usually reticent behavior to tell her anything specific.

"Ioan is... he's Carwyn's oldest son, and his biological great-grandson, I believe."

"Really?"

"Great or great-great grandson, yes. He's only about one hundred years younger than Carwyn. He's very powerful and very smart. His wife, Deirdre, is Irish and they've lived in the Wicklow Mountains for the last two hundred years or so, though they've been married for much longer."

"And they're both Carwyn's children?"

He nodded. "Yes, Ioan asked his father to change Deirdre. They met when she was human. I believe he was around five hundred years old at the time."

Beatrice fell into silence, contemplating a couple that seemed suddenly very familiar.

"So, if he's so powerful, how did he disappear?" she asked in a low voice. "Is it Lorenzo?"

Giovanni shook his head. "I don't know. I think it has to be, but this attack doesn't make sense. Ioan is not political. He's one of the most compassionate vampires I've ever met. He's also a superb scientist. Some of our conversations... " His face fell, and Beatrice realized that not only had Carwyn lost a son, but Giovanni had lost a friend if they couldn't find Ioan.

"He has studied medicine for around three hundred years," he finally continued. "And he will periodically go into Dublin for free clinics at night. He treats poor families, drug users, prostitutes... He has a very deep compassion for those on the fringes of society."

"But how does that—"

"Carwyn said he disappeared from Dublin during one of these clinics. He's weaker in the city. Earth vampires usually are. They draw their strength from the ground. And if he was put into a position where humans might have been hurt if he didn't comply, Ioan would let them take him." Giovanni sighed and closed his eyes. "He wouldn't even hesitate."

She swallowed and leaned her head on his shoulder. "Do you think he's already dead?"

He shook his head. "Deirdre would know. They've shared blood for over four hundred years. She would know if he was dead."

Beatrice fell silent, suddenly aware she knew nothing of the intimacies of vampire relationships. Though she had spent months with Isabel and Gustavo, it wasn't something they discussed, and she suddenly felt like an awkward school girl.

As if sensing her discomfort, Giovanni looked down and smiled a little. "I tried to explain once... about the biting. There are different kinds of bites, Beatrice. It's not always just to drink."

"Oh," she blushed, but he just pulled her closer, refusing to let her squirm away. "Well, I know that when you bit me... I mean, it didn't hurt. It felt... good," she said in a small voice. It had felt more than 'good,' but she didn't want to dwell on the details when she was stuck in a plane with him for the next eight hours. "I guess I always assumed that if vampires bit each other, it was just for, you know, siring someone."

When he spoke again, his voice was oddly formal, and it made her more comfortable to hear his "professor voice" when he was discussing something so intimate. "There are two different kinds of bonds that vampires will form with each other. Siring and, to use an old term, mating. When a vampire is sired, their blood is drained and replaced—"

"Does it hurt?"

He shrugged. "Not unless the sire wishes it. Andros had the odd theory, based only on his own madness, that a child sired in anger or pain would become unstable, but I've never seen any reason to believe that."

"So it didn't hurt when you were turned?"

Giovanni smiled and stroked her cheek. "No, tesoro. I knew what was going to happen. I can't say I was eager to drink blood, but I didn't want to die. Andros drained me... I don't remember much after that. I woke up the next night as an immortal. It was... an adjustment. I had to get used to my new senses and abilities, and I felt a very strong attachment to Andros."

He drifted off, lost in his own thoughts, and Beatrice took a chance on his talkative mood to ask something that had bothered her for years. "You seem like you have such complicated feelings for Andros; when you talk about him, it's almost like you love him."

"I did love him."

"But you bartered with Lorenzo to kill him."

"Yes," he said, and his eyes shuttered.

She rose onto her knees and straddled his lap on the couch, forcing him to look at her.

"I don't understand."

He began several times but paused before he could speak. Finally, he continued in a whisper, "He would have used me. He was already planning something. I don't know exactly what. You see, he never counted on me controlling fire. Once he knew... I think the temptation to use me for his own ends was too great."

She stroked his face and ran her fingers through his hair. He almost seemed like a large, fierce cat as he pushed into her palm and sought comfort in her touch.

"You had him killed so he wouldn't use you."

He nodded, but his eyes were still haunted. "I loved him, but whatever he was planning I wanted no part of. And I knew... I knew he would have been able to convince me."

"You can't feel guilty, Jacopo," she said gently, using his childhood name. "He was crazy. He murdered your uncle. He held you captive for ten years."

Giovanni nodded. "Yes, and without him doing all that, I wouldn't be sitting here with you. I would never have known Carwyn or Tenzin. No one would have been there to save Caspar. Benjamin would probably never have known a better life. So how can I hate him? His cruelty brought me to the people I love, Beatrice. What price can I put on that?"

She leaned forward and placed a gentle kiss on his forehead, smoothing the lines he created with his frown. Beatrice pulled his face into the crook of her neck and he wrapped his arms around her waist. He held her for hours until she drifted to sleep.

Wicklow Mountains
Ireland

They arrived by car at the small lodge tucked into the Wicklow Mountains a few hours after dusk the next night. There was a grouping of low, whitewashed houses around a central open courtyard, where small children ran and laughed. A large farmhouse spread out from the rear of the courtyard and a sheep dog sat by the doorway. She could see two human women walking across the garden, speaking and gesturing with their hands, as they corralled the children into the glowing houses.

"There are a lot of humans here," she said quietly to Giovanni, who had grabbed their bags and began walking toward the large farmhouse.

"Yes," he said with a nod. "Deirdre and Ioan are a poorly concealed secret in this area. The human population asks no questions, and the area is safe from almost all crime and poverty. The humans that live here are mostly connected to their children in some way."

"They have a lot of kids?"

He nodded again. "They are a large clan. Probably the largest in Ireland. And very influential. Even the water vampire that controls Dublin defers to them on most matters if they desire."

"So losing Ioan—"

"Is a very, very big deal, Beatrice."

He did not knock but pushed open the door of the large house, only to be greeted by a familiar furry face as they walked in.

"Bran!" she cried and immediately reached out to pet the wolfhound who was nudging her hip in a persistent manner. He was older and obviously near the end of his life, but the large dog still wore a friendly smile.

"Och, Bran," she heard a voice call. "Who is it now?" A stout, brown-haired woman with milky-white skin walked down the hallway. The roses in her cheeks marked her as human, and she wore a flour-dusted apron over her soft blue dress.

"Gio," she said with a smile. "It's been too long."

"Sinéad," he said softly, bending down to kiss her cheek. "This is—"

"You must be B." The woman held out her hand to shake. "Carwyn said to expect you both. Gio, your usual room is ready and, B, there's one upstairs for you. Give me a second to clean up and I'll show you. Such a dreadful, sad way to see old friends. Such a sorrow. The Father is on the warpath, though. If anyone can find Ioan, it'll be him."

"They contacted Dublin?"

Sinéad nodded. "Days ago. They've both been to the city, but the reports are unclear and they've not wanted to leave the valley unprotected."

Giovanni sighed and reached for her hand. She held it tightly and stood in silence, wishing there was something useful she could do. Sinéad was looking back and forth between them with a sad smile, but Giovanni didn't seem to notice.

"B, I'll take you up to your room. Gio, make yourself at home, of course."

He nodded and let go of her hand so she could follow Sinéad up to the second floor. Beatrice was led to a cheerful yellow room at the top of the stairs with a full bed, a small desk, and a set of drawers where she set her duffel bag. She sat on the edge of the bed and stared out the window. The stars had come out, and the clock read close to nine o'clock. She wasn't tired, but she felt lost in the unfamiliar room until she caught the whiff of smoke.

She turned and saw him standing in the doorway. He looked at her with grim eyes, and she held out her hand. He crossed the room, took it, and pulled her next to him, stretching out on the small bed as he enfolded her in his arms. They lay silently, watching the stars for a few minutes before he spoke.

"I'm glad you're here, but I wish you hadn't come."

"Not an option," she murmured as she stroked his forearm.

"Beatrice—"

"If you're so worried, train me."

"I've never studied judo."

"That's not what I'm talking about." He made an incredulous sound, and she looked over her shoulder. "What?"

"Train you? To fight vampires?"

She shrugged. "I know I'll never be as strong or as fast—"

"Or have keen senses, or control an element." She leaned down and bit his arm. "Ow!" He laughed. "Do it again."

She scowled. "Hush. I just mean, something is better than nothing. And it'll give you something to do until Carwyn comes back."

"What? You want to do it now?"

"What did you have in mind to pass the time?"

He raised a speculative eyebrow. "Well… "

"Yeah," she said. "Right. I have a feeling the house mom wouldn't be too keen on that idea." She nodded toward the door where she had no doubt Sinéad's ears were tuned toward them. "Otherwise, she'd probably have put us in the same room."

"True. I still—"

He sat up so quickly she almost fell off the bed.

"Carwyn's here," he said before he flew down the stairs.

Beatrice sat up and looked out the window, where she could just see the red hair of the priest as Giovanni embraced him at the edge of the road. She saw a blur streak by them both and the front door slammed shut. In the next heartbeat, a tall warrior of a woman stood in front of her, examining her with burning, blue eyes.

"Are you Giovanni's woman?"

Well, Beatrice almost said, it's kind of complicated. She thought better of it when she saw the fierce expression on the woman's face.

"I'm Beatrice."

"Your scent is unfamiliar."

"I didn't mean to surprise you."

"You didn't."

"Oh."

Deirdre seemed to take a step back. "I am Deirdre Mac Cuille. You are welcome in this house as long as you mean no harm to my own. You'll forgive me if I'm not a proper host to you."

Though she knew Ioan was Carwyn's blood relative, Deirdre looked like his daughter in every way. She shared the flaming auburn hair of the priest and stood at an impressive height. The planes of her pale face were regal as she stared down her nose.

Beatrice shook her head. "No, of course you wouldn't be. I'm so sorry about your husband."

Deirdre cocked her head. "He is not dead. Save your condolences, girl."

Just then, she heard a rushing on the stairs, and Giovanni appeared next to Deirdre in the doorway. They nodded toward each other, and Deirdre departed, leaving Beatrice staring in her wake.

"She's kind of scary."

He nodded. "Yes, she is. You would be too, if... well, if it was someone you cared about," he said quietly.

She looked at him standing in the door, and the wave of emotion almost overwhelmed her. She stood and walked to him. "If it were you," she whispered, knowing he could hear. "I'd be that way if it were you, Giovanni."

He said nothing as she slipped down the stairs.

Carwyn was far from the cheerful vampire she remembered from his last visit in May. She sat with him in the large farm kitchen as he ate the steak Sinéad had cooked for him. He tore into the bloody meat, not waiting for anyone to join him and barely speaking to her. Various members of the family, human and vampire, milled around him, but no one spoke.

"Carwyn," she heard Giovanni's voice as he walked into the kitchen. The crowd around the priest parted at his voice, and he came to sit beside his old friend. "Where's Deirdre?"

"She was in the garden for a bit, trying to scent him, but she couldn't pick anything up. They must know they're blood-bound and are keeping him away from open earth. I believe she's feeding right now."

Giovanni lowered his voice. "Human? I know she doesn't usually, but—"

"Yes, human. One of the farmhands. She knows she needs the strength."

"And you?"

Carwyn glared at Giovanni. "I'll not change who I am because of a madman. I cast no judgment, but—"

"For God's sake, Carwyn—"

"Do not take His name in vain among my people, di Spada!" the priest roared, standing up from the table and meeting Giovanni nose-to-nose as they squared off against each other.

"Fine," Giovanni spit out, "but I'm going to feed, as well. I've no interest in principle over survival."

Giovanni stormed out, leaving Beatrice gaping at them both as Carwyn sat down again, staring at the half-eaten meal in front of him. The humans and vampires in the kitchen dispersed and Beatrice sat silently, at a loss for what to say.

"I'm truly an ass sometimes, aren't I?" Carwyn finally muttered.

"He's worried about you. And I think he feels guilty."

"Why?" He began eating again. "I'm the one that agreed to help him get you back. Isn't it my fault? Oh, wait, you're the one we rescued, so maybe it's your fault." Beatrice felt tears spring to her eyes as she watched the surly vampire. "No... not your fault, after all, you were only targeted because of your father, so perhaps it's Stephen De Novo's fault after all."

"Carw—"

"Or," he finally looked up at her with a fierce expression in his blue eyes. "It's the fault of the man who kidnapped my son. Yes... " He nodded and took a gulp from the mug that Sinéad set by his elbow. "I'm sticking with this being Lorenzo's fault. Because that's the vampire I'm going to kill if I don't get my Ioan back." He wiped the blood from the corner of his mouth, smearing it across his jaw in an ominous red streak before he continued inhaling his food.

"What are you doing?"

She turned to see Deirdre walking toward her in the garden as she practiced her tai chi forms in the twilight. They had been in Wicklow for a week with little to no change in the situation. Giovanni and Carwyn had gone to Dublin the night before to meet with the leader of the city, and she had stayed in Wicklow with Deirdre, who refused to venture far from her home, worried that more of her family might be targeted.

"It's tai chi. Martial arts. I study in L.A."

"It's quite beautiful. Why is it so slow?"

"Sometimes it's faster. But Tenzin told me when I practice forms, I should concentrate on the flow of energy and meditation so my movements are precise. It's relaxing that way, too."

"Tenzin?" Deirdre said. "How very... interesting."

She frowned as Deirdre sat next to her on the grass, taking a deep breath and sinking her hands into the soil of the garden that overlooked the green valley. Stands of trees lay in the creases where streams cut through, and a small herd of deer broke into a run as they scented danger at the edge of the forest. Beatrice could hear the sharp bark of the dogs and the lowing cows as the farmhands brought them in for the night.

She continued with her forms, moving slowly and trying to let the tense waves of energy from Deirdre wash over and around her. She heard the vampire take a deep breath.

"Why did Carwyn say you were trying to scent Ioan? Isn't he too far away?"

She saw Deirdre smirk at her out of the corner of her eye.

"You don't know much about vampire relationships, do you?"

She blushed but continued practicing.

"Doesn't Gio tell you anything?"

"We're not—" Beatrice faltered. "It's not like that with us." Yet.

"He's in love with you. Don't you love him? You look at him like you do."

She frowned. "You know, forgive me if I don't feel like getting into the details with someone I hardly know."

Deirdre snorted. "Fine. Forget I asked."

Beatrice pushed down her irritation and focused on the slow and steady movement of her body. She could feel Deirdre still watching her.

"Sit down and talk to me, girl. It's not like I've never had this discussion with any of my daughters before. Ioan, despite being a doctor, has always been squeamish about these things. Typical male."

"I'm well aware of the birds and the bees, thanks very much."

"You asked how I could scent my husband, and I'll tell you how. It's either ask me or Giovanni eventually." Beatrice turned and Deirdre raised an eyebrow. "Well?"

She huffed and came to sit next to her on the grass, stretching out her sore muscles.

"Okay," Beatrice asked, "what's the big deal with smelling?"

Deirdre smiled. "You are amusing. I imagine you drive him mad in the best way. He has always taken himself too seriously."

Beatrice remained silent, at a loss for something to say to the vampire next to her, who looked younger but whose eyes held a kind of infinite wisdom she couldn't wrap her mind around.

"You know how our kind are sired, do you not?"

"Yes."

"When mates... when two vampires exchange blood in small amounts over long periods of time, a different bond is formed."

"A sexual bond?"

She shook her head. "Much more than sexual. You can have sex without exchanging blood, but when you do... "

"Yeah?"

Deirdre gazed out over the valley, still digging her hands into the earth. Her mood had shifted, and Beatrice could tell she was thinking of Ioan. "Blood exchanged in love and passion for hundreds of years. Over and over until it is so mingled... "

Beatrice's heart raced. "What?"

"We are two halves of a whole," Deirdre whispered. "Four hundred years we have been together. That's why I know he still lives. If he was dead, my own blood would cry out. There would be no question."

"So, when they said you could 'scent' him—"

"Our blood calls to each other if we are apart. I will be able to scent him because, if even a drop of his blood touches open earth, it will call to me."

Beatrice was silent, staring into the distance as the stars came out around them.

"I can't even imagine what you must be feeling right now."

Deirdre turned her head sharply. "Do you want to?"

"What?"

"You cannot look at him the way you do and not have thought about sharing this life with him."

She felt the tears spring to her eyes. "It's... too much. I can't—"

"You have to."

"Do you think so?" She remembered Giovanni had said Ioan

asked Carwyn to change Deirdre when she was human. "You made the choice. Has it been worth it?"

Deirdre's blue eyes were wells of sorrow, as if she was staring into a grave.

"I have shared his blood for four hundred years. What do you think?"

ELEVEN

Giovanni rang in the New Year watching a young water vampire twist into a smoldering pile of ash.

"He's created all these children," Carwyn muttered. "Almost indiscriminately. But none of them know anything."

They were standing in a warehouse on the edge of the River Liffey that was thick with the scent of Ioan's blood and Giovanni's son, but other than faint brown smudges on the concrete floor, there was no sign of the missing doctor.

Giovanni pulled on his shirt after killing Lorenzo's useless minion. "Did you call Deirdre tonight?"

Carwyn nodded as he watched Patrick Murphy's people sweep the ashes out the open door of the warehouse.

"Gentleman," said the solemn vampire in the three-piece suit. "We've come to the end of my leads. This warehouse was the last of the information my people had gleaned. We'll still keep our ears and eyes open, of course. The loss of Ioan—"

"Has not been confirmed in any way," Giovanni muttered, watching Carwyn pace at the other end of the warehouse.

Murphy tugged at the black curls on his head, obviously

nervous. "If there is any further assistance I can offer to either of you while you are here..."

"It's fine, Murphy," he heard Carwyn spit out across the room. "I'll expect your cooperation in the future, but if we've ended our leads here, I want to go back to my daughter."

Giovanni tried not to sigh in relief. Though he knew Beatrice was perfectly safe in Wicklow, he still felt uncomfortable being without her.

"Boats," Murphy said. "My best guess would be boats. Lorenzo is a water vampire, and he would have the resources to transport him by boat. This warehouse has river access, and we are not far from the port."

Giovanni nodded. "We'll keep you informed."

"Please do. And safe travels to you both."

They drove Ioan's old car back to Wicklow, having located it near a church where he'd been running a clinic the night he disappeared. As they swerved through the hedgerows and over the bumpy roads on their way to the lodge, he could feel the weight of Carwyn's worry as if it was another passenger in the car.

"I think he is dead."

"You don't know that, Father. And Deirdre would have sensed it."

"She might not. Not if he was taken far away and never touched the ground."

"Carwyn—"

"What if he is in water? Or unable to touch the earth? Oh, my son," he whispered, gripping the wheel. "My Ioan. I don't want to contemplate this life without my boy."

Giovanni clenched his jaw, willing the road to smooth before them.

He saw Beatrice in the front garden, practicing her tai chi forms in the dark. He nodded toward the silent guard Deirdre must have assigned to her; the young vampire nodded back before disappearing into the night. Giovanni crept toward her, not wanting to disturb her silent meditation, and watched her for a few moments in the moonlight.

She was beautiful. And so much stronger than he ever could have anticipated. Though Beatrice was still weaker than him physically, it was the strength of her mind and her determination that impressed him. She was no longer afraid to stand up to him, their argument before leaving Texas a prime example. He loved her all the more for it.

A mischievous smile crossed his lips, and he snuck up behind her. Before he could anticipate it, she stepped back, shoved her hip into his groin, and threw him off balance. Beatrice reached around, grabbing his waist and sweeping her leg through one of his as she flipped him onto his back and landed on his chest.

He blinked, looking up at her with a shocked face before he roared in laughter.

"Oh," she said with a snicker. "It's you."

"Hello to you, too."

"Don't sneak up on me, vampire."

He was still laughing when he brushed away the lock of hair that had fallen into her eyes. "That was marvelous."

"I try."

"I'll be expecting it next time, so you better watch out."

A twinkle came to her eye. "Oh yeah? What are you going to do—"

She broke off when he reared up and jerked her neck to the side. His fangs were bared and he let them scrape lightly across the skin of her neck before he licked up to her ear.

"Just remember, never pin a vampire face-to-face." He rolled them over so she was lying under him, and she looked up with hungry eyes. "Unless you want this to happen."

"I'll keep that in mind," she choked out.

He bent his head down and brushed a kiss across her flushed lips.

"It's been on my mind for a while now."

He helped her up and they walked arm in arm back to the farmhouse. Giovanni was filling her in on what had transpired in Dublin when a blood-curdling scream rent the air.

Giovanni halted, a feeling of dread washing over him. He picked Beatrice up and rushed back to the house, setting her near the young guard as he sped toward the back garden. He felt the force of Deirdre's amnis slam into him as she wailed in Carwyn's arms. Giovanni almost fell to his knees, but he felt Beatrice come behind him and grab his hand. He pulled her into his arms and buried his face in her hair as he rocked her back and forth.

"He's dead," Beatrice whispered, holding him close. "He's dead, isn't he?"

Giovanni nodded. Nothing but the grief of losing half of yourself could tear a person in two the way that Deirdre Mac Cuille had been. Her screams were hardly that of a woman; they more closely resembled the death keen of the mythical banshee. She tore at her hair while Carwyn shouted, "Where, Deirdre? Where?" over and over again. She was unintelligible, gnashing her teeth and rocking back and forth as she dug her hands into the earth.

Finally, she shoved her father away, tore off her clothes, and stretched herself upon the ground. Giovanni felt the sudden jolt and sigh as the earth opened up and swallowed her whole.

Before dawn, letters were sent and calls made. Though Deirdre had not yet reappeared, some of their clan had already arrived, emerging from the valley confused and angry. Deirdre and Ioan's children converged on their parent's home as the scent of their father's blood travelled through the earth from which he had drawn his power.

Giovanni took refuge from his grief in the small stone room under the mountain. He pulled Beatrice with him, and the two retreated from the overwhelming sorrow of Ioan and Deirdre's family. Carwyn was surrounded by his children's children, both comforting and being comforted by his kin.

He held Beatrice for the rest of the night, and she lay with him, quietly stroking his hair the way she knew he loved, old wounds overtaken by the ache of new loss. He fell into his day rest next to her and when he woke she remained, staring at him with her deep brown eyes.

"There are so many vampires here."

He nodded. "Deirdre and Ioan sired or fostered many children over the years. They would take in anyone that needed a home unless they were dangerous. All their children had children, and so forth. Their clan numbers in the hundreds, probably."

Giovanni knew it had only begun. Soon, the trickle of friends and allies would become a flood as Ioan and Deirdre's people returned to the quiet mountain their parents had called home.

"Why did they all come? I mean, what do vampires do when… "

"When Deirdre returns and the family is gathered, Carwyn will say a funeral mass."

"I can't—" Beatrice choked and wiped at her eyes. "How will he be able to do that?"

Giovanni took a deep breath and hugged her closer. "It's the last thing he can do for his son."

He could feel her tears wet on her cheeks as she lay her head on his arm.

"Tell me about him."

He pulled her closer. She had been handling herself extremely well, considering how recently and dramatically her world had changed. For the past week and a half, she had been surrounded by humans and vampires she didn't know, and he had left her alone for much of the time, consumed by the need to search for his friend.

"Ioan was kind. Intelligent. Wise. He had a kind of wisdom about life and family I could only hope to gain." He noticed the lines of stress that creased her brow. "Beatrice, there will be many vampires here and not all of them will be Carwyn's people. Some of the water vampires who run Dublin will be here, as well as others from around the country. They do not have the same attitude toward humans that we do, so make sure you stay close to me. It will be somewhat overwhelming. It could be dangerous if tempers run high."

"Since I don't want to be a beverage during the vampire version of an Irish wake, I'll keep that in mind."

He tried to stifle a laugh, but couldn't.

"Sorry." She closed her eyes in embarrassment. "Too crass?"

He shook his head and leaned over, brushing a soft kiss across her temple. "I was just thinking how Ioan would have laughed at that. Having married an Irishwoman, jokes about his adopted homeland were some of his favorites. No one loves a joke like a Welshman."

"Will she survive?" she whispered. "Deirdre? How do you recover from something like that?"

He swallowed the lump in his throat. "You learn to deal with loss the longer you live. I have lost many people I cared for."

"But not like him. Not even you expected Ioan could die. I could tell. You all thought you'd be able to get him back somehow."

He frowned, thinking about her words, and realized she was right.

"Yes," he finally said. "It is difficult to think that someone so powerful could be cut down."

"This is Lorenzo, isn't it? He did this. Or someone he hired."

He pushed back the useless well of guilt. "It has to be. First he attacked someone important to you, then the child he knew would pain Carwyn the most."

"Is he—I don't know the right term—herding us? We were spread out before and now Carwyn, you, and I are together. If he wanted to attack us—"

"He won't be that direct, I don't think. He's not strong enough. He's going after the people we care about to distract us and throw me off balance."

"Should we warn Tenzin?"

He said, "Tenzin has four beings she cares for enough that Lorenzo might target them. Three are in this house, and the other is more protected than you could imagine. Don't worry about Tenzin. Lorenzo should be the one worried. Tenzin was... fond of Ioan."

He broke off, overwhelmed as grief ambushed him again. He gripped Beatrice against his chest, more afraid of loss than he had been in hundreds of years. If he could have allowed himself to weep, he would have at that moment. "I should call Caspar and check in, make sure everything is all right," he said hoarsely.

"I called my grandma a few hours ago," she said. "They're fine. In the mountains and hidden. Ben isn't causing any problems."

He relaxed a little. "Thank you."

"You don't have to do everything yourself, you know."

He smiled ruefully. "I'm not used to asking for help."

"Well... " She faltered a little before she continued in a quiet voice, "Get used to it."

He wanted to see her eyes in that moment, when her heart was racing and her face was flushed, but she was turned away, so he simply kissed the top of her head.

"Beatrice—"

Suddenly the air churned with the scent of power, and Giovanni turned toward the flurry of activity in the hall. He leapt up and opened the door. Beatrice peered out from underneath his cautious arm.

"Deirdre, wait!" Carwyn shouted in the corridor.

The scent of blood and dirt hit his nose as he saw Deirdre stride toward them, carrying what was left of Ioan's body wrapped in a dusty sheet. She walked down the narrow hall, still naked and covered with earth as she headed toward the chamber she had shared with her husband for over two hundred years.

She paused briefly and her eyes glanced over his shoulder where Beatrice stood behind him in the small stone room. The widow's eyes searched his out, and he shuddered at the utter desolation.

So quiet even he could barely hear her, Deirdre breathed out, "Are you sure?" Then she turned the corner, and he heard a door slam shut. Soon afterward, Carwyn walked down the hall and Giovanni could hear him enter the room. Then the low keening wail started again, and he pressed the door closed.

Four days later, the majority of Ioan's clan, his friends, and those who had known him had gathered on the small mountain. Carwyn and his daughter emerged the night after she brought Ioan's body home, the priest carrying the small wooden box of earth that contained all that was left of the nine-hundred-year-old vampire he had sired.

The mood on the mountain was cautious and confused. Ioan had been known not only as a powerful and ancient earth vampire, but as a scholar and a humanitarian. The idea of any immortal targeting him was seen by most of his friends and allies as supremely wasteful and far from shrewd, considering his alliances.

The moon was almost full, and the night was crisp and clear when Carwyn returned the remains of his last blood relative to the earth. Giovanni stood silently, grieving as his friend spoke the ancient rite over his child, and all those gathered felt the surge of energy as the clan reached down and touched the mountain together as the earth he had loved became Ioan's final resting place.

The following night, the clan of Ioan ap Carywn and Deirdre Mac Cuille gathered on the hilltop to grieve, as Carwyn and Giovanni met in the library of the main house with Deirdre and Beatrice to talk about what steps they needed to take. Deirdre had found Ioan's beheaded remains on the bank of the Liffey River, dumped by whoever had killed him.

"Murphy still has his people looking in the city and the port, and my people are scouring the coast of Wales to make sure they didn't escape in that direction," Carwyn said.

"The humans whose memories were tampered with were here," Giovanni pointed to a location on the map of Dublin spread out before them. "But the warehouse is here. Now that warehouse backs up to the port, so it's also likely that Murphy is right, and whoever did this is already out of our reach for right now. Beatrice?"

"Yes?"

"Is it possible for you to search online to see what ships were in the port the night Ioan died and where they went?"

"Absolutely." She nodded. "I just need an internet connection."

"Good, you do that and I'll give you the number of Murphy's day people so you can contact them if you run into any problems. He's offered the use of any of his resources—"

"Damn right he has," Carwyn muttered, obviously still unhappy with the water vampire who controlled the city where his son had been killed.

"—to catch whoever took Ioan."

"We know who took him," Deirdre said with a sigh. "We know who it is, Gio. Why are you wasting time?"

Giovanni's shoulders tensed when he heard her hollow voice; he braced himself for her recrimination, but her empty gaze was fixated on a canvas she had painted of Ioan, which hung on the wall near the small fireplace in the corner of the library. He looked at the painting, which had captured his friend's lively smile and the wicked humor he had inherited from his father.

"Deirdre—"

"I'll not be leaving the mountain, Gio. Not right now. There is too much to do and too many defenses to shore up. Our people need me here, so I'll depend on you and Father to kill him for me."

He nodded. "I understand."

"Though I'd rip his heart out of his body and feed it to the dogs," Deirdre said in a low voice, "just to rip it out again when it grew back."

The intense guilt from his son's actions almost threatened to overwhelm him, but Giovanni stood, stoically meeting Deirdre's vicious gaze.

"Kill him, Giovanni di Spada. I will not have you take his sin on your shoulders, but I do expect you to rid the world of this monster."

"I will," he whispered, as he fixed her burning blue eyes in his mind.

"I demand it of you."

"The right is yours, Deirdre, and I will honor it."

"For me, for Ioan, and for your woman as well."

He saw Beatrice's lip twitch minutely when Deirdre called her "his woman" and the grieving widow must have seen it as well, because she turned to Beatrice.

"Do I offend your modern sensibilities, Beatrice De Novo, to call you 'his woman?'"

An embarrassed flush rose in Beatrice's cheeks, and she opened her mouth to speak, but Deirdre continued, scorn dripping from her words.

"This immortal," she said, pointing to Giovanni, "who has never claimed a human woman in five hundred years, is not worthy of calling you 'his?' This vampire who wields the fiercest of elements with iron control is the one you dismiss?"

"Deirdre," Giovanni cautioned, but she brushed him aside with a careless wave.

"You foolish girl!" she bit out. "Why do you hesitate?"

"I know you're grieving," Beatrice said as she glared at Deirdre, "but our lives are none—"

"Do you think you have forever?" Deirdre finally choked and blood tinged tears rolled down her face. "Not even we had forever. And I only seek to live now that I may care for my people, otherwise I would join my husband in the grave."

"Daughter, that's enough," Carwyn murmured as he walked across to gather her up and hold her as she shook with silent sobs.

Giovanni watched Beatrice from across the room, noting her pale face as she watched Deirdre's grief. The fear in her eyes matched that which slashed at his own heart, and he fought back a wave of hot panic at the thought of being parted from her.

Deirdre finally wiped her eyes and pulled away from her father. She gave Beatrice a hard look, but before Giovanni could rebuke the widow, some unspoken communication seemed to pass between the women and the tension drained from the room. Deirdre turned to him with a veiled expression.

"Giovanni, forgive my outburst. I will leave you so that I may see to my family."

"Deirdre—"

"And you, Beatrice, thank you for helping to find those who killed my Ioan."

"Of course."

Carwyn and Deirdre walked out of the library to join the vampires who surrounded a bonfire lit in remembrance of their kinsman. Giovanni watched them through the window until he heard a quiet sniff behind him, and he turned. "Beatrice?"

"Is that what you want?" Tears were in her eyes, and her arms were folded across her chest.

"What—"

"Is that what you want for us? For me to give up my human life and be tied to you like that? So connected that either of us would want to die if something happened to the other?"

Yes.

No matter how painful Deirdre's loss was, Giovanni had also seen the incredible joy her bond with Ioan brought. "You know my feelings for you. And what I want."

"To become a vampire. Like you. To live in the dark and watch all my family and friends die around me." She dashed the tears from her eyes. "But I'd have you, right? And what if I lost you? Or what if you left me again?" Her eyes flashed out the window toward Deirdre. "What then?"

"I won't leave you again," he said gently, walking across the library. "And you see only the sadness, but what if we could have a thousand years together? More? Even if we had only one hundred years together, isn't that more than a mortal man could give you?" He stood in front of her, gripping her shoulders and willing her to see the devotion in his eyes. "What if we had ten? Or only one? Do you think Deirdre regrets any of her time with Ioan because of her grief now?"

"I don't know," Beatrice whispered. "It's too much, Gio. Everything's changing so fast. This is not my world. And it's so much bigger than anything I could have imagined."

He shook his head. "We live on the same Earth, Beatrice. The world has not changed, only your perception of it."

"I don't know what I want," she whispered.

"And I finally do." He embraced her, feeling the race of her heart against his chest. "I've spent five hundred years waiting to feel toward anyone the way I feel toward you." He clenched his jaw when he spoke again. "I know you want to be cautious, but remember that, too."

Beatrice's pulse began to even out as she calmed herself, taking deep breaths until her shoulders relaxed. She took a step back and her hands unclenched.

"I feel like I'm falling sometimes. I feel like my life is out of control, and I don't know my way around." She shrugged helplessly. "I'm a stranger here."

He reached his hand out and she took it. "You're not a stranger to me."

TWELVE

North Wales

A week later, Beatrice and Giovanni travelled by horseback through the rugged mountains of Snowdonia in northern Wales. They followed Carwyn, who was hospitable enough to travel above ground for the benefit of his guests. They were stopping in Carwyn's house in Wales for a few nights before continuing on to London to meet with his daughter and her fiancé, a water vampire who ran London and had extensive contacts throughout Britain and the continent.

The leads into Ioan's death had dead-ended in Dublin, but Beatrice had found two boats in the port that were owned by shadow corporations that looked promising. One was headed to London, and the other had been tracked to Le Havre. Either could have been Lorenzo, but they would have to go to London before they could find out more.

"I'm sorry you're visiting my home for the first time under these circumstances."

Beatrice looked over and smiled at Carwyn. "Don't apologize. I'm sorry I've been so moody lately."

He pulled his mount back and kept pace with her as they made their way along the trail. Giovanni had ridden ahead, familiar with the terrain and, she suspected, wanting to give her and Carwyn some time alone to talk.

He shrugged. "It's a crazy world you've found yourself in, darling girl. I can hardly blame you for not feeling entirely yourself."

"I'm glad to be visiting anyway."

"How's the bike?"

"Good," she smiled. "I'm happy you convinced me to buy the Triumph."

Carwyn nodded. "Anyone looking after things? While you're away?"

"Well, officially I'm still on my vacation time, though Dez and Matt know what's really going on and are watching the house. I'm going to have to figure out something to do about work, though."

"Ah, so Dez is finally in on the secret, is she?"

Beatrice nodded. "She is. And she and Matt are dating now."

"About bloody time," he muttered.

"Hey, watch the language, Father. Don't you have parishioners around here?"

Carwyn smiled and looked around the snowy valley. "That I do, though I hardly think any of them are out on a night like this."

Though she was bundled in the warm woolen clothes she had bought in Ireland, Beatrice still shivered as they made their way through the cold, desolate hills leading toward Carwyn's mountain home.

"So Matt and Dez are finally together," he continued.

"Yep."

"And you and Gio?"

She fell silent and looked sideways at him. "What about us?"

Carwyn shrugged and gave a wry smile. "Distract an old man with some juicy gossip. What's going on with you two? I know you and Mano broke up."

"Yeah," she said quietly, surprised by how much it still hurt, "we did."

"And you and Gio are obviously more than friends. You always were. Anything else is pure denial. So why aren't you two together now?" She may have been glaring at him, but the priest only offered a wink.

"He left me, Carwyn. For five years he stayed away, and he knew where I was the whole time. Am I supposed to just forget all that time because he comes back and tells me he loves me?"

Carwyn lifted an eyebrow. "He told you he loves you?"

She shrugged and looked at the mounded cairns that started to appear at regular intervals along the path.

"Do you love him?"

She wouldn't have answered for anyone but him, but Carwyn was one of the people she trusted most in the world.

"Honestly? I don't know. I think part of me never stopped, but the other part of me doesn't quite trust him to stick around."

They rode in silence for a while longer.

"I understand where you're coming from, B—and heaven knows I told him he was wrong to stay away for so long—but at the same time, I do understand why he did it."

Beatrice scowled at him. "You know, I'm pretty sick of everyone thinking they know what I want more than I do."

Carwyn chuckled and brushed at the red hair that fell in his eyes. "I'm sure you are, but let me tell you, the time you were in L.A., without him, you did a lot of growing. It was lovely to watch, you know, to see you come into yourself. Do you think you would have grown the same ways if he had been there? Or if you had stayed in Houston with him?"

She clenched her jaw. "It's not that I don't agree with what you're saying. I do, but—"

"Or what kind of life would you have had if you were traveling all over the world with him? The work he was doing, B—tracking

His hand came to rest on her left arm, and his fingertips traced gentle circles along the inside of her wrist.

"Am I the only one who calls you Jacopo?"

"You're the only one who knows my name."

Beatrice closed her eyes and gave in to the comfort of his warm hands. The low hum that always accompanied the touch of his skin on hers soothed her. As she sat in bed, enjoying the feel of him, she realized if she was robbed her sight, her hearing—of every sense she had—but could only feel his touch, she would recognize him by that alone.

She sighed and smiled, closing her eyes as she relaxed into him.

"'Tu sei tutta bella, amica mia, e non v'è difetto alcuno in te,'" he murmured.

"Hmm?" She roused herself from drifting. "What does that mean?"

He tucked her head under his chin. "It means you're beautiful."

She smiled and turned her face to press her cheek to his chest.

"Do you dream? I've always wondered that."

She heard him let out a soft chuckle. "I do sometimes. Not often though."

"What do you dream about?"

He hummed a little, still sounding sleepy as he played with the ends of her hair. "The past. The future. You."

She had no idea how to respond to that. *I dream about you a lot, too. Have for years. You're usually naked.*

"So." She cleared her throat a little. "I've been reading Ioan's book about vampire biology. I remember you said he was a doctor. It's fascinating." *Speaking of naked, did you pose for some of those diagrams? I'm pretty sure I recognize your abs.*

He reached his left arm around to the table where she had set the manuscript.

"Ah, I remember helping him with this one. Deirdre did some of the sketches. Excellent resource."

"I'm sure you get tired of answering all my questions, so I thought I'd just take advantage of the library since we have a few days here."

He smiled. "I don't get tired of answering because you ask good questions. So feel free to take advantage of me any time you like."

She swatted his arm playfully. "Haha."

He only pressed a kiss to the top of her head. "What a good little librarian you are, tesoro."

"Don't be patronizing."

"I'm not. Just teasing you a bit. So, what have you learned, Miss De Novo?"

"That you aren't immortal, but you are very hard to kill."

Giovanni nodded. "Yes we are. Fire and losing our head are the only ways I've ever heard of."

"Really? Definitely no wooden stakes, huh?"

He shook his head. "No, though that would take a long time to heal if anyone tried."

"Unless you're surrounded by your element, right? Like when you burned Lorenzo and he dove in the water, he knew he would heal faster that way."

"Yes, though burns still take years to heal completely, unless you're a fire vampire. But if Carwyn was injured, he could heal very quickly if he went to ground."

"So Tenzin—"

"Is practically impervious to serious injury unless she's buried or drowned."

"Wow."

"'Wow' is a common reaction, yes."

"And you?"

He shrugged. "Fire feeds me; fire destroys me. It's a very fine line."

"So, if you allow yourself to... what do you call it?"

Giovanni smiled. "Flame up? Manifest fire? Get sparky, as Carwyn likes to say?"

Beatrice quirked her mouth in a wry smile. "Yeah, that."

He stretched an arm against the headboard. "I'm not going to lie, when I allow the fire to take over my body, it feels... heady. It's intoxicating, and it could be very addictive. It does feed something in me and it does help me heal, but at the same time, it's very, very dangerous."

"But you control it, Gio. It doesn't control you."

He shrugged. "And oddly, we have my sire to thank for that. Without the years of discipline Andros beat into me, I would probably have destroyed myself long ago."

She paused for a moment, frowning. "I don't like feeling grateful to him."

Giovanni gave her a sad smile. "He made me who I am."

"You made yourself who you are. I've read your journals."

"I wasn't a good man for a long time. It was Carwyn and then Ioan who helped to humanize me."

"And Tenzin. Kind of."

"Kind of, yes. But nothing like Ioan. He was the finest of us," he said quietly, slouching in the rumpled bed.

Beatrice wanted to erase the grief she saw fill his eyes, but she knew she couldn't, so she pulled him over to rest his head in her lap and began running her fingers through his hair like she knew he loved.

"How did you meet him?"

He lay with his head on her thigh, and she listened as he timed his breath to match hers. Finally, he spoke in a soft voice, "My father created me to be his idea of the perfect man: a scholar, an artist, a strategist, a soldier... after he was gone, when I had to make my way in the world, there was little need for strategists, artists or scholars. But there was always a need for soldiers. Especially with the talents and training I had.

"I was a known fire vampire. I knew I needed to make a reputation quickly, and I needed to make it frightening, so I used what Andros had given me, and I became the most efficient assassin and mercenary I could be."

"Who did you kill?"

"Whoever I was hired to," he said quietly.

She took a deep breath and tried to reconcile the gentle man she knew with what he was describing. Beatrice had read his journals, but it was so much more brutal to hear the truth from his own lips.

He continued when she did not speak. "After a while, I had built a decent reputation, though I was still targeted regularly. Then I met Tenzin and she wasn't what I was expecting. At all."

"Why not?

"Well, I was hired to kill her—"

"What? Tenzin?" Beatrice laughed.

"Ridiculous, I know. She is one of the oldest and most powerful vampires I have ever heard of. But I did not know her reputation when I was hired. I was young—only fifty years old or so. I took the contract, but she is the one who hunted me."

"Why am I not surprised? Where did she find you?"

"It was in the mountains of southern Siberia, perched in the branches of an evergreen. She jumped on my back like she does, and I was too shocked by her appearance to do anything but try to run away."

"But she caught you?"

"Oh yes. She laughed and told me that she'd seen me long ago. That we were fated to be great friends, and that we would work together." He raised an eyebrow. "We would be more powerful than any other vampires walking the earth."

"Talk about appealing to your ego."

"I didn't believe her about fate, but she was persuasive, and I could see how powerful she was. She's always known how to get me to do what she wants me to. And then, well, she just knew things. It was Tenzin who took the contract in London that led us to Carwyn. She always seemed to know the exact moment to get out of one situation or into another. Tenzin always... Well, she always... "

He drifted off and she noticed an odd, almost childlike, look on his face.

"Gio? What were you saying about—"

"Why did I go to the library where you worked?"

"What? You went to transcribe that manuscript, remember?"

"Yes." His eyes lit up. "The manuscript for Tenzin. The one she just had to have copied."

"Gio?" she whispered, but he could only stare at her in wonder as his head lay on her lap. He reached up to smooth away the frown that had gathered on her forehead and slowly pulled her face down to feather a kiss across her mouth.

"You are my balance in this life. In every life," he murmured against her lips.

"Gio?"

"Tu sei il mio amore," he said with a brilliant smile.

"I finally learn Latin and you switch to Italian on me, Jacopo? No fair." She frowned against his insistent lips.

"I don't want you to get bored."

"Because that's so likely, isn't it?"

He just grinned at her. "Were you bored without me?"

Beatrice didn't want to answer but knew she should considering how open he was being.

"Never mind," he said. "It's not my business. It's your—"

"Yes."

Giovanni cocked his head, as if surprised she had responded.

"I was bored without you," she continued. "I had a good life, but it wasn't anything... " It was monochrome instead of color.

"I hated being away from you, Beatrice. Even when I convinced myself it was necessary."

She blinked away the tears that tried to surface and pulled away from him. He still lay in her lap, looking up at her with an unguarded expression.

"What are we doing, Gio? I had so many questions for so many years. Why is everything suddenly not a secret?"

"Don't you know?" he murmured.

She looked into his eyes, which had once been veiled and enigmatic. Now, they were open, and Beatrice was beginning to realize that everything she thought she knew about the previous five years might have been wrong.

"I think... I'm starting to know," she finally said.

He shook his head; she could see the disappointment.

"Tell me more," she begged. "When did you meet Carwyn?"

A smile touched the corner of his mouth.

"I was a little over two hundred years old. Tenzin and I were still working together, but I had grown weary of it, no matter how efficient we were."

"You were tired of killing vampires."

"I was tired of killing anything. I mentioned a contract that Tenzin found. We'd taken a job from the old guard, the vampires that used to control London. There was a band of rogues that was terrorizing the human population in Cornwall, and we were hired to get rid of them and clean up the mess they'd left. By the time we got there, Carwyn and Ioan had already taken care of most of the problem. Carwyn had killed the young vampires and Ioan was altering all the memories of their human victims and healing those he could. It had been going on for quite some time, so there was still a lot we were able to do.

"Tenzin and I offered to share the bounty with them for the vampires they had killed, but they both refused. It intrigued us both, and we went to spend some time with them in Wales. Eventually, I decided to stay with them and leave mercenary work. I was exhausted."

"Was Tenzin mad?"

"Not really. She had begun to attract more attention than she normally liked, so she was ready to lie low for a few hundred years to let the rumors die down."

"Just a little while, huh?"

He smiled. "I told you, she's very old. I stayed with Carwyn's family for a time and slowly remembered what it was like not to spend every night looking for who would attack me next. I remembered how much I loved books, and music, and quiet. Eventually, I became convinced that I could choose to live another way. Carwyn and Ioan helped me see that."

"I'm sorry I'll never meet him," she whispered and rested her hand against his cheek.

"I'm sorry too."

"What happens when vampires die? The book was kind of vague."

He took her hand and knit their fingers together before he rested them on his chest. "If we're not burned, we return to our elements. What was left of Ioan's body lingered for a few days and then crumbled into earth. Water vampires almost melt away, but again, it's not instantaneous. And wind... well, they just disintegrate. Eventually, there is no trace of them."

"And fire?"

He shrugged. "I've never beheaded a fire vampire. I don't know. Usually, we burn."

She paused. "Why did you leave me your journals in Cochamó?"

"I wanted you to know everything. Like when I told you to tell Dez about your life. There can be no future with that many secrets, tesoro."

"But why didn't you tell me all that before?" she asked gently. "You always held back with me."

He sat up and moved to her side, looking into her eyes when he answered.

"When we first met, I didn't know if I could trust you. And when you left for Los Angeles, I wasn't sure you wanted to be part of my world. Which I understood. So I tried to shield you, Beatrice. There was no reason for you to be burdened with all of this if you were only going to touch the edges of it."

"Gio." She shook her head. "I think it's pretty obvious at this point... "

She didn't finish, and he leaned forward. "What? What's obvious?"

She stopped short of admitting she loved him. She still wondered, when the current mystery was solved, whether he would disappear from her life again. This time, she knew the hole she felt from his absence when she was younger would be dwarfed by the immense vacuum another departure would leave.

He reached over to nudge her chin toward him so she was forced to meet his eyes. "I take nothing for granted, but I will not have you make any decision blindly. I'll not have you resent me for hiding things from you."

"I don't want you to."

"Then why—"

"Are you going to leave me again?"

He drew back as if she had struck him. "What?"

"If we find Lorenzo—"

"When we find him."

Beatrice looked away. "Fine, when we find him. After he's been killed. After you find my father, will you leave again? What if you decide you don't want to feel grief like Deirdre's? What if I choose not to become a vampire? What if—"

"You'll have to be far better at evasion than even your father to lose me at this point, Beatrice De Novo."

She looked at him, and his eyes begged for her to believe him. She wanted to, she realized. More than anything, but five years still hung between them. "Are you sure? About me? About this?"

He cocked his head.

"What?" she looked down nervously, wondering at his expression.

"Deirdre asked me the same question," he said softly. "When she brought Ioan's body back. She asked me, 'Are you sure?' I didn't really understand what she meant at the time."

A memory of the fearsome woman carrying the body of her husband flashed to Beatrice's mind. "What did you answer her?"

"I never got the chance."

She swallowed the lump in her throat. "Will you answer me?"

Giovanni grasped the back of her neck and pulled her into a hard kiss; she felt the force of it down to her toes. Finally, his mouth traveled to her ear and there was no mistaking his answer.

"I am sure of the fire that runs through me. I am sure of the earth I stand on. And I am sure of you."

THIRTEEN

"When are you coming home?"

"I'm not sure yet, Benjamin. I want to come home, but it's more important that I make everyone safe first."

"From Lorenzo?"

"Yes."

He heard the boy sigh over the telephone and knew that he was probably rolling his eyes as well.

"Tell me what you and Caspar and Isadora have been doing," Giovanni said to distract him.

"Lots of stuff. They're pretty cool for old people."

He chuckled. "They are. Has Caspar taught you how to shoot yet? He thought it would be good for you to learn. He's a very good shot, so make sure you pay attention when he teaches you."

"At first I thought it was going to be really cool, but then he made me clean all the rifles after we finished." Giovanni grinned. "And that wasn't cool at all. But we shot some cans for target practice, and he said I was pretty good."

"Excellent. And how is the rest of your schooling?"

Ben huffed on the other end of the line. "Dude, Caspar isn't very good at Latin anymore, Gio."

"Well," he said and laughed, "you can be his teacher then. And how is Beatrice's grandmother? Are you getting along?"

"Other than the cleaning stuff, yeah."

"Cleaning stuff?"

"She wants me to clean my room here, like, all the time."

He frowned. "Well, I'm fairly lax on that, so pay attention to her. Your room at home is something of a disaster area."

"She's a good cook, though. I'm gonna get fat hanging out with them, Gio. They both cook really good."

"They both cook very well, and see if Isadora will give you lessons while you're staying with them, will you?"

"If it means I'll have to help her clean up the kitchen, I think she'll be okay with it."

He smiled and sat back in the chair, feeling more relaxed than he had in days. Giovanni sat in the library at Carwyn's house, enjoying the fire and listening to the wind whipping outside. Beatrice had already fallen asleep, so he had taken advantage of the time difference to call Ben in Texas.

He was surprised by how much he missed the boy and his quick humor, though he was pleased Ben was getting along so well with Caspar and Isadora.

"Caspar said your friend died."

"Yes, he did."

"Did he have kids?"

Thinking of all the children Ioan and Deirdre had sired or fostered over the years, he nodded. "He did. He had a large family."

"I'm really sorry. Tell Carwyn I'm really sorry."

"Thank you, I will."

He could almost hear the wheels turning in Ben's small head, so he wasn't surprised by the next question.

"Are you going to get hurt? I thought you couldn't die."

"Benjamin, I will do everything in my power to prevent anything happening to Beatrice and myself."

"Can't you guys just come home and hide here with us?" he asked in a small voice.

He closed his eyes and thought how he wanted to answer.

"You know, Ben, in my own way, I hid for years. I minded my own business and tried to keep out of sight so I could live my life in peace. But sometimes, minding your own business isn't the right thing to do. Sometimes, you need to confront the evil in the world. I tried to ignore that for too long and people got hurt."

"Like B? When Lorenzo took her?"

"Yes."

"And your friend? Is that because of Lorenzo, too?"

The guilt and grief threatened to overwhelm him, but he cleared his throat and answered, "Yes, that was also because of Lorenzo."

"But you're going to get him, right?"

"Yes, I'm going to make sure he can't hurt anyone else."

"And find B's dad, too, right?"

He nodded, even though he was alone. "I'm going to find her father. Eventually."

"Good, 'cause he sounds like a good guy and she misses him."

He smiled, happy to hear the more relaxed tone of the boy's voice on the other line. He could hear Caspar and Isadora talking in the background, and Giovanni wished he and Beatrice could be relaxing with them in the Texas hill country instead of stuck at an old stone house in the cold Welsh mountains.

"So, is B your girlfriend yet?"

He frowned. "I'm working on it."

"Still?"

"I think I'm still on probation. She's making sure I'm really going to stick around."

Ben was quiet for a long time before he spoke again. "I guess that makes sense. You did go away for a long time."

Giovanni sipped at the scotch he'd poured before he sat down. "I did. I thought I was doing the right thing for her."

"Did you say you're sorry?"

He sighed. "I'm not sure what to say. I still think it was necessary to leave her, so I'm not sorry I did that."

"But you hurt her feelings!"

"I know," he said sadly.

"So you should say you're sorry for hurting her feelings then."

Giovanni frowned. He hadn't thought of doing that. Sometimes children really did see things more clearly.

"—and then ask her to marry you so she knows you're not going to leave again."

He inhaled his scotch. "Wh—what?"

"Well, you want to marry her and everything, right? I mean, you love her and all that stuff, and you don't want her to go anywhere, and you want her to know you aren't going anywhere again, so... you should just ask her, and then she'll know you aren't going to leave."

His mind whirled. Strangely, the thought of marrying Beatrice hadn't occurred to him, though he knew he wanted to spend the rest of his life with her. Suddenly, Ben seemed like a genius. After all, she couldn't ignore the inherent commitment in the request, could she?

"Ben, I'll consider that, my friend."

"Good. I think she's cool. She'd be an awesome fake aunt."

He smiled. "I should let you get back to your math work. Tell Caspar and Isadora I said hello."

"Okay," Ben sighed. "Tell B and Carwyn I said hi, too."

"I will see you as soon as I am able, fake nephew."

"I miss you and my basketball court, fake uncle."

He grinned and said goodbye. His ears perked up when he heard Beatrice stirring in their bed. Carwyn had muttered about them sharing a room while they were under his roof, and his housekeeper, Sister Maggie, had glared, but he and Beatrice ignored them. He suspected that Beatrice was afraid her night-mares might return, and he didn't like risking her peace of mind to appease the priest or the nun.

Besides, he thought, they were being frustratingly celibate.

Giovanni thought of how she looked curled into his side while she slept and the alluring scent of her blood when she woke, warm and sleepy as she stretched next to him.

He had gone longer without sex in his five hundred years—much longer at times if it was necessary—but he wasn't going to lie and say he enjoyed it. Especially when the object of his desire slept next to him every night and inflamed his preternatural senses with her every pulse.

Feeling his fangs descend, he decided that he should brave the cold and hunt. There was little wildlife to choose from this time of year, and Sister Maggie had stocked donated blood for him in the kitchen, but he needed the exertion of the chase.

So he gritted his teeth and braced himself for the sour taste of mountain goat.

He walked down the hall to check on Beatrice and put on a shirt, only to find her twisted in the covers, her eyes darting behind her lids in the beginning of a nightmare. He quickly slipped into the bed behind her and pulled her to his chest, murmuring soothing words and stroking the hair back from her face.

She started and turned in his arms.

"Gio?"

"You were having a bad dream," he murmured. "Do you remember?"

She took a deep breath and relaxed. "I... kind of. I remember hearing the ocean. It was echoing like it did when I was in Greece. The waves always echoed... "

She drifted off, sighing quietly as she relived the weeks she had spent as a captive under Lorenzo's control. The water vampire had kept her isolated and alone in his compound in the middle of the Aegean Sea. Beatrice told Giovanni later she had never felt more trapped than in the small room that faced the ocean. It was why she chose to live in the hills in Los Angeles instead of on the beach. The sound of waves, though soothing to most, gave her nightmares at times.

He held her tightly, humming a tune he remembered from his human childhood. It was a song about a cricket that Giuliana had sung to him in the garden of her home in Arezzo. He remembered her lilting voice and the sun as it reflected off the water of the fountain.

"Gio?"

"Hmm?"

"What is that song?"

"'Il Grillo.' It's a song about a cricket."

"I like it. I didn't know you could sing."

"Hmm," he breathed in her scent and pulled her closer. "My uncle liked it when I sang. Andros required it. I don't really sing anymore."

"It's nice."

"Thank you."

She was quiet, but he could tell she had woken from her slumber, at least for a while. She normally had trouble getting back to sleep if she woke in the middle of the night. Ironically, she often slept better during the day.

"Gio?"

"Hmm?"

"Did you call home?"

He nodded. "Ben said hello." *And that I should ask you to marry me. What do you think?*

"How's Grandma and Cas?"

"Doing well and pestering him about cleaning up his room."

She laughed quietly, and the shaking of her body against his reminded him why he had come to the room to begin with. The feel of her curves was starting to make his blood pulse.

"Beatrice, I need to go out."

"No," she murmured and pulled his arms more securely around her waist. "I'm too comfy here. Stay."

"Tesoro," Giovanni groaned quietly and took a deep breath. It didn't help, he only managed to make his throat burn all the more and his desire spiked. "I need to go. I need to... hunt."

She stilled, and her fingers dug into his forearm.

"You're hungry?"

"Yes, I need to go out and hunt something. I need... I just need to hunt." He tried to pull away, but she clung to his arms and his jaw clenched in frustration. "Beatri—"

"Drink from me."

His blood roared when he heard her quiet voice and his fangs descended. "Are... are you sure?"

Beatrice rolled over and looked at him. "Yes. Will it be like before?"

"I won't drink too much," he whispered. "I promise." He could feel his skin heat and his heart begin to beat.

She blushed, and Giovanni stifled a low growl as the heat flooded her face. "Not that. I mean, I don't want to... you know. We probably shouldn't—"

"If you tell me 'no,' I'll stop." Giovanni clamped down his self-control. "No matter what."

"Okay," she whispered and tilted her head to the side, brushing the hair away from her neck. The scent of her skin washed over him, and he swallowed a groan. His hands reached under the camisole she wore, splaying across her back as his mouth dipped down to her neck.

He nosed against her pulse, rubbing his cheek across the delicate skin of her collar and reveling in the scent of her pounding blood. His tongue flicked out and began tracing the artery. He could feel the amnis that ran under his skin spread over her everywhere their flesh touched.

Her bare shoulders. The small of her back. Everywhere his hands went, her skin prickled in awareness. He could scent her arousal and he struggled to control his own. He fought the urge to plunge his fangs into her neck, determined to enjoy the rare pleasure of her blood and skin for as long as he could.

"Gio?" she panted, arching against him. "Are you going to—"

"Shh," he whispered. "Let me... " His tongue fluttered against the pulse point in her neck. "I don't want to rush."

"Oh," she breathed out and reached up to run her hands through the hair at the nape of his neck. Giovanni trailed his fangs along her skin. He closed his eyes and held her for a moment, feeling the beat of her heart against his chest.

"I love you," he whispered, as his hands stroked her back. He pulled her closer, but kept himself in check, determined to only take what she was offering.

He could, however, give her a taste of what she was missing.

Giovanni rolled over her, and his lips closed over her neck. He nipped at it, savoring the rush of blood to the surface. His fangs pierced around her artery, and she gasped in pleasure as the sensation of his bite combined with the electric current that ran from his lips and over her skin.

He was determined to drink slowly, but she cried out when he bit and her hands pressed his head to her neck. She arched under him as her rich blood filled his mouth. He moved against her, letting his hands roam as her blood ran down his throat, soothing and inflaming him at the same time.

It was nothing like the empty feeling Giovanni had experienced when he drank from random humans. Beatrice's touch, her smell, everything about her drew him in. When he moved, it was in time to her breath and pulse. It was need. Love. Nothing could compare to it.

He felt his amnis snap when she peaked, and her body shuddered underneath his. Her heartbeat hammered against his lips and he took one last draw from her neck before he pulled away. Their bodies slowed as he licked the last of the blood from her neck and sealed the small wounds. His hands stroked her hair, her shoulders, and down over the curve of her hips.

"Gio," she panted. "That was... "

Even as her blood coursed through his system, Giovanni hungered for more. Pushing down his own desire, he pressed her to his chest and breathed deeply, deliberately slowing the rush of his blood as he held her.

"Thank you, Beatrice."

"You're welcome. Did you get enough?" She was already falling asleep in his arms.

He smiled. "For now."

She rubbed her face into his chest and released a sigh. "Don't leave, okay? Stay with me. Just... stay."

He closed his eyes and sent up a silent prayer that she would do the same.

"Always."

"I can't believe you told her the story about me and the bear," Giovanni muttered to Carwyn as the priest piloted the Range Rover through the twisting mountain roads.

Carwyn gaped at him. "I can't believe you didn't. I thought you were trying to impress this woman."

"I hardly think that story impressed her, you idiot."

"Well," Carwyn shrugged. "It made her laugh, anyway."

Giovanni glanced at Beatrice, who had fallen asleep in the back of the vehicle as they made their way to London. "I love hearing her laugh."

"She has a great laugh, doesn't she? Did she tell you the story about when she fell off the motorcycle when I was teaching her to ride? She was so terrible at first! She broke two fingers, and we had to wait six months for her hand to be strong enough to shift again. She had such a good sense of humor about the whole thing."

Giovanni glared at him. "You broke two of my woman's fingers?"

Carwyn cocked an eyebrow at him. "Careful now, you'd been gone for two years at that point. I doubt she'd appreciate you calling her 'yours.'"

Giovanni crossed his arms over his chest. "You knew better. You knew I was coming back."

"Oh, aye, but she didn't, did she?"

He was silent for a few minutes before he muttered, "Benjamin says I need to apologize to her."

Carwyn's eyes popped open. "You've not apologized to her? For leaving for five years? Why on God's earth is she even talking to you?"

He glared at the priest. "I've explained to her—"

"I want to punch you right now, di Spada. I really do," he whispered. "That's quite childish of you." Carwyn drove in silence for a few more minutes with a frown plastered to his face. "You don't deserve her."

"What?"

"You don't! For heaven's sake, is it that hard to say you're sorry? I've not been married for a thousand years, and I know that much."

"Can we talk about something else, please? This really isn't any of your business."

"Fine. But for the record, you're lucky she's even talking to you. And don't think I can't smell her all over you or see that flush in your cheeks."

"Drop it, Father. I'll not be leaving her again," he muttered, glancing over his shoulder to make sure she was still sleeping. "I don't even think I could at this point."

Carwyn glanced between them, muttering something in Welsh, a language Giovanni had never wrapped his brain around sufficiently, before he looked back to the dark road ahead. "Let's talk about London."

"Fine. What have Terrance's people found out?"

Carwyn shrugged. "It's been vague, but there seem to be enough reports of your boy lingering to make Terry think he's still around. It's a large port and with easy access to the French coast, it makes it harder to get a handle on him."

"Lorenzo had allies in Le Havre at one point. Has that been investigated?"

"It has, but not thoroughly. You know how tricky the French can be. Also, they're water clans in that area, so they're tight lipped to any that aren't their own."

Giovanni racked his memory, trying to think of some connection he might use to get more information. "I could always ask Livia. One more favor to add to the growing list."

Carwyn said, "Do you have time for that? Besides, you know how she is. She'll not give you anything unless you come to Rome, and I doubt you want to take a side trip right now. Would you bring B? That would be interesting."

Giovanni sighed. "They'll have to meet eventually, and Beatrice handled the meeting with the Alvarezes in Los Angeles quite well."

"Ernesto Alvarez is a friendly guppy compared to the sharks that swim in Livia's sea. Don't dump her into that until you have to."

"I think you're underestimating Beatrice, Carwyn. She's a fast learner and I have a feeling that she'll have a knack for the political side of our life."

"Well, one of us should. I hate that stuff, and you piss people off too quickly. Don't get me started on Tenzin."

"Tenzin said something about Beatrice being my balance," he murmured.

Carwyn frowned. "You're not thinking—"

"I'm not thinking anything at this point. It's not an issue yet. She's handled herself extremely well so far. Ernesto was incredibly impressed with her. You could almost see him salivating at her potential." He looked over his shoulder at the young woman who still slept peacefully. "We'll see how she does in London. Meeting Terry and Gemma ought to be interesting."

"Does she know about you and Gemma?"

He paused, thinking about Carwyn's daughter, who was also a former lover. "I've told her we were involved, and that we are still friendly."

He heard Carwyn chuckle quietly before the Welshman laughed out loud.

"What?" Giovanni's voice dripped in irritation.

"You make it sound like the two of you were study partners at university!"

"Beatrice knows that I love her." He glanced at the sleeping woman in the backseat. "There was no need to go into detail."

"Well, don't let her imagine the worst. And she doesn't need to hear about your sporadic relationship with my daughter from someone else, either, so make sure it's from you."

"Gemma and I were never serious."

"I know that, but you two danced around each other for almost two hundred years, so don't just dismiss it."

"I can't believe she's marrying Terry. I would never have put them together."

"Well, sometimes we find our match in the most unexpected places, don't we?"

Giovanni turned to stare at Beatrice. Her head was slumped to the side of the car, and she was curled up with his coat covering her in the back seat. He had the urge to crawl next to her so she was lying against his side as she slept.

"I've never felt for any woman what I feel for her, Carwyn," he said quietly. "It's somewhat terrifying at times."

He heard his friend start to speak a few times, but he kept pausing. Finally, he heard him mutter under his breath.

"You're a lucky bastard, Giovanni Vecchio."

Giovanni was reminded why he hated London as soon as they arrived, but he tried to enjoy it through Beatrice's eyes. Carwyn had woken her as soon as they crossed into the city and started pointing out the sights. She smiled and bounced, enjoying the historic town as he tried to smother his own displeasure.

He hated the city. The streets were too crowded. The traffic too rushed. Too many people pressed against him if he tried to walk around, and there was too much noise. The air quality may have improved, but he remembered when coal smoke hung over the dreary town and soured the air. More than anything, Giovanni hated the cold damp that reminded him of the school in Crotone where Andros had held him against his will for so many years.

"Don't be such an old man," she teased him. "How long are we staying, anyway?"

"As long as we need to. I may not be very fond of London, but Gemma and Terrance are close allies and this is the best place to start looking for Lorenzo. If the information you found is correct, he's still in England or France. Between the three of us and all of their contacts, we have a very good chance of finding him. It may only take a few weeks if we're lucky."

She fell silent; finally, he heard her heave a great sigh.

"Beatrice?" He turned to look at her grim face.

"I'm going to have to quit my job."

Giovanni turned around so she didn't see his satisfied smirk. "Oh no. Whatever will you do?"

She pinched his ear. "Shut up and don't gloat. I'm quite capable of surviving without a job, thanks to my superior embezzling skills. I haven't agreed to work for you yet."

Carwyn snorted, but Giovanni just grinned.

"Yet."

Fourteen

London, England

"Another glass of wine... *B*?"

Gemma arched an eyebrow at her in the formal sitting room of the house in Mayfair. They had arrived at the home of Terrance Ramsay only an hour before and been immediately welcomed by more household staff than Beatrice had ever seen outside a period film.

"No, thank you."

"Perhaps some tea?"

"No," she smiled stiffly at the extremely elegant vampire sitting across from her. "Thank you."

Gemma Melcombe may have been Carwyn's oldest daughter and second child, but her manners, accent, and wardrobe revealed none of what Beatrice suspected were probably humble origins. It wasn't just the staff that seemed to belong in a period film. Gemma's delicate features, gold-spun hair, and tinkling laugh made it hard not to imagine her in lace and petticoats, riding in a carriage to a ball.

Which she had most likely done on more than one occasion. Possibly in Giovanni's company.

Casually involved, my ass. Beatrice plastered a pleasant smile on her face.

"What do you mean, you were involved? She's an old girlfriend or something?"

"Nothing that serious, tesoro. I just wanted to let you know. We're friendly now. She's apparently quite happy with her fiancé."

"Oh."

"What?"

"Nothing."

"Are you jealous?"

"Why would I be jealous? You said it was years ago."

"A vampire can hope, can't he?"

Beatrice hadn't asked more about their involvement, and she pushed away the cold lick of jealousy, knowing it was unreasonable. Giovanni, for all his keen intellect, could be startlingly obtuse about human nature at times. Because whatever he thought about their friendship, Gemma Melcombe was completely in love with him.

"Perhaps I should show you to your room," Gemma said with a polite smile. "I've prepared one of our guest suites for you. The windows are east-facing, so you'll be able to enjoy the morning—"

"Beatrice will share my room, Gemma," Giovanni murmured.

He had been sitting next to her on the small sofa, lost in his thoughts and absently playing with the ends of her hair. Upon their arrival, Carwyn and Gemma had taken a few moments together, presumably to talk about Ioan, before Terry and Carwyn had retreated to the study to speak to Terry's lieutenant about the current political situation, leaving Giovanni, Gemma, and Beatrice in the elegant sitting room to become acquainted.

Giovanni's skin, Beatrice observed with perverse satisfaction, was still flushed from feeding from her the night before, and she noticed he seemed quicker than he had been in weeks. His amnis was stronger, as well; she wondered how much his diet of donated blood had been affecting his health.

"You want her to share your room in the basement?" Gemma laughed, cutting her eyes toward Beatrice. "Surely she will want something brighter, Gio."

"We always share a room. We both rest better that way." Beatrice tried not to sound smug, but she remembered Giovanni telling her years ago that no one had seen him sleep in hundreds of years, so she knew Gemma was probably included in that. She placed a proprietary hand on his thigh and smiled.

"Well—" Gemma's blue eyes frosted. "—I'm sure that will be fine."

"Tesoro, if you want to rest, I will meet with Carwyn and Terry and fill you in at first dark. Gemma, will you be joining us in the study?"

"Of course," Gemma said. "Terry always asks for my opinion. It's what makes us such excellent partners."

"I forgot to offer my congratulations on your engagement. You and Terrance are a wonderful couple."

Beatrice could see the flash of hurt in Gemma's eyes and wondered again how Giovanni could be so dense.

"Thank you. We're very happy. I'm sure you can imagine how pleased Father is, as well."

"Congratulations," Beatrice added. "If you could show me to a phone, I have a few calls to make before I turn in." She turned to Giovanni, still resting a hand on his thigh. "I need to talk to Dez, and I'll call Dr. Stevens this afternoon."

He frowned and reached up to trace her cheek. "All joking aside, I am sorry about your job. I never intended—"

"Oh, yes you did," Beatrice laughed. "Don't lie. You wouldn't have forced the issue, but don't pretend like you're not pleased."

He winked at her and tugged at a lock of her hair. Beatrice saw Gemma watching them out of the corner of her eye.

"Sorry," she said. "I'm having job issues. If you could show me to a phone, it would be great."

"Of course." Gemma smiled politely. "Giovanni, I'll meet you in the study. Make yourself at home. You know where everything is."

"Of course."

They stood, and he leaned down to place a quick kiss on Beatrice's cheek before he stepped out of the room. Beatrice turned to her hostess, who had a hand held toward the door.

"I'll show you to Gio's room. We keep one for him since he visits so often. It's almost like a second home for him."

"I'm sure." Beatrice smiled and tried not to grit her teeth.

"There's a phone on the desk in his room."

They walked down the hall, and Gemma opened a door that lead to a small landing and a set of stairs that curved down to the plush basement level of the house. Gemma walked at a leisurely pace, gliding down with preternatural grace while Beatrice felt like an awkward young girl trailing after her.

"Do tell me what dietary accommodation my cook will need for Gio. She's stocked some of the blood type he prefers, but let us know—"

"Oh, he won't be needing anything," Beatrice said. "He's taken care of."

Gemma halted on the stairs and raised a lofty eyebrow. "Is that so?"

"Very so," Beatrice said as she stepped past Gemma and continued down the stairwell. She halted at the foot of the stairs and turned with her hands in her pockets, tapping her boot on the floor as she waited for Gemma to reach her.

"So," she said, looking up and down the rich gold hallway. "Which room is ours?"

"Cat fight! Hiss hiss hiss," Dez said. "Wish I was there to see it. Damn, how do you get all these good looking men nuts about you? Tell me your secret."

"My secret?" Beatrice rolled her eyes. "I don't know. I smell good? At least Gio seems to think so. What about Matt? I thought Ken and Barbie were ready for their dream house."

"Shut up, you smelly man-magnet. We're not moving in together. And I'm just joking. Matt... " Dez gave a dreamy sigh. "He's so great. He's so fun and smart. I even met his parents at Christmas time and they're really cool, too. I can't believe he was into me for so long and I never knew about it."

"Yeah, imagine that. I've only been telling you to ask him out for three years now. I can't imagine what I was thinking. Who would have thought?"

"You know, some people say that sarcasm is not an attractive feature in a woman, Beatrice De Novo."

"Luckily, I don't give a shit about any of those people."

Dez laughed before suddenly turning serious. "So, I'm not going to be seeing you any time soon, am I?"

Beatrice settled back into the four-poster bed in Giovanni's chamber. It was decorated in dark burgundy and navy stripes, and rich mahogany furniture graced the room. There was an old-fashioned rotary phone on the bedside table, so she had kicked off her Docs and stretched out on the bed to call her best friend.

"I don't think so. It's not good. I don't know how much Matt's told you—"

"He told me that Lorenzo is back in business. And that he killed one of Carwyn's kids."

"Yeah," she sighed, relieved that Giovanni had kept Matt informed about the danger. "I want you to make sure you're not out by yourself at night, Dezi. I couldn't take losing a friend right now. I'm just... " She pinched the bridge of her nose as she began to feel the tension and exhaustion catch up with her. "I feel like my life is so crazy right now. I need to remind myself that the real world still exists."

"What are you talking about?"

"What?"

"What are you talking about 'the real world?' Have you been swept into another dimension? No one told me about that part if you have been."

"No," Beatrice frowned. "You know what I mean." She paused, looking around the dim, windowless room. "You know, you and Matt are part of my real life and—"

Dez laughed. "What are you talking about, your 'real life?'"

"Just all the non-vampire stuff. I know it's kind of crazy."

"Well, I don't know," Dez said. "I'm not an expert in any of this, but how is this not your real life?"

Beatrice said, "Maybe because there's vampires and villains and mysterious books and constant turmoil and danger?"

There was a long pause before Dez spoke again. "You could have stayed here, B. Matt told me Gio was having him watch you and all the security he had in place and even about the water vampires you're related to and everything—which, by the way, seems really cool, you should have told me about that—"

"What are you trying to say?"

She heard Dez take a deep breath. "You could have stayed here. None of this was forced on you. Gio didn't drag you away with him—you went. In fact, if I know you, you insisted on going."

Beatrice shifted on the richly appointed bed. "Yeah? So?"

"I just mean, I know you're human and that hasn't changed, but your world is bigger." Dez paused. "It has been for a while. You just weren't admitting it."

"So, you're saying—"

"Vampires and villains, danger and mystery... that is your real world. I mean, if you could forget all this and go back to the life you had before, would you even want to?"

"I don't know," Beatrice murmured.

"If it meant losing Gio? And Carwyn? Or missing the chance to find your dad someday?"

"No," she whispered. "I'd never choose that."

"Then I think you know what your 'real life' is, don't you? It's not the Huntington and the harmless boyfriend and a house in the suburbs."

She rolled her eyes. "Setting aside the suburbs comment, I know what you're saying, but I don't want to lose you, Dez."

"Please," she said. "Like you could. This shit is so damn cool, I'm dragging myself along with you."

Beatrice laughed, wiping tears from her eyes and swallowing the lump that had formed in her throat. "Oh, Dez, thanks for the perspective. I have to call and quit my job later today and I know that's not going to go well."

"Quitting over the phone from thousands of miles away? Nope, I don't think you're going to get a shining reference after that."

"No kidding. Well, I'm going to tell them it's an emergency, and it can't be helped. That's the best I can do. I have no idea when I'm going to be back in the States."

"Tell them it's a family emergency. Because it is."

"Yeah." Beatrice smiled, looking at Giovanni's coat, which lay on the back of a chair, tangled with her own. "I think it is."

They talked for another half an hour, chatting about mundane details like bills, houseplants, and cleaning out offices; but when Beatrice hung up the phone with her best friend, she felt like she had a new outlook on her life.

On her real, supernatural, hanging out with dangerous immortals, running from danger, plotting to kill, searching for elusive fathers and hidden books life.

And she finally felt like she could handle that.

"I want you to teach me how to fight better."

Giovanni arched his eyebrow at her as he stretched on the bed. "I'm not sure that's a good idea. You already have good self-defense skills; that's enough."

She sat up and crossed her arms over her chest. She had fallen asleep after an upsetting phone call with her former boss. Though she understood the woman's anger, Beatrice was longing for her kickboxing class; she really wanted to punch something.

"Why shouldn't I learn how to fight?"

He sat up next to her, raking his hands through his hair before he crossed his arms across his chest. "In what way are you equipped to fight a vampire, Beatrice? You are not as strong nor as fast. You don't have any elemental—"

"I know all that, all right?"

"So unless you're ready to talk about possibly turning—"

"So not ready for that discussion, Gio." She glared at him.

Giovanni examined her, looking every bit the five-hundred-year old, stubborn man that he was before he shrugged. "Then you learning how to fight vampires is a moot point."

"It wasn't a vampire who kidnapped me from the library. That was an old man with a gun that scared me to death and caught me by surprise."

"Beatrice—"

"It wasn't a vampire who guarded me on Lorenzo's island. It was a bunch of humans who were doing his work during the day."

He remained silent, staring into the fire with a stubborn set to his jaw.

"During the day," she reasoned, "I can be as strong, or stronger, than anything in this world, mortal or immortal. But I need to know more. I have self-defense training, but I don't know much about weapons or offensive fighting. You know about all that stuff, and I want you to teach me."

Giovanni didn't say anything, and she was beginning to think he was going to just ignore her request.

"I cannot help you learn to fight."

"Why not?"

He turned with a clenched jaw. "Because the mere thought of harming you, even while practicing, goes against every natural instinct I have! You cannot ask me to try to hurt you when everything in my being tells me to protect you. It is not an option for me, Beatrice."

She took a deep breath and lifted a hand to stroke his hair, calming him until she could no longer feel the flair of heat coming off his body.

"And don't ask Carwyn to help you. I would end up hurting him, and I don't want that."

She rolled her eyes but continued to stroke his hair, moving further down his bare back as she soothed him. A thought occurred to her. It wasn't pleasant, but she gritted her teeth and forced herself to ask.

"What about Gemma?"

"Have Gemma train you?" She could see him tilt his head as he considered it. "Well," he began, "that idea has some merit. I suppose if I told her to be very careful... If you're going to insist on it, she would be the person to ask. She's a fierce fighter, but I know she wouldn't be too harsh with you."

Beatrice forced herself to hold in the snort and focus on her goals. If anyone in the house would go easy on her, it most definitely would not be Gemma.

"Again!"

Beatrice blinked back the tears that dripped from her eyes and forced herself up to her knees. Even after years of martial arts training and a week with the vampire, she felt as if she was hitting a rock wall every time she came at her opponent. Gemma may have looked like a "lady of the manor," but her fighting style was far more "hooligan in the pub." It was nothing like she had imagined, and she was rethinking her determination to improve her fighting skills.

"Stand up and come at me, girl. Don't be so obvious in your attack next time. I saw that punch coming from a mile away. Go for the dirty punch. Always. And hit your opponent when they're down. There is no such thing as a fair fight."

"Fine," Beatrice muttered as she struggled to stand. Every muscle in her body ached and she tasted the blood in her mouth. She told Gemma not to bruise her in obvious places that Giovanni would see, but she was grateful it was wintertime. If he could see the series of bruises she was hiding under her clothes, Beatrice knew he would have lost it.

"You think you can take on a vampire? Currently, my lady's maid has better fighting skills." Gemma stood across from her, looking fresh and young in baby blue workout clothes that belied her ferocity. It was no wonder she had survived for over seven hundred years; the woman was lethal. Beatrice forced herself into position again.

"Remember, throw your attacker off-balance. It's the only way your small size can be used to your advantage."

"Got it."

They circled each other, both eyeing the other for weaknesses.

"I imagine Gio has to be quite careful with you, doesn't he?"

"What—" She ducked to the left as Gemma's arm shot out. "Are you talking about?"

Beatrice winced as Gemma landed a punishing fist to the shoulder. "Oh, you must know. He was always quite... vigorous if I remember correctly." The vampire gave her a wicked, knowing grin.

Bitch, Beatrice thought, dodging the blow Gemma aimed at

her chest, only to miss the one that struck her abdomen. She doubled over for a second before she stood, trying to keep a clear eye on the vampire.

"Well, he certainly doesn't seem to have any complaints," Beatrice panted. "At least, he didn't last night." When we did nothing but sleep because I was sore and could barely handle an arm around me.

Gemma grinned as if she could read her mind. "You're such a sweet little thing. I'm sure you'll miss him when he's gone to France."

"Yeah," she grunted as she managed to block a swift kick to her knee. "Because God knows I was waiting in my bedroom, crying, for the five years we were apart."

Gemma cocked an eyebrow at her before she flipped backward over Beatrice's head.

"Hey!" Beatrice said as she spun around and avoided Gemma trying to sweep her leg. "I thought you were keeping it to human speed." She darted to the side and grabbed the edge of Gemma's shorts, pulling the vampire closer as she tried to throw her off-balance.

"And I thought," Gemma laughed. "That you wanted to learn how to fight vampires, little girl."

"Fine." Beatrice grunted when Gemma punched her side. Even though she was only using half her strength, the blow caused tears to spring to her eyes.

Gemma stepped back and wiped at a spot of blood Beatrice had spilled on her arm, allowing the human to catch her breath.

"I forget sometimes that you two are only recently reunited. Terry hasn't left my side in twenty years, at least." She darted in and landed a kick to Beatrice's hamstring. "He's so devoted."

Okay, that one hurt a little. Beatrice was determined not to show any mental weakness before the woman, even if physical fortitude wasn't an option.

"You need to toughen up," Gemma continued. "And you need

to get faster. Watch me." Gemma attacked one of the training dummies in the large studio on the second floor of Terry's house. Beatrice watched in awe as Gemma laid a flurry of punches, elbows, and even a few head-butts to the dummy in the corner. Though she had slowed to human speed, Beatrice still recognized the utter ruthlessness of the attack.

"Now, try that on the dummy, and then you can try it on me. After that, you need to run some more; your stamina is still not up to snuff. And be quicker. Make yourself so fast they can't grab you. If they do, you're dead."

"Fine," she grunted, approaching the dummy in the corner. Beatrice had been training for over two hours that night. She was exhausted but tried to rouse herself so she didn't meet Gemma's mocking eyes when she finished.

She imagined the face of her old boss for a moment, but that didn't raise as much ire as it had the week before. Then she imagined Gemma's face, but not even the sneering blonde could raise her out of her exhaustion.

Finally, she imagined the look on Deirdre's face when she felt Ioan's death. She remembered the howl of her cries before the ground swallowed her; then she imagined pale hands restraining Giovanni.

A cold calm settled as she cleared her mind and focused the way Tenzin had practiced with her. She sprang, first into the combination Gemma had shown her, but she couldn't stop. She rained down blows over and over until she felt her knuckles slip wet against the plastic skin. Beatrice paused to catch her breath, leaning down and bracing her hands on her knees. As she wiped the sweat from her eyes, she realized her knuckles were bloody and the skin of her knees was torn.

Beatrice glanced over her shoulder to look for Gemma and found the blond woman watching her with narrowed blue eyes. Her stance was relaxed and a small smile played on her porcelain face.

"You'll do fine," she said. "Now run."

"Ow, ow, ow," Beatrice whined as she sank into the bathtub. She was exhausted, sore, bloody at the joints, but relieved as well. She was finally getting a little less battered every night. Beatrice and Gemma had been training together for over two weeks, and as much as Beatrice resented her, she had to admit the vampire was giving her a lot of precious time.

Beatrice had realized soon after she learned Giovanni was a vampire that, as much as their strength and speed gave them physical advantages, the fact that vampires were housebound for half of the day put severe limitations on their immortal lives. Even older immortals like Carwyn who could be awake for much of the day were groggy and weak, exhibiting barely human strength and even less speed.

For Gemma to devote as much of her limited night hours to training Beatrice as she had—no matter how much satisfaction she got from beating her up on a regular basis—was not something Beatrice could forget, and she was reluctantly grateful.

She relaxed into the heat of the bath, wishing that she could share how sore she was with Giovanni, but knowing instinctively that he would not react well. He and Carwyn had been in France for a week, trying to determine what connections Lorenzo still had and meeting with possible allies. It was a delicate balancing act, since most of the French immortals seemed to hate Terry, Gemma, and all their people simply because they were English.

"Vampire drama," she muttered. It still reminded her a little bit of high school.

She heard the door to the bedroom open and Giovanni's voice when he walked in. Her eyes popped open. He was back early.

"Shit," she whispered and stuck her bloodied hands under the water.

"Beatrice? I'm back."

"Hey, just taking a bath. I was training tonight," she called through the door.

Shit, shit, shit.

"How are you feeling? Gemma was quite complimentary of your determination when I talked to her. She says your speed is improving as well."

He sounded impressed, and she hoped he wasn't breathing too deeply.

"That's good to hear," she said and ran the soap over her knees, trying to clean the blood from her skin even though it made her wince.

Owwwwww.

"Beatrice?"

No!

She panicked and ducked under the water, remembering all the blood that had stained her hair from her broken knuckles. She heard him snarl from the other room.

"Why do I smell so much blood?"

Too late.

She surfaced to see an irate vampire standing over her.

"I'm naked, Gio! Naked! Get out of here."

He ignored her, his eyes raking over her bruised form and bloody joints.

"What the hell is going on?" he roared. "You look like you've been attacked."

"I was. On purpose. That's kind of the point, isn't it?"

She sat up in the bathtub and crossed her arms over her bare breasts.

"What has Gemma been doing to you? She was supposed to take care of you. She was supposed to make sure—"

"We've been training. And I don't want her to go easy on me, that's not helpful. Now will you—"

"I told her not to hurt you!" he yelled. "I told her to temper herself and make sure—"

"The last person in this house that's going to temper herself around me is Gemma! That's the only reason—"

"What is that supposed to mean?"

She finally realized he wasn't going to leave the bathroom while they were arguing, so she swallowed her embarrassment and continued washing up.

"Do you really not know she's in love with you, Gio?" she whispered, conscious of the sensitive ears that filled the house. She rinsed out her hair as Giovanni stood over her, glowering. "Gemma is in love with you. And you love me and she's not going to cut me any slack in the training room. That's the only reason I suggested training with her."

He wore a furious expression when he finally spoke. "You're being ridiculous and jealous, Beatrice. And this is beneath you."

She stood up, water sloshing out of the tub as she grabbed a towel from the stand.

"I am not. Stop being a pretentious ass and get out of the bathroom right now." She shoved his chest when she caught him glancing at her breasts. "We will argue about this when I'm dressed."

He turned and stormed out of the room. She heard the bedroom door open.

"And do not go looking for Gemma right now!"

She heard a pause before the door slammed shut. His heavy footsteps paced the bedroom. Beatrice toweled off, grimacing at the broken skin on her knees, elbows, and fists. She ached badly but forced herself into her soft sleep pants and t-shirt without a sound. Finally, she grabbed her hairbrush and went to sit on the bed to work the tangles out of her knotted hair.

Giovanni had stopped pacing and was standing with his back against the door, the scent of smoke pouring off him.

"You better calm down. You'll burn that shirt if you don't."

His jaw unclenched enough for him to speak slowly. "I am not interested in the state of my wardrobe, Beatrice."

"Well, calm down anyway." She started working the brush through her hair, but he darted behind her and sat with his legs on either side, running one hand down her arm to grab the brush.

"Let me," he said in a gentle voice. "You're hurting. Just try to relax."

He started to pull the brush through her tangled hair, stopping to work out the knots as she tried not to wince. She was sore and beginning to get stiff in the cold room.

As if sensing her discomfort, Giovanni tossed small blue flames toward the grate, where they lit the wood that was waiting to be kindled. She sighed and tried to relax her shoulders.

He spoke softly as he worked. "Why do you say she's in love with me? We were involved, but it was never serious."

"Well, obviously it wasn't for you, but from the way she looks at you, it was for her."

"But I never felt for her what I feel for you. I have an affection for her; I consider her a friend."

"And I'm not trying to interfere with that, Gio. I understand, I'm just—"

"Did she beat you like this because I love you?" he asked in a whisper.

Beatrice stopped his hands and turned so she could look him in the eye. She placed one hand on his cheek. "No. We were sparring, and she's a good teacher. My sensei in L.A. would have treated me just the same. Well, if he was a vampire." She shook her head. "It wouldn't do me any favors for her to go easy on me. I need to know how to fight." She turned back around to face the fire, and he continued to brush her hair out.

He finally spoke again. "Is this because you don't trust me to stay? The fighting? Is it because you think I'll leave you again?"

Was it? It was a fair question, but the more she thought about it, the more she realized that even if Giovanni didn't leave, she would still feel like she needed to be able to defend herself.

"You can't be with me all the time. You have to sleep during the day, and I don't want you following me around all night, either. We'd both go nuts."

He put the brush down and laid his hands lightly on her waist.

"Maybe I'll lock you in with me during the day," he said in a teasing voice, pinching her waist and putting his chin on her shoulder. "I think I could keep you occupied."

She rolled her eyes. "You wouldn't dare. I would draw all over your face while you slept. I'd write, 'I'm a pretentious ass' on your forehead."

Beatrice felt him chuckle and his skin was cool, so she knew he was no longer angry.

"Where does it hurt? Let me help."

"Can your blood do anything? What if I drink a little?"

"Unfortunately, it only works on open wounds for humans." He turned her and rolled her pants up to her torn knees. He bit his finger and started rubbing the blood into the cuts. She felt a tingle as it spread over her skin; then she saw the wounds start to knit together before her eyes.

"That is wicked cool."

He smirked. "If you were a vampire, some of my blood would help heal your bruises, too. But your human metabolism would break it down before it could take effect. It will help on any open wounds, though. Give me your hands." He held out his hands and she placed her palms into them as he bit his thumbs and spread the healing blood over the cuts there, as well.

"Thanks."

He shrugged and finished looking over her arms, healing, then cleaning any wounds he found. Finally, he tilted her face up and she saw him pierce his tongue. He licked from her chin, mending the cut there before he traced along her bottom lip. She could feel the tingling before he caught her lips in a gentle kiss.

Giovanni sighed into her mouth and wrapped his arms around her. Even though his embrace was gentle, Beatrice winced when he touched her shoulder, and he backed away.

"Sorry, sorry," she muttered. "I'm still pretty sore."

He picked her up and laid her down on the bed, stretching out beside her and rolling up her shirt.

"Don't apologize. Just tell me where it hurts."

"What are you—"

"Heating pads for hands, remember? Tell me where it hurts."

She slowly relaxed as he kneaded her sore body, making his hands almost painfully hot at times to treat the battered muscles. By the time he was finished, she was limp as a rag and half-asleep.

"Tell me what happened in France," she murmured.

"Shhh. Tomorrow, Beatrice. I'll be here when you wake up."

"Okay... night."

He wrapped his warm arms around her, and she drifted away.

FIFTEEN

The Swan with Two Necks was not a pub where tourists would venture. In fact, as Giovanni looked around, he thought even the fiercest of immortals would balk at entering the dark bar in London's Docklands, if for no other reason than to avoid tasting a human with Hepatitis, which was never a pleasant experience.

But the dark pub was the known meeting place for the canny water vampire he and Gemma were finally meeting that night. Tywyll only had one name, as far as anyone knew. And his name was the only thing most humans or vampires knew about the dark vampire whose skiff moved up and down the River Thames, trading and controlling the valuable flow of information Giovanni needed to access.

He had brought Gemma along because Terry had jokingly informed him the night before that Tywyll had a rather unexpected, and very unrequited, infatuation with his old friend. He had been avoiding spending time alone with Gemma since Beatrice's revelation of Gemma's feelings for him.

"So, ye' want to know whether yer boy ha' been on the river, do ye'?"

Tywyll took a gulp of the porter in front of him. He was a small, dark man with an enigmatic middle-aged face that indicated he could have been turned anywhere between ages twenty and fifty, depending on when he had lived his mortal life.

Giovanni had long suspected Tywyll could give Tenzin competition in the age department. He glanced at Gemma, nodding toward the old vampire.

"If you had any information about Lorenzo, Tywyll, we'd be most grateful for it." She smiled. Gemma was perched precariously on the bench in the small booth where they had found the man, and her legs were pressed to his as she scowled at Giovanni across the table.

"Eh, lass, I'm sure you and yer man would be most grateful, but what of the Italian next to ye'? Is he wantin' the goods as well?"

Tywyll stared at Giovanni with hooded eyes. He knew that Giovanni wanted the information, but what he needed to know was if the fire vampire recognized the favor that would be owed for his cooperation.

Giovanni nodded. "I would be grateful for any information you could obtain about my son's whereabouts or activities, Tywyll."

Understanding offered, Tywyll sat back in the booth and took another sip of his pint. He eyed Giovanni with dark delight, happy to be doing a favor for the feared immortal.

"I'll not lie to ye', he's not been upriver that I've heard. And I'd know. I might be makin' my way down to the mouth of the river in the next week or so. If I hear anything of value, I'll let ye' know."

It was as close to a promise of investigation as they would get from the old vampire. Tywyll had a reputation as a loner, which was unusual for a water vampire, but Giovanni had long suspected that, like Tenzin, the vampire was simply too old to comfortably socialize with others more steeped in the modern world.

Instead, he maintained an extensive list of contacts up and

down the river who owed him favors of one sort or another. If Lorenzo was in London, he was probably in a boat. If he was in a boat, then Tywyll would be able to locate him.

"Thank you ever so much, Tywyll," Gemma started. "As always, it's a pleasure to see you. Of course—"

"We'll be staying to finish our drinks," Giovanni added quickly. "I'm living near the water now and I'm considering buying a boat of some kind. I'd greatly appreciate any insight you could give me."

The old vampire grinned and glanced at Gemma from the corner of his eye, keen to play along with Gemma's discomfort if it meant he could spend more time with her.

"Well, now... it all depends on what yer wantin' the vessel for, doesn't it?"

"You know, Giovanni, I used to consider you a friend. That time has passed."

He laughed and twisted the woolen scarf around his neck as he and Gemma walked the damp streets. They had left the car and driver in one of the more recently gentrified areas of the Docklands where the old Bentley wouldn't be as conspicuous.

"Whatever could you mean, my dear? He was a delightful companion for drinks. If I lived in the area, I'd surely make a habit of meeting him for a beer now and then."

"You're a miserable, spiteful man, Giovanni Vecchio. And if it was your knee he was not-so-subtly brushing against, you'd be humming a different tune."

"I'm sure I wouldn't be humming at all." He grinned as they approached the car. "Nonetheless, I'm grateful you came. I doubt he would have trusted to meet with me otherwise. I know I don't have the best reputation here."

"If you hadn't have been so damn lethal during the sixteenth century, people might have forgotten by now."

"Fair enough. I appreciate the favor."

He opened the car door for her and she immediately raised the privacy screen Terry installed in all his vehicles. Not only did it provide complete sound insulation, it also protected the mechanics of the car more effectively from the energy that coursed through the vehicle if more than one vampire was present.

"So," he asked. "How is Beatrice's training going? She's very close-mouthed about the whole business with me."

"Probably because she knows how overprotective you are."

"Protective, not overprotective."

She fluttered a dismissive hand. "Beatrice is doing quite well for a human. I'm glad she's meeting with Terry tonight for firearms training. She's ready for it. I have a feeling she'll be an excellent markswoman."

He nodded with a smile on his face. Sometime after they had arrived in London and she had quit her job, Beatrice seemed to gain a new sense of resolve. As much as he disliked it initially, she had thrown herself into her training with Gemma; she had also taken an active part in the search for Lorenzo, which he did appreciate. Though Giovanni hated that she was constantly bruised, he sensed her physical confidence growing.

She was also becoming more affectionate with him, and Giovanni often rose in the evening to find her curled into his side sleeping or reading a book. He couldn't forget the picture she had made under the water, naked and floating in the large tub with her hair drifting around her. Though he had seen her in damp clothes more than once and had a good imagination, it was the first time he had seen her completely bare and, if not for the bruises covering her body, he would have had a hard time controlling himself at the sight.

Thinking of their argument that night, he looked at the woman next to him and frowned; Gemma caught his eye and squirmed.

"Gio?"

"Hmm?"

"I've been wondering... are you angry with me for training

her?" Giovanni looked at Gemma's hands, which were twisted in her lap. "I know you're not pleased about her fighting, but it really is her choice. I don't want you to be angry."

She's always been so supremely confident with everyone but me. Gemma's age, her strength, and her intelligence made her a force to be reckoned with, but she had always seemed to lose her nerve around Giovanni at odd times.

And he suddenly realized why.

"Are you in love with me?"

She stared at him with wide blue eyes.

"What are you talking about? I'm marrying—"

"Are you in love with me, Gemma?"

Her eyes narrowed and grew colder.

"You really are a right bastard," she said harshly, her cultured accent slipping in anger. "You have no idea, do you?"

"You are," he muttered with a frown. "You are, and I had no idea. She's right, I'm really quite obtuse at times, aren't I?"

Gemma curled her lip. "Well, that's something your perceptive little human and I agree on, Giovanni." Then she shrugged and faced forward, crossing her arms across her dove-grey suit and lifting her chin.

"Why are you marrying Terry?"

"Because he's a good man, an excellent partner, and he knows me and cares for me as I am."

He frowned. "Do you love him?"

Giovanni saw her roll her eyes. "For a five-hundred-year old vampire, you're remarkably sentimental at times, do you know that? Perhaps it's because you were raised during the Renaissance." She shook her head. "For most of human history, marriages were arranged and almost none of them were based on love. I have a huge amount of respect for my fiancé, a real affection for him, and the sex is surprisingly good. Nothing explosive like we were, but for long-term prospects, I doubt I'll see better. I foresee Terry and I working well together for hundreds of years. Past that?" She shrugged. "Who knows? Nothing is permanent in this life. If we choose to part ways after that, then I'm sure we can reach an amicable arrangement. We're both very pragmatic people."

"But Deirdre and Ioan—"

"Had something very few people ever find." She cut her eyes toward him. "Don't tell me about my brother and sister. What they had... " She turned away, but not before he could see the sheen of tears in her eyes. "What they had was unique. I've never... even what I may feel for you is nothing like what they had. Ioan and Deirdre were special, Gio."

A single tear slipped down her cheek, and he reached across the car to take her hand in his.

"I know, Gemma." He squeezed her fingers. "I know. I miss him, too."

They sat in silence the rest of the drive to the house, and Giovanni knew they would never speak of her feelings for him again.

Beatrice straightened his tie for him before they went upstairs for dinner.

"As long as you've lived," she muttered, "and you still make it crooked."

He smiled down at her. "How did you learn to tie a necktie, tesoro? Was it a rebellious fashion statement in grad school that I never caught wind of?"

"My grandfather, you goof," she said as she continued to tie the perfect Windsor knot. If he was purposefully making them subpar so she would fix them... well, he decided she didn't need to know. He enjoyed her fussing over him too much.

"My Grandpa Hector was a plumber, but he loved dressing up. He would take Grandma for dinner and dancing every month."

She smiled wistfully. "It was their thing. And he always dressed in a suit for church on Sunday. He was..."

"What?" She hardly ever talked about her grandfather, and he knew they had been very close.

"He was my ideal man," she said with a soft smile.

"You loved him very much."

She sniffed and wiped at the tear in the corner of her eye. "I adored him."

Beatrice finished up with his tie and then went to the bathroom to change into the deep burgundy dress she had bought the day before. It was high necked and long-sleeved, which would cover the bruises that still dotted her pale skin.

Giovanni was happy to see her injuries gradually decreasing as she gained strength and speed. She had also acquired the faint smell of cordite and gun oil since learning to shoot with Terry. According to their host, she had a natural and "typically American" affinity for firearms and was becoming a very good shot.

"Speaking of grandfathers, did you call Ernesto today?"

"I did," she said through the bathroom door. "Why did you want me to talk to him again?"

"He requested that I keep him updated on our progress, and I thought he would enjoy talking to you, as well. Keep in mind, he's a powerful vampire who has a real affection for you. That's not something to take for granted."

She peeked her head out the door and he caught a tantalizing glimpse of bare shoulder. "I just met him that one time. I don't want him to think I'm looking for anything from him." She shut the door and continued her preparations.

"You should. He would expect you to." He came to sit on the edge of the bed closest to the bathroom and picked up a long, dark hair that lay on her pillow, twining it around his finger as they talked.

"What do you mean, he expects it?"

"He considers you family, remember? He will enjoy providing connections for you. He'll consider it a privilege."

"That seems kind of opportunistic."

Giovanni chuckled. "Trust me, he'll use his connection to me now if he needs it, and I'm happy to give it to him. He won't get anything I'm not willing to give."

"So why—"

"He's a powerful and wealthy man. Part of his wealth is his connections. He offers you connections and... pedigree, if you want to call it that. You offer him connection to me, to Carwyn, to Gemma and Terry now... even to the legendary Tenzin. It's all part of how the game is played."

The door cracked open and she stood with a hand on her hip, which was cocked ever so slightly in his direction. He pushed down the satisfied rumble that wanted to leave his chest as he stared at the luscious curve he knew would be pressed against him when he rested later.

"Gio."

"Hmm?"

"Up here."

His eyes moved up her body to meet her amused gaze.

"Yes," he said with an innocent smile.

She only rolled her eyes. "So, what you're saying is, don't be afraid to drop names at dinner."

"Name dropping is an art in immortal society, particularly among water vampires. So no, drop away."

"Good to know."

"Happy to tell you."

She left the door open, and his eyes traced the lines of her body through the form-fitting dress. He darted over to rest his chin on her shoulder as she applied make-up in the mirror. He disliked when she put anything over her skin, but he enjoyed the brush of gold that accented her dark eyes.

Giovanni placed his hands on her waist and bent down to nose along the nape of her neck where she had pulled her hair up in a simple ponytail.

"You look beautiful."

"Thanks." She winked in the mirror and reached back to tug his tie. "You look pretty good yourself."

J ean Desmarais had controlled the ports of Le Havre and Marseilles for over two hundred years. His ruthless ascension on the French coast bore witness to both his canny political skills and his ferocity as a fighter. He was renowned for his business acumen and his negotiating skills; his wealth and connections were some of the best in France.

What Giovanni hadn't counted on was his charm.

"Surely, mademoiselle, they cannot pretend to make wine in Texas. California, I grant you, may have some passable vines, but Texas? How could a cowboy produce something so fine?"

Beatrice laughed along with him.

"I don't know, Jean, some of the Chardonnays I've had from the Hill Country have been pretty fantastic."

"Far be it from me to disagree with such a charming recommendation." He winked and sipped his glass of red from the bottle he had brought for dinner.

Jean was decidedly rakish in his appeal and appeared to have been turned in his mid-thirties. His brown hair and dark eyes spoke to as much Spanish blood as French, and the ladies at the table seemed to melt when he flashed them his roguish grin.

When Giovanni and Carwyn had wrangled a meeting with the busy water vampire over a month before, he had agreed to come and meet with Terry and Gemma in their home, which was a testament to both Jean's confidence and his curiosity. The French and the English, like their human counterparts, did not often agree.

But since the swarthy vampire had arrived, he had charmed the party with his wit and humor.

Giovanni stared at Beatrice from across the table. She had been nervous at first, glancing at him as if checking for proper protocol, but he only nodded and shrugged, curious how the evening might progress.

In very short order, she had the shipping mogul eating out of the palm of her hand.

"I haven't seen him eye her neck once." Carwyn leaned over and murmured into his ear. "He's playing this very well."

"As is she," Giovanni said. "I told you, she has a knack for this. She doesn't even realize she's doing it."

"—so I was riding through the hills and I had my helmet on. Now, granted, it was winter and I was wearing a bulky jacket."

"Winter? In Hollywood? I thought you only had sunshine and palm trees?"

They both laughed and Giovanni smirked, pleased to see others appreciating her quick wit and humor.

"We get a little bit cold. Nothing like here, of course—"

"My own home is quite damp. Perhaps I need to come to California to see the surfers."

She smiled. "Perhaps you should."

"Please, continue my dear."

"So I was riding my bike and my helmet was down. I pull up to the stoplight and no less than three girls in a convertible—don't ask me why they had a convertible in December, they were probably tourists—start cat-calling me!"

"Cat-calling?"

"Oh, you know, 'Hey, handsome, I'll give you a ride,' stuff like that."

"They thought you were a man?" he asked, finally catching on before he started chuckling.

"I didn't know whether to be insulted or flattered, Jean."

The whole table seemed to find the story amusing, and the

small side-conversations continued as the roast beef was served. Giovanni bypassed it, never caring much for roast meat, which reminded him too much of his days as a mercenary. He focused quietly on Beatrice and the Frenchman across from him.

"Di Spada," Jean called. "How were you so lucky to find this lovely woman, and why does she pay you any attention?"

"I must have been born under an auspicious star." Giovanni winked at Beatrice, smiling when he saw the slight blush on her cheeks.

"Truly, you must have been. Now, Mademoiselle De Novo, if I were to visit Los Angeles, what must I see?"

"Well, it all depends on your interests... "

She continued to explain the various sights in Southern California as the table hummed around him. Giovanni exchanged cautious nods with Jean's silent enforcer, who sat near the door to the dining room and glanced occasionally at Terry who, he noticed, was also observing Beatrice and Jean. Gemma caught his eye, and he saw a small smile cross her face. Despite their initial dislike, he had seen a grudging respect grow between the two women in the weeks they had spent in London.

"My daughter would love to meet you," he heard the Frenchman say.

"Oh?"

"She was born during the twenties, my Louise. She absolutely adores the cinema. And anything American, for that matter. She even talks about acting on the screen, but that, of course, is impossible."

"Is she interested in other aspects of working in film? I'm sure there are a lot of things she could do that wouldn't be in front of the camera."

Jean gave a typically Gallic shrug. "She has expressed an interest in costumes; but of course, there is nothing like that in Marseilles. And the vampires in Paris and Lyon... They are not particular friends of mine. No, French cinema is not for my Louise, I'm afraid."

Giovanni saw the minute Beatrice recognized the opportunity, and he suppressed a smile.

"Has she considered moving?"

"Out of France? My dear Beatrice, where could she go where I would be assured of her welcome and safety? I am very fond of my daughter. She is my youngest child."

"I wonder... are you familiar with my grandfather, Don Ernesto Alvarez?"

A slow smile spread across the Frenchman's face. "What are you proposing?"

"You were brilliant." He shoved the door closed and reached for her, pulling her to his chest and kissing her passionately before he drew her to the chair in the corner of their bedroom.

"That was kind of fun," she said when he finally let her up for air. She was perched in his lap, and he was running his hands over her waist and kissing her neck, tasting behind her ear as he pulled the tie from her hair.

"I knew you'd be a natural at this."

"I kind of am, aren't I? It's like a big game board. Or a puzzle. You just have to figure out how everyone is connected."

"Mmmhmm," he murmured as his lips wandered over her collarbone.

"And you're sure Ernesto won't mind?"

"He'll consider it an honor to introduce the girl to Hollywood if it means Jean's cooperation on the French coast, I'm sure of it."

"And you think Jean will help us look for Lorenzo?"

He nodded and ran his fingers through the hair that fell down her back. She hadn't cut it since they had been reunited, and he wondered if she knew how much he liked the length. "He's in shipping, smuggling, all the same circles. They were allies of a sort, for a while. If Lorenzo goes to France, he'll call Jean."

"Okay then. Yay me."

He pulled her closer, and his mouth moved along her neck as his fangs ran out. "Yay you, indeed," he said as his tongue fluttered against her racing pulse.

"Go ahead," she whispered and pulled him toward her neck, tilting her head as his fangs pierced the skin.

He moaned and pulled as the sweet blood entered his mouth. Giovanni pulled her hip against him, knowing she could feel his arousal.

"Gio," she whispered. "Wait—"

"Can you feel how much I want you?"

He licked at her neck, sealing the wounds after a few quick drinks that slaked one hunger while feeding another.

She gasped, "Gio—"

"Let me make love to you, Beatrice. I've wanted to for so long. I love you. Let me show you." One hand pressed at the small of her back, while the other stroked over her breasts. Her arms lifted and she clutched at his shoulders.

"I don't... " She whimpered in pleasure. "Not here."

"What?" He blinked and pulled away.

"Not in Gemma and Terry's house. I just... " He saw the blush flood her face and he only imagined it spreading further down her body. "And... it's too soon."

He sat back and let his arms drop to the side.

"Too soon? For what? For this? For us?"

"We've only been... together for a few weeks now," she stammered. "I mean, we've never even talked about—"

He pushed her off his lap and stood up to pace the room. "What? What do you want to talk about?"

"Well—" she was still blushing. "—us, I guess."

"I love you." He crossed his arms as he leaned against the desk.

"I've made it quite clear what I want, Beatrice. If anyone should have doubts about our relationship, it's me."

She stood as her jaw dropped. "Excuse me?"

"You are the one holding back. You've held back for months when I know how attracted you are to me. I know how aroused you are right now. Why do you push me away?"

"I told you—"

"You tell me… " He broke off and lowered his voice, which had risen as they argued. "You tell me nothing. I know nothing of your feelings for me because you refuse to tell me anything."

She stood gaping at him, furious as she struggled for words.

"You—you haven't even apologized."

"For what?"

Her face flushed with anger. "If you don't know, then I'm not going to tell you, you stubborn ass."

Giovanni walked over and sidled next to her. "You know, you talk a lot about me being an ass: a pretentious ass, a stubborn ass. Seems like you think about my ass a lot, Beatrice." He yanked her hips to his and pressed their bodies together, pulling her arms around to place them on the ass he'd just mentioned. She trembled, and her breath came in quick pants. He could sense her arousal through her fury.

"What are you—"

"Are you missing something?" He leaned down and purred in her ear. "Something you know I could give you? Don't be coy, tesoro."

Giovanni was frustrated and angry, but he still wanted her.

"Stop it," she hissed. "Not like this. Not—"

"Not good enough for you? I think you might be surprised. I've had a few hundred years to practice—"

"Stop it!" She pushed away from him and walked across the room, standing by her side of the bed. "Why are you being like this?"

He forced down the snarl that wanted to erupt. *Because I've been the equivalent of a monk for almost six years, and you're driving me crazy. Especially when you've been flirting with another vampire for the better part of the night.*

He didn't say it. Giovanni only frowned and shook his head. Beatrice's face was pale, and she looked angry and on the verge of crying. He took a deep breath and shook his head. "This... this is a mistake. I'll find another room."

Giovanni spun on his heel and walked toward the door but stopped when he heard her heart go wild. He turned to see a hollow look on her face, and she started to shake. He suddenly realized the rash words he had uttered.

"No!" He rushed to her side. "I'm not leaving you. Not like that. I would never... I just meant that I am frustrated tonight, and you're angry—"

"Don't leave me," she whispered as the tears sprang to her eyes. "Don't. I don't think I could handle it again. You left me and... "

He grabbed her, wrapping her tightly in his arms. "I won't. I promise."

"Everyone leaves."

"What?" He frowned and pulled away so he could see her face. "What do you mean?"

"Everyone. Dad left. Grandpa. My own mom never even wanted me."

Her small voice tore at his heart, and Giovanni finally realized the enormity of his actions five years before.

"And then I left you." His chest ached when he pulled her against it, pressing her against his heart as if it could heal the wound.

"I don't want to be left again."

"I won't. I'm sorry I even said it. I'm so sorry...."

She looked up at him with tear-filled eyes, and he brushed at the shining tracks that ran down her cheeks.

"I am sorry, Beatrice. I am sorry I was so arrogant. I'm sorry for hurting you when I left."

She gripped his waist as he held her, sighing before she pressed her cheek to his chest. Finally, she nodded. "Okay," she whispered. "Okay."

He stood, rocking them back and forth before they lay down in bed, still in their dress clothes. He didn't want to release her, even to take off his shoes. Giovanni finally felt her retreat into sleep an hour before dawn took him.

He woke the next night to the clamor of the old phone in their room. He was still wearing his dress shirt and slacks, though his shoes, coat and tie had been removed sometime during the day. He saw Beatrice's burgundy dress hanging on the back of the chair, but he did not sense her nearby.

He reached over and picked up the phone.

"Is this the Italian?" Tywyll's creaky voice greeted him on the other end of the line.

"It is. Do you have information for me?"

"I have a question for ye', fire-starter."

"What is it?" He rubbed his bleary eyes.

"Do ye' know where yer woman is?"

Sixteen

" S tupid, stupid, stupid,"
Beatrice chanted, punctuating each utterance with a quick kick to the side of the small room where she had been stashed. The four walls seemed to close in on her with each passing hour. She glanced at the fading light through the porthole.

She guessed that she was on a freighter of some kind, after being snatched from the streets of Mayfair while shopping on Thursday morning. Now it was nearing Thursday evening, from the look of the sun, and she braced herself for her inevitable appointment.

It just figured that the one time she left Gemma and Terry's house without her guard was the day she would be kidnapped.

"Stupid, stupid, stupid."

She just couldn't stand the idea of the rough-looking thug they'd hired to tail her during the day following her to the lingerie shop on Conduit Street.

Beatrice had been shaken by her argument with Giovanni the night before. She'd thought they'd been doing well, and her trust in him had been growing each night they spent together. When his frustration boiled over, she had been unprepared.

Not that she wasn't frustrated, too.

He was right—she was attracted to him; that had never changed. And it was maddening to sleep next to him every night and morning knowing how he felt about her. Knowing that he wanted her. Knowing that making love to him would be amazing. She'd certainly had a taste of his passion during the infrequent feedings they shared. He never seemed to take much, but just the touch of his lips at her neck sent her shuddering toward release.

But Beatrice had held back, not wanting their physical attraction to overwhelm what she knew was the most important part of their relationship. She still needed to trust him.

"Stupid, stupid, stupid," she chanted as angry tears gathered in her eyes.

In the dim light of morning, when she'd finally removed her rumpled dress, she forced herself to confront her feelings for the vampire she shared a bed with every night.

She sat next to him in her robe, stroking his face before she rolled him over and removed his jacket. Her hands pressed against the iron weight of his chest, and she lifted his muscular arms to pull it off.

This immortal being that slept next to her every night was almost unimaginably powerful. His hands could snap her like a twig if he wanted. Even more, one simple touch from him could render her malleable to any whim he could imagine. Yet, Giovanni knew how she feared mental manipulation and had always restrained himself.

"Don't you realize how I adore you? I wanted you to have a choice."

He was waiting for her. He had been waiting for months. He had never wavered in his promise not to leave her again, and he had done everything in his power to make himself a permanent fixture in her life.

"I will earn the woman's love, if I have lost the girl's."

She pulled his shoes off and set them at the foot of the bed before she leaned over to remove his tie. He purposely made it crooked so she would fix it. Such a small, human thing. He did it purely for her attention.

"Why do you call me by my human name?"

"Because I love you, Jacopo," she whispered.

Beatrice felt tears on her face as the walls she had carefully constructed for the past five years fell, and she finally let herself imagine a future with Giovanni. Could she give up the life she knew to join him? Even more, could she imagine a future without him?

She curled next to him in bed, wishing for the sun to fall faster so he could be with her again. She lay next to him and considered trying to wake him but decided it would just be frustrating. She had tried more than once to rouse him during the afternoon to give him some important message, only to be disappointed when he had no memory of it when he woke.

And now, she sat in the bowels of the creaking ship, banging her head against the wall.

"Stupid, stupid, stupid." Just letting him wake up next to you naked probably would have been a better idea than new lingerie, Beatrice.

They must have used chloroform or something similar, because she hardly remembered anything besides thick arms and something soft covering her nose and mouth. Then she'd woken in the swaying boat, alone and unharmed, which probably meant she was due for a visitor as soon as the sun set.

She stood up, pacing the room and trying to imagine any form of escape. There had to be something. There had to be someone. Someone she could plead with. Someone she could bribe. Someone who...

Her attention was drawn to the porthole. The sky was deep blue, and the setting sun turned the clouds gold.

In the distance, she could see land, closer than she would have expected for such a large ship, but then, she really didn't know much about boats. She stopped pacing and started jogging in place, trying to loosen her stiff muscles and think.

Beatrice muttered to herself, "No way in hell am I spending another month of my life under this sick bastard's control."

She knew he wouldn't hurt her, which dispelled some of the fear she'd felt five years before and gave her renewed confidence. No doubt the humans he had guarding her were under orders not to harm her either. She walked to the small bathroom in the corner of the room, relieved herself, and prepared to do everything possible to make keeping her a major annoyance.

She jumped up and down, doing as many of her warm-up exercises as she could in the limited amount of space. She mentally ran through the throws she had learned in her judo class, the hits and kicks she had learned from Gemma, and tried to quiet her mind the way Tenzin had always advised her. She hoped one of the humans had guns; she might be able to steal one.

As the sky darkened, she realized that the possibility of avoiding a vampire was probably non-existent. She sat on the bed, closed her eyes, and listened for the approaching footsteps. In the back of her mind, she realized that Giovanni would be waking soon. He would realize she was gone, but would he have any idea where she had been taken?

Beatrice heard footsteps coming toward her room. She could tell it was more than one person, but she couldn't tell how many. The door swung open, but she remained on the bed, trying her best to look calm. A young, dark-haired vampire of medium build walked in and looked around, only glancing at her as his eyes swept the room. He was completely unremarkable except for the twin fangs she could see in his mouth. He murmured something over his shoulder in a low voice. She had noticed Giovanni and Carwyn using the same tone when they didn't want her to hear something.

With some ceremony that was probably meant to frighten her, Lorenzo swept into the room. His blond curls were shorter than she remembered, and his Botticelli face bore the smudges of healing scars around his mouth and left eye. He was still wearing the ridiculous white wardrobe he had favored in Greece, though he was dressed for the colder winter weather of Northern Europe.

"Beatrice, my dear, it has been too long," he said as he looked down his nose.

"You look like a ski bunny. Nice sweater."

"Ah!" his face brightened. "You have regained your delightful sense of humor. Excellent. You were so dreadfully dull when we parted in Greece."

"You mean when your dad came and spanked your ass with his two friends? Yeah, that was awesome. Nice scars. You getting a Phantom of the Opera mask to go with those? They're white too, if I remember correctly."

He smiled, his cold blue eyes examining her as he leaned against the open doorway.

"That lovely De Novo sarcasm. I do so miss that about your father. And now that I know how much Giovanni loves you," he sneered, "I'll enjoy torturing you as well. As soon as we've secured Stephen, of course. You see—" He darted over and leaned down so she could feel his cold breath against her neck when he spoke. "—I'm going to find him first."

"Good luck with that," she choked out, disgusted by the chill that seemed to course over her skin at his proximity. "Even Gio—"

"Does not have the resources I do when it comes to finding people," he said with a condescending smile. "He's too virtuous. And once you tell me exactly what he knows about your father from his search, the combined information should be enough to put me well ahead in the race."

"Don't count on it. What makes you think I'm going to tell you—"

She choked on the words when his cold fingers grasped her neck, and she began to shake when she realized he was right. She would tell him anything.

Anything he wanted.

He knelt before her and let the cruel smile twist his lips as he forced his influence on her.

"No wasting time with friendly banter, Beatrice. I've been waiting too long to get what is mine, and I have little faith that our location is a well-kept secret. I need that book your father has. I've made promises that some are starting to doubt. And I will not—" She winced when his grip around her neck tightened. "—be denied any longer."

His touch was not the soft caress of Giovanni or even the sick, teasing touch she remembered from the last time he'd held her. It was the cold burn of ice that gripped her throat; the sensation quickly spread over her skin and nausea turned her stomach.

The ache spread from his fingers, around her neck, and up to the base of her skull as she stared into his frigid, blue eyes. She couldn't speak, but her teeth began to chatter and the goose bumps spread down her body. It was as if his touch had frozen her and, as the creeping cold slipped into her mind, Beatrice knew she was powerless to stop the invasion.

"Where is your father?"

Her teeth chattered when she answered. "I—I don't know."

"Has Giovanni been in contact with him?"

Her mind screamed at her to tell him nothing, but she couldn't stop the words as they tumbled out of her mouth.

"Postcards."

"Explain."

"Dad left clues for Gio, and he sent me... postcards."

"Who sent you postcards, Beatrice?"

"G—G—io sent me postcards," she rattled. "From the places he f—found clues."

Beatrice could feel the tears trickling down her cheeks, and she was surprised that they didn't freeze against her cold skin. But as she saw the spotted condensation on the porthole, she realized that no one in the room was cold except her. In fact, if someone touched her skin, she imagined it would still be its normal temperature. But Lorenzo told her nerve endings she was freezing, and her body reacted accordingly.

"What kind of clues?"

"He—he wouldn't tell me." Beatrice wondered if the knowledge of her vulnerability was what had caused Giovanni to hold back the information, and she was suddenly grateful for his stubborn, determined, forward-thinking ass.

"He sent you the postcards?"

"Yes."

"From where? I want every location he sent a postcard from. List them all."

And with trembling lips and tears in her eyes, Beatrice gave Lorenzo the location of every place Giovanni had found a clue left by Stephen De Novo in the previous five years.

Warsaw.

Johannesburg.

Lima.

San Francisco.

Tripoli. Santiago. Shanghai. Stockholm. Budapest. Novosibirsk.

She told him everything she knew.

And as she told him, Lorenzo came to sit next to her on the small bed, putting an arm around her as he played with her hair. He twisted it in his right hand while his left hand played with her fingers.

"Your skin is so lovely, Beatrice. Have I ever told you that?"

"N—no."

"It is. It's no wonder he likes you. I can see his bite marks on your neck now." He bent down to run his lips against her skin, inhaling deeply. "Do you like it? When he bites you?"

She wanted to pull away. To strike him. But she was utterly frozen and had no choice but to answer as the cold fingers of Lorenzo's amnis stroked her mind.

"Yes."

"Does his bite make you come?" he purred into her ear.

Beatrice tried to resist. She pictured walls going up in her mind, blocking the creep of his influence, but the twisted fingers flowed over and around the walls, forcing her to answer.

"Y—yes," she whispered.

"How delicious you smell. Sweet, but not overpowering. Very much like I remember your father tasting. Maybe I should have kept him like my father keeps you. Quite convenient having a regular meal."

The angry tears still fell down her face as she realized how powerless she was.

"Of course," he whispered her hidden fear as his fingers slid up her arm. "I could just keep you. Maybe my father is on to something with his human women. Who cares if you bruise a little when I'm done with you? If you're interesting enough to keep him occupied, perhaps you are worth my time."

"N—no!" Just the thought churned her gut. "I don't want—" And yet it didn't seem to matter what she wanted. She could feel the suggestion take root in her mind, and her arm lifted until her fingers were nestled in the soft golden curls on his head. She stroked them, and he hissed in pleasure.

"Such lovely, delicate hands, Beatrice. Why are your knuckles so bruised, precious girl? Surely you haven't been practicing your ridiculous martial arts like you did in California. Surely you know... " His lips brushed against her cheek, and he whispered into her ear, "You cannot fight me."

He snickered a little and pierced her earlobe with one fang, quickly lapping at the blood with his cold tongue before he rose and straightened his clothes. She immediately felt the chill leave her, and Beatrice resisted the urge to shake.

"Delicious. You are a treat, my dear. I've already fed this evening, but hopefully we'll have time tomorrow night."

"Where are you taking me?" she asked, shrugging the tension from her body and drying her eyes with the back of her sleeve. He thought she was going to wait around to let him feed on her? In his dreams.

"Don't be silly. It's very possible that Giovanni will have found you by tomorrow night, and I don't want to give him any new information."

She glared at the monster in front of her.

"Why did you kill Ioan?"

He giggled and looked around the room. Beatrice finally noticed that there were four other vampires present beside Lorenzo and no other humans beside herself. All of Lorenzo's men were dressed in black, and none of them seemed remarkable in the least.

Lorenzo finally stopped his ridiculous giggling. "One, I did not kill the kindly doctor, these lovely gentlemen did. Two, the reason I killed Ioan is between Ioan and myself. So you'll have to ask one of us, and since I'm not telling, and he's little bits of dust at this point, I suppose you'll just have to live with disappointment."

In that moment, Beatrice De Novo decided that she would become a vampire. If for no other reason than to kill the evil creature in front of her, who shattered lives on a whim. A cool calm settled over her, and a smile flickered across her face.

"I am going to kill you, Lorenzo."

He only laughed. "You're precious. Now, will my father kill me?" He shrugged. "Perhaps. He's definitely powerful enough. The problem for him is, he lacks a certain... we'll call it 'devious intent,' that allows me to be far more ruthless. Oh, he's quite violent when provoked, as my lovely house on the island can attest, but he doesn't really enjoy it like I do. Now you... " He lifted a curious eyebrow. "You might be a force to be reckoned with, Beatrice De Novo."

The smile fell from his face, and he cocked his head to the side. "I can see the calculation in your eyes, and it's very intriguing. What could you accomplish with power? It's almost worth changing you to find out."

The thought of his blood running through her veins sickened her, and she curled her lip. He quickly plastered on a sick smile.

"Oh! You're so darling. I missed you."

"I can't say I feel the same, Paulo."

She didn't even see the slap coming. His quick backhand would have knocked her unconscious if she hadn't become accustomed to Gemma's even more ruthless blows during their training. Lorenzo was eyeing her with a new light in his eyes.

"So, my darling Papá confided my human name to you, did he? What else did he confide?"

Beatrice kept her expression neutral, suddenly aware that she'd made a horrible mistake. No one had known how much she knew about Giovanni, and she realized that his secrets were completely open to any vampire that wanted them if they could get their hands on her.

The same thought seemed to occur to Lorenzo, but he didn't put his hands on her. Instead, he smirked and blew her a kiss before he swept out of the room with his entourage. Beatrice released a breath when she was alone again and settled into the bed to rest and wait for dawn.

SEVENTEEN

The sun was pouring through the porthole when she woke, and small droplets of condensation cast tiny rainbows around the small room. Beatrice remembered Giovanni's favorite waterfall in Cochamó and how it looked during the day with the sun reflecting off the spraying mist. It would be late summer right now, and she decided that if she could pick one place to be, it would be at their house in the valley with him.

They would wake in the early evening and make love in front of the fireplace in their bedroom, the flecks of mica sparkling in the hewn granite wall. She would sleep next to him all day and spend the night riding through the meadows in the moonlight. Maybe there would be wildflowers. She would have to remember to see as much of the valley as she could in the sunlight and take pictures for after she had turned. Since it was summer, maybe they would implement a no clothing rule in the house. She knew Giovanni wouldn't mind.

Beatrice rubbed her eyes and stretched. She was going to get out of the room today. She wasn't sure how, but it was daytime. Granted, it was morning, which meant that some of the vampires could still be awake if they stayed out of sunlight, but by afternoon, she knew they would be sleeping. That meant anyone up and walking around would be human. And she was pretty sure if she could land the odd blow on Gemma, she could kick some human ass.

Hours later, when the sun was hanging lower in the sky, she beat on the thick metal door.

"Hey!" she shouted. "Anyone?"

She paused to hear if there was any movement.

"Anyone out there? I've been in here all day, you gonna feed me?" She pounded some more. "Hey, I'm starving!"

She wasn't starving, she was sickeningly nervous, but she needed someone to open the door.

"Open up! I need some food."

She finally heard steps approaching, and Beatrice stepped back, grasping the sheet she had twisted into a thick rope.

"Hello?" an accented voice called. "You are hungry?"

"Yeah, I'm starving, all right? Will you feed me already?" She braced herself on the corner of the bed. When the door opened, whoever came through would see her immediately, there was no avoiding it, so she stepped up on the small bed, knowing that she would get one chance for surprise.

"Okay. I get food," the voice called. She felt a brief pang at the thought of harming the voice, which sounded fairly friendly, but there was no way in hell she was going to show mercy to her captors when Lorenzo was waiting at sundown.

The footsteps walked away, and she put down her sheet to take off the jacket she had been wearing. It was cold on the ship, and she knew it was cold outside, but the jacket was too bulky for her to move freely, and she knew that the less an attacker had to grab, the better.

Beatrice took deep breaths, preparing her mind for the rush at the door. She focused on her hand-to-hand training with Gemma and all the advice the woman had given her over the past month.

"Go for the dirty punch. Always. And hit them when they're down."

"Throw your attacker off balance. It's the only way your small size can be used to your advantage."

"Be quick! Quicker. Make yourself so fast they can't grab you. If they do, you're dead."

She took a deep breath.

The footsteps approached.

She heard a key in the lock.

The door cracked open.

She saw a tray.

Spotting her opportunity, Beatrice braced her arms on the narrow walls and kicked up, knocking the tray into her captor's face as she swung the twisted bed sheet around his neck and, holding it securely, jumped off the bed.

The force of her momentum knocked the large man off balance and he stumbled into the wall. She aimed her boot at his groin and kicked him as hard as she could. Then she kicked him again.

He was on the ground, grunting in pain, so she stomped.

Beatrice was surprised how little noise he made. She must have knocked the wind out of him. After the first low grunt, the crewman curled into himself while she continued battering his kidney area with her boot the way Gemma had taught her. She shoved the door mostly closed and paused to survey the writhing man at her feet.

There was a gun in his belt. Score.

She reached down to his doughy waist and grabbed it. It was a Heckler and Koch nine millimeter, exactly like the one she had practiced with the previous week.

"God bless you, Terry," she muttered as she popped the magazine out and checked the ammunition. The crewman hadn't fired his weapon since he'd loaded it, so she slammed it back, racked a bullet into the chamber, and took the safety off.

She aimed it at the belly of the large man who was looking at her with wide eyes.

"Funny thing, guns. Six foot tall man with a nine millimeter, five foot tall woman with a nine millimeter... pretty much the same, aren't they?"

He didn't speak, but he was panting and she saw his mouth start to open. She kicked him in the kidneys again.

"You stay quiet. You yell? Everyone's going to know I'm busting out, and I'll have no reason not to just shoot you. Noise is noise, right? I don't particularly want to shoot you, but I really hate the creepy asshole that put me in here, so if I have to, I will. Is this making sense?"

The silent crewman nodded and closed his mouth.

"Good, what language do you speak?"

"Español," he whispered.

"Fine." She switched to Spanish. "I want off this boat. Like I said, I don't particularly want to shoot you, but I will if it'll get me off the boat. Is that a cell phone?" She nodded toward his pocket, where she could see a slight bulge.

"Yes."

"Give it to me. One hand, in your pocket. No sudden moves, or I'll shoot you."

"Yes," he said as he reached down. "Please, I just work here. I don't want to hurt you. I don't even know—"

"Shut up."

"My name is—"

"Shut. Up." If she had to shoot him later, she sure as hell didn't want to know his name. She didn't know if she could kill him, but the thought of shooting his legs didn't bother her at all.

The more Beatrice examined the nameless crewman, the more she realized that he looked like a normal guy. He didn't react or assess the room like someone trained in security, and she smiled a little when she realized she had lucked out.

It also made her feel slightly bad about scaring the shit out of him—she could smell that he had peed his pants—but she wasn't going to back down.

Let him think she was a big badass; Beatrice was feeling like it at the moment.

He handed her his phone and she stuck it in her pocket. "Thanks. Now, where are we, and how far are we from land?"

"We're still in the Channel. We had to stop in Le Havre before dawn. We are... maybe fifteen miles off the coast of France? Near Cherbourg. I'm not sure." His voice shook just a little.

"Shit." The land didn't look that far away. She was going need a boat. "Where are the lifeboats?"

Would a lifeboat be enough on the English Channel in the middle of February? She had a sudden thought. "This is a freighter, right?"

He nodded, looking confused when she smiled. "So it's got those big, orange life rafts with navigation and engines and all that stuff? The contained ones?"

"Yes."

Thank you, Discovery Channel. She shoved the gun closer. "You ever launch one?"

"I—I've seen the drills, but there's never been an emergency—"

"Good enough for me. We're headed for the lifeboat, mister. If you try to get away, I'll shoot you. If you try to yell for help, I'll shoot you. I don't really have a lot to lose at this point, and I'm sure the creepy, blond asshole that hired you told me you can't hurt me, so don't even try."

She nodded toward the door and the crewman scrambled up, still clutching his groin from where she had kicked him.

Beatrice hadn't heard anyone pass in the hall, which fit with the deserted feeling she'd gotten from the ship through most of the morning. She nudged the large man in front of her with the barrel of the H&K, taking comfort in the sturdy grip in her hand. She snagged her thick jacket on the way out the door.

Nameless Crewman walked in front of her.

"Where are you taking me?"

"The lifeboats, remember?"

"Honestly, I've seen the drills, but there's never been an emergency, so I don't know—"

"Feel this?" She nudged his back with the barrel of the gun. "This is an emergency. You're launching it, and you're taking me to the nearest stretch of land. And I suggest we get there before nightfall, 'cause that's when the monsters come out."

"Monsters?" She could hear his voice quiver a little, and she shoved down the flicker of sympathy.

"Yeah, monsters. And my boyfriend? He's the scariest one, so as long as you help me get out of here, you'll be fine."

They wound through the corridors of the creaking ship, heading upward at a steady pace. Nameless Crewman didn't halt and seemed to be cooperating, so they reached the deck in short order. She could smell the fresh sea air when he stopped by the last door.

"Wait, Miss. Let me check outside to see if anyone—"

"I will have this gun at your back the whole time, do you understand? If I think you're messing with me, I'll shoot you." Beatrice was impressed by how firm her voice sounded. She was probably going to fall apart later, but at the moment, the adrenaline and the firearm were making her feel like Superwoman.

He nodded and cracked open the door, only to close it almost immediately.

"There are men out there I do not recognize! With guns. Lots of guns," he said in a panic. "What is going on? The captain has been acting so strange; he never used to—"

"Shut up! Men? What did they look like?" Giovanni couldn't have found her already; she had seen the crack of sunlight at the door. Would Lorenzo have hired security that Nameless Crewman didn't recognize?

She crowded him, shoving the gun into his belly. "Do you

know everyone on this boat? What about passengers? Are there any?"

He frowned. "There are the strange people renting the interior cabins. They are odd and they come and go at night while I am off duty—"

"Okay, but the guys out there aren't them?"

"No. And they're speaking French. This is a Spanish vessel. We all speak Spanish."

"French?" Her eyes lit up.

Jean.

She remembered him bragging about his extensive human staff when he gave her his card.

"Day or night, B. If you are in France, call these numbers and someone will help you. I have people everywhere," he'd said proudly.

She wracked her brain for the numbers he had given her and pulled out Nameless Crewman's phone. The signal was faint, but it might just be enough. She punched one in and practically cried in relief when she heard the phone ringing on the other end.

"Allo?" a polite woman answered.

"Do you speak English? This is Beatrice De Novo, and Jean Demarais—"

"Ah! Madmoiselle De Novo," she tumbled off a ridiculously fast stream of French before Beatrice heard another voice on the line.

"Miss De Novo?" a deep voice asked. "Am I speaking with Beatrice De Novo?"

"Yes, you are. I met your boss a few nights ago, and I had a quick question."

"We have been looking for you since this morning, where—"

"Do you happen to have a whole bunch of guys looking for me on the deck of a freighter in the English Channel right now?"

There was a deep chuckle. "As a matter of fact... "

She sighed in relief but gasped when she felt the cold barrel of a gun at her neck. She dropped the phone when she heard a low voice hiss in Spanish, "You're not supposed to be out of your cabin, are you?"

Beatrice turned to Nameless Crewman, who was staring in horror at the group of men gathered behind them. He looked at her in panic right before one of the crewmen raised a gun and shot him in the chest. She cried out when the man slumped forward and the pool of blood spread under him.

"No!" *I'm sorry... I'm so sorry.*

It was Beatrice's last thought before she felt something strike her temple, and she blacked out.

EIGHTEEN

The freighter's hatch started to glow, and the heat radiated from the center of the panel until the metal was cherry red. The steel turned the consistency of wet cardboard as it slumped in his hands. Giovanni pushed aside the soft metal, blocking the three vampires behind him as Terry sent a blast of cold water to cool it.

Jean's human assault team had remained, standing alert on deck to grab any humans they found. The team had already secured the bridge but had been told not to go belowdecks until Giovanni, Carwyn, Gemma, and Terry arrived at first dark. When they had, the team leader gladly let the silent immortals dressed in black take the lead.

Giovanni reached down the dark passageway with his senses, stretching his hearing and sense of smell to detect any danger. He could smell the faint scent of honeysuckle near the top of the stairs, along with the scent of adrenaline that made the blue flames jump on his bare torso.

He felt Terry's cool hand on his shoulder, dousing the flames as the salt air was drawn to him.

"Watch yourself. Narrow corridors. Flammable cargo. We don't know what's down there."

"Beatrice is down there," he said.

"So she is, and we're getting her back tonight."

Giovanni touched the melted edges of the door, nodding as he ducked his tall frame through the opening. He could hear Terry, Carwyn, and Gemma crawl through behind him. He walked down the corridor and halted at the top of a stairwell.

He could hear a scuffle somewhere in the bowels of the ship, as if humans were scrambling, and he heard the soft shush of immortals as they swept through the ship at inhuman speed.

"Father and I will go forward," Gemma murmured. "You and Terry go to the rear of the ship; with this damp air, he'll have no trouble extinguishing you if things get dangerous."

"Just stay behind me, Terry."

"Right."

She nodded. "We've all seen the layout of this ship from Jean's man, but I think it's important to note that many of the small interior cabins could be good hiding spots, as well."

Carwyn said, "We're sending humans above if they cooperate—"

"And it doesn't waste too much time," Giovanni added.

"Fine, and let's remember that there are twenty men listed in this crew, and only four of them are being held above," Carwyn said.

"And we don't know how many vampires Lorenzo has with him," Terry added.

"Is he here?" Gemma looked to Giovanni. "Do you get any sense of him, Gio?"

"Not of Lorenzo, but there are four other energy signatures. Young, not very strong."

Though all vampires could sense electricity, much as sharks could in the water, Giovanni's senses had always been more keen than most. Since his particular element made him highly reactive to electronics, he could also sense vampire signatures at far greater distances than even most ancient vampires. It was one of the reasons he and Tenzin had been such effective mercenaries.

"Lorenzo's scent is here, but I don't feel him. He might have left."

"Rats do tend to flee when they smell fire," Carwyn muttered.

"Let's go," Terry said. "No need to be quiet if we find them." He leaned over and pulled Gemma toward him, planting a rough kiss on her mouth before chucking her chin. "Make sure you leave some for the rest of us, luv."

The four nodded toward each other before breaking apart to search. Giovanni clamped down the instinctive rage and forced himself to think rationally. Beatrice was smart and brave, and he knew Lorenzo needed her unharmed as bait for her father. If she was still on the ship, she would be fine. She had to be.

He traced the scent of honeysuckle and adrenaline down to the starboard side of the ship, halting before a small cabin where the smell was strongest. Terry caught up with him just before he cracked open the door.

"Here." Giovanni stepped through the door, almost falling to his knees at the scent of her panic and a faint trace of blood. A cocktail of Lorenzo's scent and cloying energy combined with the smell of blood, adrenaline, and Beatrice. Blue flames burst out over his body. Giovanni heard his growl echo through the small room, and his fangs punched through his lower lip.

He felt Terry slap at his burning shoulder and steam rose. "Gio, focus. I smell blood, too, but it's not much. Calm down and track her." The water vampire sent a cooling blanket of air over his torso, extinguishing the flames as Giovanni wiped the blood dripping from his chin.

He walked back to the corridor, focusing his senses on the scent of Beatrice and a male human. It drew him down the hall and through twisting corridors, slowly working its way toward the top deck.

"She had a man with her," Terry noted. "A pissing scared one, at that."

"Caught that, did you?"

"She's no wilting flower, your girl."

"Neither's yours."

Beatrice's scent stopped right before a steel door that he knew led to the top deck, and he caught the thick musk of four male humans along with the stronger scent of human blood. It was not hers. He looked down to the pool of blood on the floor, following the trail to a small supply closet where a large body had been stowed.

Terry peered in. "This is the one she took up from her cabin by the smell of him. Look at his holster, empty. I bet she took his gun. That's why he pissed himself. Good girl, B."

"But they were intercepted. Beatrice wouldn't have shot him in the chest if he was cooperating. Other humans must have found them."

"Rough smelling ones at that."

"Let's go." Giovanni turned. "Their scent leads down this way."

They moved down to the lower decks, and Terry let a sharp whistle echo down one corridor. In a few seconds, Carwyn and Gemma had joined them, and all four snuck through the freighter, following behind Giovanni.

There was a scuffle in the cabin to their right. Carwyn turned and ripped the door off its hinges, throwing it to the side.

Terry caught the first crewman who tried to scurry out, tossing him to Giovanni while Gemma found the other trying to hide in a closet. The man was trembling in fear, so she used her amnis to calm him and send him to the top deck with his hands on his head.

"Where is the girl?" Giovanni growled, as he held the small man up by the throat. Flames flared on his shoulders, and the crewman's horrified gaze flicked farther down the hallway to a pair of large, steel doors.

"Forward cargo hold," Terry murmured before Giovanni squeezed the man's neck and sent the human into unconsciousness before dropping him on the floor.

The four approached the door cautiously, Giovanni reaching out with his senses, searching for Beatrice's distinctive scent in the confused mass of immortal energy, human scent, and growing commotion behind the steel doors. The flames flared on his arms as his frustration grew.

"Carwyn... "

"Focus on her, Gio. Is she in there?"

"Yes," he hissed and reached for the door. His hands were already flaming as he placed them on the metal, but Carwyn put a firm hand on his shoulder, halting him.

"We don't know what's on the other side of that. Hold back the fire, my friend. Now, what's behind there?"

He closed his eyes and focused. "Beatrice is there. Four vampires... too many humans. More than ten, that's all I can tell."

"Is she frightened?"

"Everyone is frightened. I can't tell where she is." His patience snapped. "Just get the damn door open before I melt it!"

Terry pulled him back from the doorway and let Carwyn forward.

"Hold back, mate. We'll take care of the rest. You just find your girl."

Carwyn placed his ear on the door and closed his eyes before nodding with satisfaction. He reared back and punched both hands through the layers of steel, ripping them apart and pulling the door off its hinges as it broke apart.

All four rushed into the room, darting around the confused humans, who were running to one corner of the cavernous hold where boxes were stacked in a kind of barricade. The four vampires rushed toward them, and Gemma and Terry confronted them as Carwyn began knocking out humans who darted by and tossing them in a pile.

Giovanni only looked for one thing.

"Gio!"

He heard her call his name, but he could not see her in the confusion. One of the vampires escaped Gemma and rushed him, sending a blanket of wet air and extinguishing his flames before he could send them out. The young water vampire drew a sword and slashed at him but only succeeded in cutting Giovanni's arm before he was grabbed by the throat.

Giovanni eyed him, trying to determine whether he was worth interrogating. The vampire sneered, and Giovanni almost snapped his neck, but Carwyn reached over and snatched him away.

"No. This one feels the oldest. I want to question him."

Giovanni grunted as he continued stalking toward the corner with the boxes. He saw Beatrice peek out before she was pulled back by a large human holding a gun on her.

"Gio!" she shrieked again before the human tugged her behind a stack of crates. He heard her yell, "Let me go, you bastard!"

Giovanni was tracking her so intently that he barely registered when one of the human crew members to his right pulled a handgun and shot him in the chest.

The blast punched through him, but missed his heart, which would have knocked him over. Giovanni grunted and reached over to grab the man, annoyed as he twisted his neck and let him fall to the ground. He strode to the crates where the human had taken Beatrice only to find her twisting away from her captor. He watched as she drove her elbow into the large man's gut and her knee into his groin. She had already disarmed him, and the gun lay on the ground as they struggled.

Giovanni rushed over, grabbed the human by the neck, and squeezed. The man's face turned red as he struggled helplessly in his iron grip. Beatrice reached down to grab the nine millimeter and aim it at the dangling human. He examined her quickly.

She was pale and had bruises on her arms, several cuts to her face, and a swollen knee. She also had the beginning of a black eye and an ugly bruise spread over her temple, but her hands were steady.

"Tesoro, are you all right?"

"Fine. I'll be fine. I'm really glad to see you guys, though." He saw her glance over his shoulder. "There's four vampires here. They came down as soon as the sun set, but they didn't say anything to me. They just herded us down here and told this guy to keep me quiet."

"Gemma, Terry, and Carwyn are taking care of them."

"You're bleeding a lot," she said in a shaky voice as she glanced at his chest.

"I was shot. It missed the heart, so it shouldn't take long to heal." In fact, he could already feel the wound beginning to close, so he reached in his chest with his fingers, grunting until he had pulled the bullet from the torn flesh.

"Oh, Gio!" she cried as she watched him toss the bullet to the ground and wipe at the bleeding cavity. "Are you going to be okay?"

"I'll be fine. Did this human hurt you?" The man was barely conscious, but his eyes widened when he heard Giovanni.

He saw her clench her jaw from the corner of his eye. "He's the one that hit me. He was trying for something else, but my boot met his balls."

The man desperately tried to pry Giovanni's fingers from his throat. His terror-stricken eyes met the vampire's gaze when he cocked his head and spoke in a low voice.

"Did you lay your hands on my woman? That was very foolish. You're going to wish she had killed you now. She would have been quicker than me."

His heart began a slow thud of anticipation, but Giovanni wanted to be fair.

"Beatrice, do you wish to kill him yourself?"

His green eyes remained locked on the struggling human's, and he refused to allow any amnis to spread over him to soften the terror.

"No," he heard her murmur. "You need the blood."

Giovanni bared his fangs in the man's face, cutting off the human's scream as he twisted his neck to the side and sank his fangs into the soft, warm throat. He closed his eyes and took long, dragging gulps as his bloodlust collided with the pain that finally slammed into his chest.

He opened his eyes to see Beatrice looking around the cargo hold, watching for any threats. He could hear Gemma and Terry rounding up the last of the humans behind them. Beatrice came to stand in front of him as he drank, and he bit harder, piercing the carotid as the blood flooded into his mouth. His green eyes locked with hers and blood ran down his chin, but Beatrice did not flinch as she watched him drain the human who had threatened her life.

He felt the blood pumping through his system as his stomach filled, and a feral growl rumbled in his chest. The flames began to lick at his arms as his body grew stronger.

Beatrice never took her eyes off Giovanni, watching as he slowly sucked the life out of the man. Her hand reached toward him, and an instinctive snarl ripped from his throat, but she only paused for a moment before she placed a hand on his forehead, sweeping her fingers back through his hair as his eyes remained on hers. Gradually, the rage lessened, and the fire along his arms began to die down.

The human's heartbeat slowed, then stopped, and Giovanni dropped the dead man on the ground, wiping his mouth on his forearm before he stepped toward Beatrice, gripped the back of her neck, and let his bloody mouth crash down on hers.

He almost expected her to push him away, disgusted by his animalistic display, but she did not. She wrapped her arms around his waist and pressed close, careful to avoid his chest wound. He pierced his tongue and licked at the cut on her chin and at the corner of her mouth until they were sealed and healing.

"Gio," she finally murmured as he buried his face in her hair, inhaling her scent and holding her as his heartbeat slowed. "You came for me."

"I will always come for you. I love you," he murmured as he nuzzled his face into her neck, covering her in his scent before the smell of blood and Lorenzo hit him.

"What did he do?" he hissed and brushed back her hair searching for the source of the blood. He saw a small wound that looked like a piercing on her earlobe, and he looked at her. "Did he hurt you, Beatrice?"

She took a deep breath and lifted a hand to his hair, soothing him with her touch. "Just that. He bit my ear, but that's all. Other than that, it was just mind games again."

"If there was only a way to kill him more than once," he muttered as he pierced his tongue again and sucked her earlobe into his mouth to clean and heal the small wound.

He held her for a few more minutes until he heard Terry walk over.

"Nicely done, B. Gio, you hurt?"

"Nothing serious. The vampires?"

"Gemma killed two. Carwyn and I grabbed the others so we could question them."

"And the humans?" Beatrice asked.

"Most of them are dead. A few surrendered willingly, and Carwyn sent them up to Jean's men."

"I need to heal myself," Giovanni said as he pushed away from Beatrice. "Terry, you and Gemma take the vampires up to the deck and wait for me there. Beatrice, go to Carwyn." He could sense the earth vampire hovering nearby.

Terry nodded and crossed the hold, grabbing the other vampire that Gemma held before they walked out. Carwyn walked over to the corner.

Beatrice just stared at his bleeding chest. "How do you heal yourself?"

"Stand back," he said as he turned and nodded toward Carwyn, who reached out his hand to Beatrice and drew her away toward the far side of the hold.

"How do you heal yourself?" she asked again.

"I need to let it take me. Father, keep her away."

"You're going to set yourself on fire?" Beatrice was starting to sound panicked.

"Darling girl," Carwyn soothed her. "Come stand with me. Did you get shot, Gio? You're getting slow in your old age."

He closed his eyes, trying to focus on something other than the pain in his chest. "Keep her away. Maybe you should both go up on deck."

"No," they said together.

"I won't leave you," she said.

Giovanni thought about the resolute look in her eyes as she watched him drain the human and nodded before he stepped to the far corner of the empty compartment. He stood motionless and lowered his head, taking deep breaths before he allowed the static electricity to start snapping along his skin. After a moment, he began pacing, keeping one eye near the door where Carwyn and Beatrice stood. They were at least ten meters away, but he was still cautious, which was, no doubt, part of Carwyn's plan in keeping them close by.

He flexed his arms and curled his shoulders in, focusing his energy to run along his skin and push outward as he felt the flames begin to lick along his chest and arms. He could feel himself start to walk the thin edge between control and chaos. The last of his clothes burned away, and he stood naked as the blue fire covered his body.

As Giovanni's energy grew and the flames rose, he could feel his chest ache and start to knit together. He glanced up to see Carwyn holding onto Beatrice with an iron grip. He turned and faced her, focusing on her dark eyes as he stood motionless and let the fire wash his injuries away.

He heard the hiss as his hair singed, and the acrid scent drifted to his nose. He kept himself focused on the sour smell of burning hair to counteract the heady sensation of power that threatened to overwhelm him. The blood rushed through his body and his heart raced, but the higher the flames grew, the stronger he became.

His power peaked, and Giovanni could feel his chest muscles stretch and smooth out. He flexed them, feeling only an edge of pain. He continued to stare at Beatrice as he let the fire fall back and finally dissipate into the cold salt air.

He gave a quiet grunt and fell to his knees as they rushed over. Beatrice put her arms around him, flinching from the heat that still radiated off his skin, but she only pulled him closer and rocked him as her hands tangled in his singed hair.

"That was… " She sniffed. "It was—"

"Cracking as always, Gio," Carwyn said with a laugh. "By God, you'll manage to kill me someday, but that's absolutely brilliant."

Giovanni sighed and slumped against Beatrice, burying his face in the cool skin at her throat and wrapping his arms around her waist.

"I hate getting shot."

NINETEEN

"Just the two left?"

"We were lucky to save those before Gemma got her hands on them."

"And no trace of my son?"

"No, but he left his lackeys here. And he must have known we would take them."

"Interesting and deliberate."

Giovanni and Carwyn were walking up the stairs, Giovanni growing stronger with every step. He wanted to feed again, but didn't want to weaken Beatrice more by asking. She was still limping, and her bruises were more vivid. It irritated him that he could do nothing more to heal her. She had been handling herself extraordinarily well, but he could tell she was starting to crash.

"Tesoro," he said as he slipped a hand around her shoulders while clutching the blanket wrapped around his waist. "Will you stay with Jean's men on the top deck while we question them? I'm sure you could handle it, but—"

"I'm okay with skipping the torture part, thanks."

He nodded, relieved she had not insisted on being present for what would be, no doubt, a brutal interrogation.

As they walked through the melted door and onto the open deck, he saw Jean's men securing what was left of the crew, and Gemma held two battered, young vampires by the throat. Terry tossed him a pair of black pants he found somewhere, and Giovanni turned to Beatrice as he saw the three vampires walk away with the captives.

He leaned down and kissed her. "I'll be back soon."

She threw her arms around his neck and whispered in his ear, "Don't be too long. There are things to say."

He nodded and gave her one more lingering kiss before he walked away.

The injured vampires were obviously disposable; Giovanni wondered why Lorenzo had even left them on the ship. They dragged them to the rear deck among the maze of containers the freighter carried.

"No one else?" he asked as he slipped on the borrowed pants.

Terry and Carwyn shook their heads.

"Jean's men searched all the containers," Gemma said, pounding on one that echoed in the dark. "Nothing. Not even a drained human or a bit of clothing."

"Cazzo," he muttered and turned his attention back to the vampires at Gemma's feet. "Why did he leave you?"

"Are you the master's father?" One croaked and took a deep breath of the salt air. Giovanni suspected they were both water vampires, turned by Lorenzo to replace the personal army he and Tenzin had destroyed in Greece. Both looked to be in their early twenties. One had an American accent, and the other sounded Irish.

Giovanni knelt down and braced one arm on his knee. "I am Lorenzo's sire."

"We have a message for you," the American said.

"Thought you might." He let the blue flames flare on his torso as the young vampires watched. The American, a young blond man with brown eyes and an innocent face, looked at Giovanni as if he had never seen anything more terrifying. The other wore a placid expression, and his hard, blue eyes did not flinch. "Well?"

It was the Irishman who spoke up. "Lorenzo says he will burn your books, take your woman, turn your child, and one day, you will call him master... and you will love him."

Giovanni cocked his head. "He sacrifices your lives to boast?"

The young American vampire could not seem to look away as the fire grew. Again, it was the other that spoke for them. "We are his humble servants."

Giovanni stared into the young one's frigid blue eyes. He whispered, "Did you kill Ioan ap Carwyn?" He could feel Gemma and Carwyn looking over his shoulders. "Did you kill my friend?"

The young vampire's calm mask finally faltered, and he stuttered when he answered.

"W—we are his humble servants."

Giovanni grabbed him by the neck and took the knife that Terry held out. "You are nothing. But you will tell me everything you know."

He slashed the vampire across the neck and the side, placing his burning hands on the wounds as the young one began to scream.

G iovanni interrogated them for hours, Terry reviving both with seawater when they fainted.

The two vampires confessed to luring Ioan away from the clinic he had been running in the slums of Dublin. The young Irish vampire, named Sean, had been a patient of Ioan's as a child and used the connection to put the doctor at ease. Then the other vampires, two of whom Gemma had killed in the cargo hold, kidnapped three children who had come to the clinic, threatening to kill them unless Ioan cooperated.

As Giovanni had suspected, his compassionate friend had not hesitated to sacrifice his freedom for the innocent girls. It was the American boy with the guilty brown eyes named Josh who finally broke down and confessed how Ioan had been killed.

Lorenzo met them at the old warehouse, where he tortured the doctor for days about some kind of research he had been conducting on vampire blood types. None of it made sense to the young ones, and Josh broke down sobbing when he confessed that he and his friends had drained the little girls instead of letting them go.

By the time Giovanni finished, he could hear Gemma sniffing quietly in Carwyn's arms as Josh explained how Lorenzo forced Sean to behead Ioan before he tossed his body onto the riverbank on their way out of Dublin. It was the only time the young Irishman showed any sign of guilt.

Giovanni continued questioning them about Lorenzo's plans, but the young water vampires knew nothing of value. Terry checked the time on the reinforced pocket watch he carried and glanced at him.

"We're wasting time. They don't know anything else."

Giovanni left the crumpled vampires twisting on the deck and walked over to Carwyn and Gemma.

"They are yours. Finish them for Deirdre."

He watched stoically as Gemma and Carwyn walked over to the two boys, forcing them down on bloody knees as Josh sobbed. Sean lifted his head defiantly. Carwyn twisted Sean's head off first, tossing it into the ocean before he kicked the body over the railing. The priest stood over the sobbing American boy for a few minutes before his shoulders slumped. Finally, Carwyn knelt down and quietly offered the boy last rites.

Giovanni turned his head away as the boy finished confessing his sins and asking for forgiveness. Carwyn walked away, and Gemma twisted Josh's head off and tossed his remains into the ocean before rushing into Terry's waiting arms.

The four vampires walked back to the front of the boat, using one of the deck showers to wash off the worst of the blood so they didn't startle Beatrice.

"Gio?" Terry called. He was walking behind Giovanni with an arm around Gemma.

"Yes?"

"Your boy knew we were coming."

"Yes."

"Why didn't he take her?"

Giovanni shook his head at the question that had plagued him since they failed to find any trace of his son on the ship. "There is something he wants more than Beatrice at the moment. That is my only guess."

"He's traveling light," Carwyn said. "Only four other vampires with him."

"And now none."

Giovanni muttered, "Who knows where he is? I can't do anything about it right now. I need to see Beatrice."

Carwyn nodded. "Go. We'll question the crew."

He sped across the deck, only slowing when he had her in sight. He walked to a small metal table where she sat huddled, blinking back tears from the wind, which whipped her dark hair into her face. He waved Jean's men away, picked her up, and settled her on his lap as he tried to block the wind.

She sighed and laid her head on his chest before she pulled away. "Oh! Is it okay?"

"It's fine." He drew her back and tucked her under his chin.

"Lorenzo?"

"They knew nothing."

"Did they kill Ioan?"

"They helped."

"Are they dead?"

"Yes."

She paused for a moment before she squeezed his waist and whispered, "Good."

They sat silent for a few moments. He drank in her scent and rocked her when she hugged his waist.

"I told him things, Gio. About my father. About you. I couldn't help it."

It was nothing he hadn't been expecting.

"It's all right. What you knew is not... it's fine. Your father's location is still a mystery to me, so I doubt it will make much sense to Lorenzo, either."

"I thought maybe you hadn't told me everything because you worried about him taking me again."

"There were a few things I held back, but not much."

Giovanni could feel her start to shake, and he held her securely as he examined her, stroking his hands along her limbs and torso, noting every minute flinch or hint of tension. Soon, the shivers overcame her, and he knew the adrenaline that had fueled her for hours was wearing off. The aftershock collided with the stress of the day and caused her to shake.

"Shhh," he soothed her, sending a mild current through his hands to relax her muscles. He rocked her in his warm arms until her breathing had returned to normal and her heart no longer raced.

"I... shit, Gio. I thought... " She sniffed, stuttering for a moment until she took a deep breath. "I thought he was going to bite me. Maybe turn me. He threatened—"

"I'll kill him." He kissed her forehead and tilted her chin up. "As many times as I can."

She snorted before he heard her mutter, "Not if I kill him first."

Giovanni smiled as she placed her cheek over his heart. "That's the spirit of competition, my bloodthirsty girl."

They sat in silence for a few more minutes, rocking in the cool night air.

"Man, I am glad you're here," she said in a shaky voice. "I'm exhausted."

"You are extraordinary. I saw you disarm that man. You didn't even need me there."

He felt her smile. "The librarian finally kicked some ass, didn't she?"

"She most certainly did. And I'm sure you've made Terry and Gemma quite proud." He winked when she looked up.

"And you?"

He shrugged. "I've always been proud of you. I always knew you were extraordinary."

She smiled and relaxed back into his chest. "I slipped and called Lorenzo by his human name. He knows you've told me about your life."

"Don't worry about it."

"Why did you tell me? Why?" She almost looked a little angry. "You knew I would be vulnerable to any vampire who got his hands on me. Why did you tell me?"

He simply smiled. "Because you asked."

"What?" She looked up at him, blinking as the wind made her eyes tear up again.

He leaned down and brushed at the tears. "I told you. I can't deny you anything. You asked. I answered. I like that you know. It's good to be known."

She pressed her hands to his cheeks and looked into his eyes. "You should take the memories away so you'll be safer. I never want to—"

He stopped her with a hard kiss. "Not in a thousand years."

Beatrice stroked his cheeks and let her fingers trail to the back of his neck where she played with the singed ends of his hair.

"I love you, Jacopo."

He blinked, wondering whether he had imagined it.

"What?"

She placed her hands back on his cheeks. "I love you, Jacopo... Giovanni... whatever name you choose in a hundred years... or two hundred. I'll love you then, too. Ubi amo, ibi patria. Where I love, there is my home. You... " She blinked back tears and gave him a smile. "You are my home."

Giovanni was speechless, so he crushed her to his chest. He held Beatrice for a few moments before pulling away so he could kiss her. He kissed her over and over again, nipping at soft, swollen lips as his heart pounded. "I love you," he whispered. "Per sempre. Forever."

"I love you, too. I never really stopped. I can just admit it now."

He broke into a low chuckle that turned into a full laugh. He was happy. More. Joyful. She loved him. He kissed her again.

"I really wish we didn't have an audience right now," she finally said when they came up for air.

Giovanni tucked her head under his chin. "Someday, woman, I will have you to myself."

"We need to get away, just us. Soon. But right now... " She hugged him close. "We have a crew to interrogate and strategy to plan. We still need to murder Lorenzo and find my dad, remember?"

"Somehow, you are not any less sexy as you say this, Beatrice," he said with a smile. "I love you."

"I love you, too. Now, let's go interrogate some Spanish sailors."

"Darling girl," Carwyn walked over and embraced her. "Gemma says you disarmed a six foot man. If I promise not to make you watch wrestling anymore, will you promise not to hurt me?"

She punched Carwyn's side and smiled. "Very funny, old man."

"That'll teach you to run from your bodyguard next time you visit," Terry muttered. "I had to keep your man there from turning the poor sod into a pile of ash last night."

"I'll remember. Thanks to you both, by the way," she said, nodding at Gemma and Terry. "Thanks for beating me up, Gemma. Humans have nothing on you."

"What do you Americans say? 'It was a tough job, but someone had to do it?'"

"Right." Beatrice said and rolled her eyes.

"You should keep that gun, by the way. It's a nice piece," Terry said, nodding to the nine millimeter handgun tucked into her waistband. "Your first spoils of war, B."

"That is a good weapon," Giovanni's eyes narrowed. "Why does a Spanish sailor have an H&K?"

"Well, while some of us... " Carwyn waggled his eyebrows at the two of them. "Were snogging on the deck, others were questioning what was left of the crew. None knew anything about your son, of course."

"It seems like they took Lorenzo and his people on in Rotterdam, but they didn't really know what they were getting into," Gemma added. "Lorenzo was directing the captain off his usual route. London was not a scheduled stop, so thank God for Tywyll's informants, whoever they are."

"Where does that little bastard get his information?" Terry muttered.

Carwyn shrugged. "From looking at the ship's records, it looks like they were headed to North Africa. The details are a bit fuzzy, but Lorenzo outfitted the crew with weapons, probably thinking he could use them as fodder if he was threatened."

Giovanni looked between Carwyn and Terry. "Then why is he not here? What tipped him off?"

"Well." Terry glanced at the French humans. "It's more likely 'Who?' is the better question."

Carwyn shook his head. "Apparently, they stopped in Le Havre early this morning, just before dawn. Someone on our side or Jean's must have warned him we were sending a daylight team. There were three containers dropped off and put on trucks. Gemma called Jean. He has people at the port checking where they went, but Lorenzo could have been in any of them."

"And that explains why the bastard didn't take Beatrice," Terry said. "He would never have left himself alone with a human during the day."

"Damn, now I wish he had taken me," Beatrice muttered at his side. Giovanni put an arm around her and stroked her arm, more relieved to have her back than angry at the missed opportunity.

He bent down and kissed the top of her head. "We'll get another chance at him. The most important thing is that you are safe."

"We'll have some questions for Jean's people. And my own, for that matter. Unfortunately, it's probably the human staff," Terry said, shrugging. "They're always the most vulnerable."

"It could be a vampire," Giovanni added. "Lorenzo still has resources we don't know about."

Gemma piped up, "Anything's possible. We'll just have to keep our ears open."

Carwyn looked over at the group of humans surrounded by Jean's men. "What should we do with the crew?"

Giovanni looked at Beatrice, who only shrugged. "Let Jean look into them," he said. "If they were only being used by Lorenzo, I have no quarrel with them, as long as they did not harm Beatrice."

"All the ones who hurt me are taken care of."

The five of them looked around the deck, and Giovanni noticed that the sky was already beginning to lighten with a hint of dawn. They needed to return to Terry's secured boat in the port of Cherbourg.

"Can we go now?" Beatrice asked. "This human is cold and really, really tired."

Terry motioned toward the zodiac floating nearby, piloted by one of his sons. "Your chariot awaits, ass-kicking librarian."

"Haha," she said with a slight blush as she tugged Giovanni in the direction Terry and Gemma were walking. Carwyn walked beside them, looking out toward the sea, and Giovanni wondered whether he was thinking of the two boys who lay at the bottom of the ocean, finally dead after stealing the life of his oldest child.

His friend looked over at him, glancing between him and Beatrice with a bittersweet smile. Carwyn reached a hand over to stroke her hair. "You're safe, darling girl, you're safe."

Twenty

They took refuge an hour before dawn on the secure yacht one of Terry's lieutenants had brought to Cherbourg harbor for them. When they arrived on deck, they were greeted by a steward that informed them Jean Desmarais was waiting in the saloon, along with two of Terry's people.

"Beatrice," Jean said as she stepped through the door of the luxurious room. He rose from the leather couch, setting down a glass of something red. Whether it was blood or wine, she couldn't tell. "I'm so very relieved you are unharmed. I hope my men were helpful."

"Yes," Giovanni said as they walked across the wood paneled saloon. "It appears I am in your debt, Desmarais."

The keen water vampire cocked an eyebrow. "It was a pleasure to do a favor for a friend."

"I'm sure it was," Terry muttered from behind them. "Now, if you could inform us how exactly your old friend managed to hear we were on our way, that'd be greatly appreciated."

Jean stiffened and his narrowed eyes swept the room. "I do not care for your implication, Monsieur Ramsay."

"Like it or not," Carwyn added as he walked in with Gemma.

"Lorenzo was taken off that freighter in Le Havre. Someone told him we were coming, and he bolted. Who has the closer tie to the little bastard, hmm?"

Jean's eyes flared, and Giovanni pulled Beatrice closer to his side as the three vampires circled the Frenchman.

"I know nothing of this. I am insulted—"

"Fine," Carwyn said. "Be insulted. You'll answer our questions or we'll know why."

"Hey, guys," Beatrice held up her hands. "Let's calm down. I think we need to—"

"Yes, Jean," Gemma piped up. "Why exactly were the only vampires on that ship sacrificial lambs that died too quickly for my brother's death?"

"I offer you my help and you ambush me?" Jean glared at them. "Do you think if I am harmed you will leave this harbor alive?"

"I reckon we've got a fair shot," Terry said, crossing his arms as his men shut the door.

"As do I," Carwyn added. "Besides, what do you care? You'll be dead if you betrayed us."

Beatrice braced herself against Giovanni, clutching his hand and scanning the layout of the room. It was open, but there was no way Jean could escape. He was completely outnumbered.

"I did not betray you." Jean's chin jutted out arrogantly. "I do not dishonor myself by turning on an ally. Unlike some here, I—"

"You were allied with Lorenzo for two hundred years," Terry growled.

"Do you know why I broke ties with him?" Jean spit out. "Do you know why I am supporting you? As charming as the De Novo girl is, she's certainly not my only motivation."

Beatrice leaned forward. Jean was tense, Terry and Carwyn stood across from him with their arms crossed on their chests, and Gemma stood at the door, guarding it like some lethal angel with eyes trained on the rakish Frenchman. But when Beatrice glanced up, she noticed that Giovanni was completely relaxed. His arm slid around her waist, and he wore an almost bemused expression.

"Tell us why we should believe you," he said. "For some reason, I think I do."

Carwyn glared. "Gio—"

"He's not the only one who could have told Lorenzo," Giovanni said with a shrug. "I want to hear what he has to say."

Jean stepped toward him. "No, I did not give Lorenzo any information. Nor would I have. My daughter will forgive me for speaking of this." He glanced at Beatrice before looking away. "Louise had one child while she was still human. The boy was raised in my home, and his family was under my aegis. Louise remained very close to her son's children and grandchildren. One of her granddaughters was on holiday in Greece ten years ago."

A sick feeling began to churn in Beatrice's stomach. She saw Jean's eyes swing to hers and they locked. The truth was written on his face.

"Oh no," she whispered as the tears came to her eyes.

"Julie had met Lorenzo before, so she accepted his invitation. She thought she was safe. She was not."

Beatrice's face fell as she flashed back to the young bodies Lorenzo's men had tossed over the cliffs in Greece to be swallowed by the Aegean Sea.

"There were so many," she whispered, blinking back tears. "I believe you."

Giovanni squeezed her waist. "As do I."

At Giovanni's quiet declaration, Beatrice felt the tension drain out of the room, though all parties kept their guarded positions as the questions flew.

"Lorenzo killed a girl? One under your protection?" Gemma asked from the doorway. "Why would he be so stupid?"

"Or so arrogant?" Terry added.

Jean was staring at Giovanni. "You have been fooling yourself, di Spada, hiding away in your books. Your son has many powerful friends. In the last ten years, his influence has grown. I do not know why. It is a testament to your connections that you were given the girl five years ago." He nodded toward Beatrice. "You think you damaged him? He is still more powerful and connected than you know."

"What do you mean? What do you know?" Giovanni asked.

Jean only shook his head. "You think you have allies? Everyone has an agenda. Everyone."

"What's yours?" Beatrice asked.

The Frenchman turned. "My family. Nothing remains except family. Power. Wealth. All these change, but my family remains. My daughter was distraught. Her family lost faith in us. My own reputation was damaged to have lost one under my protection. Trust me." He looked around the room. "None in my company bear Lorenzo any goodwill."

"And I vouch for my people," Terry said.

"So where does that leave us?" Carwyn asked, looking around the room in frustration. "Someone told him. One of our humans? Someone manipulated? Bribed?"

Jean shrugged. "I will have the port checked immediately. If there is any indication where the containers went or who arranged the shipment, I will find it. I have many people in Le Havre."

"Don't most shipping containers have GPS now?" Beatrice asked.

"These wouldn't," Giovanni muttered. "I think you taught him a lesson about technology. It would be easy enough to make them untraceable, and since there were three containers—"

"He could be on any one of three trucks going to any one of three locations," Gemma sighed.

Beatrice looked around the room. "But there has to be a way of finding out more."

Everyone was silent, standing around the room with the strange blank expressions she hated, each vampire lost in their own thoughts.

"Gio?"

"Beatrice—"

"Who told you?"

He frowned. "What?"

"Who? Who told you that Lorenzo had taken me? You knew what ship I was on; Jean's team found the boat too fast for you to be looking very long. Someone told you which one I was on. I was barely there for a day. Whoever told you knew where I was and had to know you were coming for me, so who told you?"

"That little bastard," Gemma murmured.

She felt Giovanni's skin heat.

"Tywyll."

Gravesend, England

Beatrice looked around with a poorly veiled look of disdain. "This is the dirtiest pub I've ever seen."

"It definitely ranks quite high."

"Is it... floating?"

Beatrice looked at the floor, which seemed to rock and sway under their feet. She saw a beer bottle roll in the corner as the pub near the mouth of the River Thames rose with the swell of the water. Then she looked into Giovanni's taciturn face.

"Are you going to kill him? Can you?"

He thought for a long moment before he shrugged. "Doubtful, and definitely not until you get your information. I have a feeling that Tywyll has a bit to tell us."

"He's really old, isn't he?"

"I believe so. No one knows. I've never met anyone that claimed to know him before he became what he is now."

She frowned and pulled his arm to sit next to her in the dark booth with its cracked leather seats. Giovanni sat with his back to the wall and his eyes on the door as the dark pub rose and fell.

When they had returned to London just before dawn the night before, they were met at the door of the Mayfair house with a handwritten note.

Mariposa—
   Come to The Cockleshell in Gravesend with the Italian tonight at nine o'clock. I have information for you.
   —Tywyll

"What is he?"

"A trader. A conduit. And apparently, someone who knew your father."

She whispered, "My dad and my grandma are the only ones that have ever called me 'Mariposa.' And it's not something he would have shared with just anyone."

"Which is why we are meeting him alone at the dirtiest pub in Gravesend, instead of being accompanied by twenty of Terry's most vicious minions."

She smiled and tried to lighten his mood as she slipped an arm around his waist. "You should totally get some minions."

He smiled despite himself. "Isn't that what Benjamin is for? He's a minion-in-training."

She snickered and pulled him down for a kiss. Between rushing back to London, seeing a doctor for her injuries, and questioning Terry's human staff, Beatrice had little to no time alone with Giovanni, and she could tell the stress of the previous three nights was wearing on them both.

"I'm exhausted," she whispered as she laid her head on his shoulder. He pressed a kiss to her forehead.

"I know."

His restless eyes continued to scan the dark, almost empty, pub. She sat next to him and left a hand on his knee, needing the connection. Giovanni had been eager to escape the city, wanting to whisk her away somewhere safe and away from prying eyes and ears as soon as they had returned. But after they received the note, Beatrice and Carwyn had insisted it was important to meet the mysterious water vampire—even if he was the source of the betrayal—and Giovanni had reluctantly agreed.

She heard the door open and an electric current radiated up her arm. She could feel Giovanni's skin heat against hers.

"Tywyll," he said in a low voice.

"This is Stephen's girl then." She looked up. "Ay, ye' are. Look at the eyes. Just like yer father."

She stared at the unassuming man wearing dirty work clothes. To anyone else, he would have fit right in, a hardworking middle-aged man out for a pint at the pub after work. Beatrice, however, took note of his inhuman paleness, the energy that seemed to vibrate off him, and the fangs that peeked from the corners of his mouth.

"How do you know my father?"

"Can I sit without fear for meself, fire-starter? Do I have yer word?"

She could tell it was a struggle for him, but she saw Giovanni give a slight nod out of the corner of her eye.

"For now, yes."

"Fer now'll do fine." He sat across from them and raised three fingers toward the bar. "I reckon we'll stay out of each other's way after that, eh?"

"It depends very much on what you say, waterman."

"How do you know my father?" Beatrice asked again.

The old vampire turned his eyes toward her.

"Yer father is a fine one, miss. I don't like many, but I liked him. Met him at this very pub."

A shiver crossed her neck and she felt Giovanni's hand squeeze hers under the table. "My father was here?"

Tywyll paused as an old man came to set three dark pints on

the table in front of them. Tywyll took his and drank before he answered.

"He was. Ten years ago. He'd just come from the North and he was makin' his way out of the country. Needed a bit of help. Someone gave him my name. Had gold and he didn't talk too much. I like that in a vampire."

Giovanni leaned forward and passed one of the pints to Beatrice as he set the other in front of himself. The glasses were surprisingly clean.

"I heard rumors about him ten years ago," Giovanni said. "About the books he had. He was referred to me for a job, but no one seemed to be able to find him."

Tywyll's eyes almost twinkled. "Well now, that might ha' been my doin'. He was awful young then, and he didn't know much. I may ha' kept him out of the way for a bit from those lookin' for him."

"Why?" Beatrice asked. "You protected him? Why? And if you protected my father, why would you sell us out to Lorenzo?"

"Did I sell you out?" Tywyll's head tilted to the side and she could feel the heat start to radiate from Giovanni. She squeezed his knee and felt the energy in the air dissipate slightly. "You were taken, but it looks like yer here and safe to me, girl."

Giovanni's voice was taut. "Do you deny informing my son we were coming after Beatrice?"

Tywyll squinted as he took another drink. "I may have... repaid a favor, fire-starter. I always repay my favors. But I wouldn't be bringing harm to Stephen's dear girl." Tywyll's eyes darkened and Beatrice saw the cold-blooded killer beneath the unassuming demeanor of the small man. "Now my debt is repaid, so I'll ask you: were you hurt, Mariposa?"

Giovanni spit something out in a language she didn't recognize, and Tywyll glared at him before responding in kind. She didn't recognize the language, and she was beginning to get frustrated with their quick, heated exchange. She saw tension lift from

Tywyll's shoulders before his eyes shuttered closed. He fell silent and took a long drink of his beer.

"Interesting," Tywyll muttered.

"What?" She turned to Giovanni, irritated and confused. "What was that?"

"I'll tell you later. Tywyll knew your father. He hid him from Lorenzo for a time. He has an... interest in you. Nothing to be concerned about."

"Do you know where my dad is?" She turned to Tywyll, reaching across the table to grab his cold hand. She saw Giovanni start, but Tywyll only squeezed her slight fingers. "Please, do you know—"

"No, girl, I don't. I taught him well. You'll not find Stephen unless he wants to be found. That was my gift to him. In my many years, I've not considered many friends, but yer father was one."

Giovanni put a hand on her shoulder and drew her back. "Why did you tell Lorenzo we were coming for Beatrice?"

"Did the mariposa figure it out?" Tywyll asked with a small smile. "I'll bet she did. She's got the look of her father; I'll bet she has his mind, too. Ye' are the butterfly, aren't ye?" Tywyll said. "I'll be keen to see what happens with ye."

"I don't know what you're talking about," she whispered. She was lying, she knew exactly what he was talking about, and from the look in his eyes, Tywyll did too.

"Don't ye'?" Tywyll took another drink and turned to Giovanni. "Why did I tell yer son? I owed a very old favor to him, Giovanni Vecchio. One he was keen to collect. I do have a reputation to maintain, and I'll not be backing out of a favor owed. However, I don't owe him anymore. The ship he was on before I got word to him was bound for two ports—Port Said in Egypt and Shanghai, China."

Tywyll directed his words to Beatrice. "Now, I've no idea where he was goin' after that, and I don't know his location now. Not my job. But he's still after my friend, so I've got no objection to answering what ye' want to ask, if it suits my mood, and ye' ask the right questions."

Beatrice could sense the buzzing anticipation from Giovanni. She still didn't know what she wanted to ask, her mind was whirling from the night's revelations, so she looked up and nodded at him. A small smile quirked Giovanni's mouth as he began questioning Tywyll.

"What did Stephen De Novo take from my son?"

"Good question. Gold, for one. And a lot of it. Unusual stuff. Old. Some of it melted down. All unmarked, not that I minded."

She caught the minute flicker in Giovanni's eyes and she knew he recognized what the other vampire was talking about. "What about the books?"

"Books?" Tywyll cocked his head. "Not a good question."

Beatrice whispered, "Book. What about the book?"

Tywyll nodded. "Better question."

Giovanni looked confused. "Only one?"

"Only one he kept with him. Only one yer boy really wanted."

They all seemed to lean toward each other, and her heart pounded.

"What book does my son want?"

Tywyll smirked. "If I could read ancient Persian, I'd have a much better idea. Unfortunately, Stephen didn't teach me. Don't know that he could read it himself—though, I've no doubt he can by now. When he escaped yer son, he only knew that this book was the one Lorenzo guarded most carefully."

"He didn't know what it was?"

"Oh—" The old vampire's eyes twinkled. "He had an idea."

Tywyll paused to finish off his beer as Beatrice fought the urge to reach across the table and shake him. "Well?" she finally asked.

"What do you know of alchemy, Mariposa?"

Giovanni shook his head and slumped in his seat. "Spells and magic," he muttered. "Ridiculous. What does that tell us? Nothing."

"Arrogance, fire-starter. It's an old science."

Beatrice looked between them, confused by their demeanor. "Wait, isn't alchemy just an early form of chemistry?"

"Yes," Tywyll said, as Giovanni muttered, "No."

She could almost hear the "professor voice" before Giovanni opened his mouth. "Alchemy is magic, not chemistry. And most certainly not a real science. Philosopher's stones. Gold from lead. Elixir of life. Not science. Magic."

Tywyll cut his eyes toward her. "Oh... immortality, manipulation of the elements, the creation of life itself. I can't imagine why a curious vampire would find those things worthy of further study."

They all fell silent around the table while Giovanni and Tywyll exchanged looks she couldn't quite decipher. "So—" She looked back and forth between them. "—what is it? Is it science, like amnis? Something natural we just don't understand yet? Or is it magic?"

Tywyll chuckled while Giovanni looked chastened.

"Ye've nabbed yerself a smart one. You two won't bore each other anytime soon."

Giovanni shook his head. "We will have to consider what Lorenzo may have found."

"Or what my father did," she added. "If he was willing to risk himself for this book... " Beatrice felt her throat tighten up. "I have to think it's all been worth it."

Giovanni pulled her into his side and she felt him press a kiss to the top of her head. She glanced at Tywyll across the table, but the old vampire only wore a mysterious smile.

"Well," he said as he shrugged. "I'm tired of answering questions. This is the most I've talked in years. I've a mind to get home now."

Beatrice leaned into Giovanni's shoulder. "Where is home, Tywyll?"

He winked. "Here and there, girl. The river, that's my home."

Giovanni tossed a few pounds on the table and they rose to leave. They walked out of the dark pub to see their car and driver waiting a block away and a long, wooden skiff tied up to the side of the floating pub.

She looked at the cagey vampire, who had given her more clues to her father's whereabouts than she'd had in the five years she'd searched for him.

"Thank you, Tywyll."

"Yer welcome, Mariposa. He gave me that name, you know. I have a feeling he thought you might come looking for me."

"Smart man." She heard Giovanni murmur.

"Smarter vampire," Tywyll said.

The river surged beside them and Beatrice heard a glass fall to the floor and shatter inside.

"Why on Earth did you want to meet here?" Beatrice asked as she looked from the ramshackle bar to the old water vampire. "This bar is just... " She curled her lip as the strange man chuckled.

Tywyll stood on the dock, his hands tucked in his pockets, and she could feel the sudden energy that charged the air.

"Oh," he said, "it has its features."

Looking over his shoulder, Beatrice noticed the boats moored nearby begin to drift to the bank. There was a soft ripple, and a squawking rose as a flock of ducks took off from the center channel. In the distance, she saw a fishing boat begin to change course. Then Beatrice gasped as the The Cockleshell pub itself began to rise as the river pushed it up and toward them.

Beatrice could only gape as the whole of the River Thames waited at attention for the old water vampire. He rocked back and forth, and the river, and everything floating, mirrored his small movement.

"Wow," she whispered.

Finally, Tywyll shrugged and the river seemed to heave a sigh before the boats drifted back downriver, and the current flowed out toward the sea. The pub settled back into its slip and the ducks landed over the rippling reflection of the moon.

He winked at her. "I like the beer, too." Tywyll walked toward his skiff and stepped aboard. He untied the ropes and stood watching them as the boat began to drift away.

"Find yer father, Mariposa. He needs ye.' And Giovanni Vecchio, don't let your arrogance blind ye to the schemes of others."

Giovanni frowned. "What aren't you telling me, waterman?"

He smiled. "A lot." Tywyll tipped his hat toward Beatrice as she clutched Giovanni's hand. "Ye' know more than ye' realize, girl. Yer father wants ye' to find him."

Tywyll drifted away, and the moon rippled in the quiet wake. Beatrice and Giovanni stood on the dock and she wrapped her arms around him, burying her face in his chest and inhaling his dark, smoky scent. She could feel his arms embrace her, and she tilted her face up for a kiss.

"Do we believe him?" she whispered.

His eyes narrowed as he searched the inky night. "I think we do."

"We've got a lot to think about."

"Yes, we do. But not here."

She paused and held him tighter as the exhaustion ate at her. She could feel his arm holding her up as they began the walk back to the car.

"Gio?"

"Yes, tesoro?"

"I want to go home. Take me to Cochamó."

Giovanni looked down and met her tired eyes. She saw a flare of excitement in his gaze and a smile teased the corner of his mouth. He nodded. "We'll leave tonight."

Twenty-One

Santiago, Chile

He stared at her profile in the dim light of the theater, admiring how the lights from the stage caught bits of red in her hair and made her skin glow. Giovanni had seen the play before, but Beatrice had not, and she stared at the actors with a small smile flirting around her mouth.

She must have caught his gaze from the corner of her eye.

What? she mouthed.

"I finally took you on a date," he whispered.

She laughed silently, and he reached across to cup her cheek before he bent and pressed a kiss to her mouth. He felt the curl of her lips against his own as she smiled and placed her cool hand on his jaw. He pulled away so she could continue to watch the performance of the Lorca play, and she felt for his hand, laying it on her lap and knitting their fingers together.

Beatrice was stunning in a black silk dress, her neck and shoulders bare. He could see the flutter of the pulse in her neck, and a flush rose in her cheeks. He made no show of hiding his hungry stare. Her dark eyes kept glancing between his rapt face and the stage; he could hear her heartbeat quicken as his amnis reached out to her. The air was lush with her scent in their corner of the dark theater. After another twenty minutes, she silently rose from her seat and took his hand, pulling him up and out the door. As soon as they reached the dark hallway, she pressed him against the wall and lifted her mouth to his as he met her in a passionate kiss.

The blood had already begun to pulse in his veins when she whispered, "Take me back to the hotel."

Giovanni said nothing as he wrapped an arm around her waist and escorted her down the stairs of the theater and into the starlit night.

They rushed through the lively streets of the Providencia district, ignoring the flow of pedestrians and the call of music from the clubs, stopping only at lights where they kissed without thought of the people around them. It was eleven o'clock, and the warm streets of Santiago were filled with late summer crowds, but they ignored all distractions as they hurried back to the private entrance of their hotel.

Giovanni paused when they were finally alone, pulling off his jacket and taking a calming breath to cool his skin. She stood near the open terrace doors, looking out on the lights of the city. The night air was soft as he placed his hands on the bare skin of her shoulders.

"Tesoro mio," he murmured. "My Beatrice."

He bent down to kiss behind her ear and closed his eyes as he felt the heat rise between them. He brushed at her dark hair, smoothing it away as it fell loose down her back. He could feel the rush of his blood as his heart picked up pace. Giovanni struggled to control the fire that wanted to burst from his skin.

"Do you know how I love you?" she whispered.

He wrapped both his arms around her waist and held her to his chest for a few moments, breathing in her scent and listening to the rush of her pulse. His lips kissed above the single button that held the halter of her dress in place. "How do you love me?" he murmured against her skin.

Beatrice turned in his arms and placed a hand on his cheek. "I love you forever."

He paused, staring into her eyes. They no longer held even a trace of doubt. She had said that she loved him, but for the first time, as Beatrice looked at him, Giovanni felt as if he held her heart in his gaze. There was no caution. No reservation. His breath caught in his throat and his heart raced.

"Don't you know," she said with dancing eyes, "how I adore you?"

Giovanni smiled to hear his own words from so many months ago repeated on her lips.

"Do you love me?" he asked.

"You know I do."

"And do you trust me?"

A slow smile bloomed on her face. "Yes."

"Finally." Giovanni's lips swept down to meet her own, and his left hand came around her waist and pulled her away from the window. He returned to her bare shoulder, trailing his hand up to slip the button of her halter loose, then down to catch the edge of her dress.

He felt her quick intake of breath, and she gave a small cry when both his palms cupped her breasts and his mouth bent to her collarbone.

"Too long," he groaned against her skin. The current raced over his skin. "Beatrice, I—"

"I love you, Gio," he heard her whisper. "One life is not enough."

His hands slipped the rest of her dress down her body. Most of her bruises had healed, and Beatrice stood before him with nothing hiding her from his eyes.

"I have seen masterpieces," he said. "But nothing that compares to you." It was the truth, because no work of an artists' hand could compare to her when she looked at him with trust in her eyes.

Beatrice smiled and reached for his shirt, undressing him as his hands trailed along her arms and his ancient heart beat for her. Her skin was flushed, and he felt his fangs grow long in his mouth, but he was not hungry for blood.

Careful. Careful. Careful.

She was mortal, exquisitely, delectably mortal. If he let loose the full breadth of his desire, the fire would consume them both.

"I've waited so long," she murmured, running her hands over his chest. "And you are everything I ever dreamed."

Giovanni shuddered under her hands, reveling in the sight of her fingers tracing his chest. His stomach. Down to his waist...

"Enough." He lifted her in his arms and walked to the bed, setting her down, naked and spread before him.

A roar of hunger.

Careful.

He took a measured breath.

Giovanni lay down facing Beatrice and let his fingertips explore the dips and curves of her body before his mouth followed, tasting and licking along her skin, letting his amnis spread where they touched until their senses were so heightened he thought the flames would burst from his fingertips. He sated himself on the taste of her, careful not to let his fangs cut her skin.

'Love is a single soul dwelling in two bodies.'

He could feel the blood in her veins; even the tiny hairs on her arms reached for him as they embraced.

"Kiss me." She sounded as desperate as he felt.

Giovanni rose to meet her lips again; he deepened his kiss, exploring her mouth as her hands traced along his jawline and the back of his neck. She pulled him closer, her heart pounding against his heated chest.

"The heat," he panted as he pulled away to let her breath. "Is it too much?"

"I'm fine." She pulled him back down. "We're fine."

He focused on her eyes, her mouth, her breasts, and the pulsing life he held in his arms. He braced himself over her, threading his hands with hers and ducking down to taste her again before he whispered the question he had waited so many years to ask.

"Forever?"

A brilliant smile spread over her face. "Yes."

He pressed his cheek to hers when he entered her, and she cried out. The needy sound tripped some long-buried instinct and he drove in to the hilt, bucking between her hips with a barely concealed growl. He wanted to sink his fangs into her neck; he wanted to make her scream.

He held back.

Mortal, a softer voice whispered. *Mortal.*

But for how long?

Holding tight to the control that had become the law of his eternity, Giovanni focused on Beatrice. Her heat. Her heart. The catch in her breath as she approached her climax. Giovanni focused every sense on her.

"Giovanni!" she gasped as she came. "I love you. I love you so much."

Giovanni could smell the scent of smoke surrounding them when he reached his own climax, but he did not let the fire take him. If the flames took him, they would take Beatrice. And that could never, ever happen. So he clamped down on his control and let the sounds of the city mask their cries as they made love through the night.

Cochamó Valley, Chile
April 2010

"You really are a better rider."

"Told you."

He smiled at her flushed cheeks and tousled hair. Only the thought of hiding away in the Cochamó house could have pulled him away from the quiet hotel room where they spent the past week. They had scarcely come up for air. She teased him that it was a good thing he didn't have to breathe. Giovanni had to agree.

"You should see her with a rifle," Gustavo remarked as he led them into the valley. "She's an excellent shot."

"I got to be pretty good with a nine millimeter, too."

Giovanni smiled as she and Gustavo caught up on news. In many ways, Beatrice was more familiar with his friends than he was. He had spent so much time flying around the world the previous five years that he was out of touch with those he cared for most. As he looked at the woman who had captivated him, he let out a contented sigh.

"Gio," he heard Gustavo say, and he looked over to the burly earth vampire. "Tell me what the current news is. Should Isabel and I be on our guard? Should we alert our families?"

He frowned at the reminder that all was not right in his world. "The last time I talked to the Frenchman, he had tracked the three cargo containers that left the ship, but he had no idea which one Lorenzo was in. The best indications we have say he has gone east. We've already sent word to Tenzin, but until we know more—"

"And B's father? Is there any news of him?"

Giovanni glanced at her. "No." The flushed, happy look Beatrice had worn fled with the mention of her father and Lorenzo.

He sidled his horse next to hers and reached an arm around her waist. She leaned into him and allowed him to pull her across his lap. He nodded toward Gustavo, tossed him the reins, and watched as the other vampire spurred his horse, leaving them behind. They rode in silence for a few minutes as she leaned her head against his shoulder.

"I'm starting to think he's really dead."

"We have no reason to think that, tesoro."

He helped her swing a leg over and scooted back so she sat comfortably in front of him in the gaucho saddle. He handed her the reins and placed his arms around her waist. They rode in silence over the summer meadows lit by moonlight, past the rushing waterfalls, and through the dense forests on the trail to their house.

She finally spoke again. "What was your happiest time?"

"Ever?"

"Yeah? Did you like it better before electricity and all the modern stuff that trips you up?"

He only chuckled, and she looked over her shoulder.

"What?"

"My happiest time is now, woman. Isn't that obvious?"

He could see the flush creep onto her cheeks and down her neck. He smiled wider and let his chin rest on her shoulder as his hands trailed up her torso, teasing under her breasts.

"Hey now." She nudged him. "I'm not sure I'm that good at riding."

"We could find out. It's good to challenge yourself."

"No." She laughed. "Besides, you can control yourself for another couple hours until we get home."

"But can you? Remember... " He reached down to tickle the inside of her knee and she squirmed. The horse gave a disapproving whinny.

"Behave!"

"You never should have let me find out where you are ticklish. That was a strategic error, Beatrice."

"I'll figure out your weakness one of these days."

You, he thought, though he remained silent. She was, perhaps, his greatest weakness. They rode quietly for a few more minutes before she spoke again.

"Really though? Now? With the mortal danger and running everywhere?"

"Well." He frowned. "I won't miss that. But you're with me now. And you are safe."

She looked over her shoulder and lifted her mouth for a kiss. "I'm happy, too."

"How long do you want to stay?"

"How long can we?"

He shrugged. "We probably shouldn't leave Benjamin with Caspar and your grandmother for much longer, or they'll never agree to babysit again."

She burst into laughter, and he joined her. He knew she missed the boy, too. They had spoken to Ben that afternoon and he was doing well with the closest thing he had to grandparents, but he did mention that he missed his basketball hoop.

"When all this is over," she said, "if it's ever over—"

"It will be over someday, I promise you."

"When it's over, what do you want?"

"To do?"

"Yes."

He thought for a few moments. "Just to have my life back. With you. Like it was when we first met."

He felt her sigh in front of him as they crossed the last bridge before they reached the house. "I want that, too. Just working with you and being normal."

"Oh yes." He snapped his fingers and tossed a blue flame into the night. It hovered in front of them, lighting the way so she could see as they passed through the overhanging trees. "Very normal."

She smiled. "You know what I mean."

Kissing her cheek, he hugged her around the waist as they broke through the last of the trees and into the meadow that surrounded their home.

"I know what you mean."

Moonlight poured over her bare skin as she moved over him at the edge of the secluded pool. The mist from the waterfall surrounded them, cooling his skin as they made love. She was a vision as she rode him, her head thrown back in the cool night air as the water dripped down her neck. He reared up, letting his fangs scrape the valley between her breasts before he teased her neck, flicking his tongue behind her ear until she moaned.

"Yes," she panted. "More."

Giovanni felt her hands run through his damp hair and down his neck as she drew his head toward the pounding pulse in her throat. His tongue traced over her skin as they moved together, and he wrapped one arm around her back to steady her as he tugged her neck to the side, exposing the lush vein.

"Gio," she whispered. "Now."

He emitted a low growl before he sunk his fangs into her, drawing on the rich blood she offered as he felt her tense and shudder around him. She cried into the night as she came, and he grasped the ends of her dark hair as she arched back.

She didn't stop moving and he hissed when he felt the edge approaching. Her fingers bit into the thick muscle of his shoulders, and he pulled away from her neck to taste her mouth. He moaned into their kiss, then bent to lick the small wounds at her throat before he buried his face in her hair and groaned in release. He didn't pull away, but stayed linked with her, enjoying the shivers that coursed over their skin as they rocked together under the stars.

"Tesoro." He listened with satisfaction to her racing heart. "Remind me to suggest swimming more often."

"It is your favorite waterfall."

"Even more so now," he said with a grin. Making love by the waterfall had been her idea. She must have sensed him holding back. But here, surrounded by water, he could finally taste her as he'd been craving.

They were soaked, and he framed her face with his hands as the water collected on their skin, running down in rivulets as they smiled and laughed together and the moon reflected in the ripples of dark water beside them.

They stretched naked on the wool blanket she had tucked into their saddlebag, and he wrapped his body around her, chasing away the night chill. His hands explored each curve, leisurely studying her unique topography. In five hundred years, he'd had lovers he'd cared for, but none like her. Never before had one woman captured his heart, his body, and his mind as Beatrice had.

"What are you thinking right now?" she asked as his fingers traced over the soft rise of her belly.

"I am thinking, for the first time in five hundred years, I wish I could give you children. I regret that I cannot. It is not possible."

She lay back, silent as she looked up at the stars. Finally, he heard her soft voice.

"Have I ever told you about my mom?"

"Not really."

"She didn't want me. She and my dad were never married, though I think he did ask at some point. But she didn't want to be pregnant or married. She kind of... had me for my dad. Then she took off."

"She was a foolish woman."

Beatrice shrugged, and he clamped down on his instinctive anger.

"She didn't want to be a mom. She could have gotten rid of me. She could have abandoned me to some stranger, but she didn't. She gave me to my dad and my grandparents. And they loved me. So I can't be too angry with her. I was probably better off."

"My mother died of a fever. I think I was around five years old. I'm not sure. I know I was very young."

"And then your uncle found you."

"And then my uncle's friends found me—purely by chance—and apparently I was a replica of my father, so they knew I was his bastard."

"But your uncle was kind."

"Yes." He nodded. "Very kind."

"So, Jacopo... " She rolled him over on his back and laid a slender arm across his chest as she met his gaze. "We know better than anyone that family is what you make it."

"You would make a wonderful mother," he whispered.

"Maybe I will be one day... somehow," she said with a soft smile. "I think I have time."

He tucked a strand of hair behind her ear and brought his mouth to hers for a soft kiss. "Yes, you will have time."

A week later they were lying in their bed in the early evening as a fire burned in the grate and reflected off the mica in the hewn granite wall. Beatrice was watching the lights dance and laughing at a story Ben had related when she'd called him that afternoon.

"So he was reading the recipe and somehow read one quarter teaspoon as one quarter cup," she said as she held back the laughter.

"And?"

The incredulity covered her face as she looked up at him.

"Really?"

"What?"

"Haven't you ever baked?"

He cocked an eyebrow at her. "Only the bad guys."

She rolled over to fold her arms on his chest.

"Well, there was a little bit of cleaning to do when the brownies ran all over the oven."

"As long as he was the one doing the cleaning."

"I have no doubt of that. My grandma has been forcing reluctant men to clean for years. My grandpa. My dad… "

She choked, and he caught her chin between his fingers, forcing her to meet his eyes.

"Do you want to know?"

"What are you talking about?" she muttered.

"You have very carefully not asked me any more about your father. You know I was looking for him. I know you received the postcards, but you seem reluctant to ask any other questions."

She pursed her lips and wiped at a tear that had come to one eye. "I'm not sure what I thought. I guess part of me always hoped he would find me. That he would come to L.A."

"He was in San Francisco once, but that was the closest he ever came that I know of."

She thought for a few more minutes as he played with the ends of her hair.

"Okay, tell me what you found."

"Whatever tricks Tywyll taught your father, he learned them well. Combine that with a brain like yours, enhanced by better vampire processing and memory… he's stayed one step ahead of me for years."

"But you found—"

"What is the saying? Breadcrumbs, tesoro. I found breadcrumbs."

He pulled her closer as he continued. "As I told you before, in each location I found some clue. I would get a call, or a note, or some indication that he had been inquiring after one of my books or my services, something like that."

"But when you got there—"

"He would be gone. I would always find a hotel room, recently occupied, with some trace—a note, a receipt, something that would tell me it had been his."

"And that's where you sent the postcards from?"

"Yes."

"So he didn't try to hide that he'd been there."

Giovanni shook his head. "Quite the opposite. It was almost as if he was waving a flag, then ducking out of sight."

He could almost hear the wheels turning in her head.

"So what if the locations were the clue? There has to be a—a method. A pattern, some—"

"I thought the same," he said, shaking his head. "I thought the locations must be some kind of code or pattern, but there was nothing. I even played with the latitude and longitude for each city, looking for some kind of method to the seemingly random appearances."

"So why did you send the postcards?"

"In the back of my mind, I thought that perhaps the cities would mean something to you. I thought that perhaps you would see something I wasn't."

He could feel her sigh as he stroked her back to try to ease the tension building in her muscles.

"No," she finally whispered. "Those weren't even places he talked about going. I mean, some of them were, but they were all fairly major cities, so there wasn't anything that stood out."

"Yes, after that first sighting in Iraklion, all the cities were major urban—"

"Where?"

"Iraklion or Heraklion. Crete. It was the first place I got any news of him. The director of the Archaeological Museum—"

"You didn't send me a postcard from Iraklion."

He blinked. "I'm sorry. I didn't think to start sending them to you until I'd left Crete, and by then—"

She bolted up, staring into the fire, and he heard her heart begin to race.

"Crete?"

He sat up next and placed a hand on her shoulder.

"I'm sorry I didn't send one from Iraklion, but it's hardly a major city. He didn't even stay very long—"

"But it's Crete!"

He frowned. "Beatrice, I don't understand—"

"Knossos. Minos." She turned to Giovanni with burning eyes. She clasped his face between her hands. "It's Minos, Gio. The minotaur."

"Beatrice, what are you trying to tell me?"

She began shaking her head and a desperate look came to her eye.

"Not breadcrumbs. Not breadcrumbs... it's a labyrinth."

TWENTY-TWO

Beatrice's heart raced.

"Daddy! Daddy, the string game, Daddy!"

She tore out of the bedroom, searching for the unassuming reference book she'd spotted on the bottom shelf in one of the living room bookcases years ago.

"Beatrice, slow down. You're going to trip if you don't—"

"I'm going to find the treasure!"

"You think you're clever enough to solve the puzzle, Mariposa?"

She searched for the blue binding as Giovanni rushed out of the bedroom to join her. "Beatrice—"

"The string game. I called it the string game when I was little," she muttered. The book wasn't where she remembered. Her eyes raked over the shelves in the living room, searching for the familiar book as the memories poured over her.

"What?" Giovanni's voice called from the edge of the room. "The string game?"

"Stephen, are you two playing that silly game again? I'm going to trip and break my neck one of these days."
　"Relax, Mom. But don't go in the living room, okay?"
　"Grandma, I'm in the maze right now!"

She finally spotted it on the bottom shelf in the bookcase closest to the front door; she rushed over. "It used to drive my grandmother nuts. She was always tripping over the strings that we put up."

"Tesoro, what are you—"

"Theseus and the Minotaur. My dad read me the story... I don't know how many times. It was my favorite." Her hands pulled the book out and raced over to the large kitchen table, slamming it down.

"Beatrice, if you need an atlas, I have much better editions—"

"No, no, this is the one we had." She waved her hand as she opened it. "We had this one in our house. It would be this one."

"Look for the clues, Mariposa. I left you clues all over the house; find them and follow the string to the treasure."
　"Like Theseus. Follow the string out of the labyrinth."

"When I was a child, my father would read me the Greek myths. I loved them. He read them to me over and over again, but my favorite was the story of Theseus and the Minotaur."

"The minotaur in the labyrinth?"

"Yeah." She nodded. "Theseus goes to Crete, right? His father sends him to King Minos of Crete."

"In Knossus, the ancient excavation site right outside of Iraklion."

"Exactly. Theseus kills the Minotaur in the middle of the

labyrinth, but then he has to find his way out of the maze again. Luckily, he was smart. He tied a string near the entrance and held onto it so he could find his way out again."

She opened the atlas and flipped to the large map of Greece, pointing toward the island of Crete. "There's no way my father picked that location at random. It was our game; he was telling me to play the string game."

"What's the first clue?"
"'What goes up when the rain comes down?'"
"Solve the riddle, Beatrice."

Giovanni was standing in a corner of the living room, his arms crossed as he stared at her like she was a crazy person. "Can you please explain from the beginning? What is the 'string game?'"

She looked up at his beautiful, confused face and smiled. "I love mazes, always have, partly because of that story. Solving mazes, building mazes. I told my dad one time that I wanted to build a labyrinth at our house, but how do you make a maze in a little, tiny house, right?"

"... 'comes up when the rain'... An umbrella!"
"Where do we keep the umbrellas?"
"By the door!"
"Go. Find my umbrella and tie your string."

Giovanni was shaking his head. "I still don't—"

"So he made up this game, the string game. He would leave me clues to random places in the house. I would have to tie a string when I found the first clue and that would start the game. Then I'd find the next clue and tie the string there."

She began to see Giovanni's eyes light in understanding. "And you would find the clues and keep tying."

Beatrice nodded. Her heart pounded in her chest. "They could be any location in the house. There was never a pattern. Totally random locations. There would be riddles, or drawings, or... anything, really. The goal of the string game was to find the locations and tie the string—"

"And then follow it." He rushed to look over her shoulder as she found the world map in the center of the book. Her eyes raked over the pages crowded with cities, borders, latitude, and longitude.

"The cities where you found my dad were random. They were meant to be."

"But where does it lead?" He shook his head. "I stopped getting clues from him after he showed up in Santiago two years ago. I thought he had found our house here and that's why he was so close. I stayed here for months in the middle of summer that year thinking that he would show himself before I gave up and went to New York."

"Did you find it, Beatrice? Did you find the treasure?"

She grabbed his arm. "No, no, you're missing the point of the game. Once you mapped out the points and tied off the string, you had to—"

"Follow it back," he said with a smile. "Clever man. You follow the string back like Theseus out of the labyrinth, but..." His face fell.

"At one point in the web—" She held out her two index fingers and crossed them. "—the strings would touch. That's where the prize was."

"Found it, Daddy!"

"And that's where your father is," he murmured.

She shook her head and fought the tears that she felt pricking the corner of her eyes. "It was our game. I'm the only one who would be able to figure it out."

"And you would only solve it if you were cooperating with me."

"Exactly."

They both looked down at the map on the table. She grabbed a pencil from the counter, put the tip on the small island in the middle of the Mediterranean Sea, and looked at Giovanni.

"Do you remember where he went next?"

He nodded. "Budapest. The next sighting was in Budapest."

She began to drag the pencil north.

"Wait." He held up a hand. "You need something—"

"Oh, a straight edge, just give me a magazine or—"

"Got it!" He tossed her a thin book from the end of the table.

"Okay... Budapest, Hungary."

Her pencil stopped on the map, and she looked up.

"Then Warsaw."

She moved the book and her pencil tip traced a light line over the soft, pastel colors of the map, each thread drawing them closer to the mystery of her father's whereabouts.

"Stockholm."

"Novosibirsk."

She could feel his crackling energy fill the room as he listed the cities. "It will be a major city," he mused. "It's much easier to stay hidden in a major city."

Beatrice looked up at him. "Okay, next?"

"Shanghai."

"Madras."

The line dipped and traced over the world, zagging north and south as each city was reached, slowly working east, then south.

"Johannesburg."

"Lima."

"San Francisco, right?"

"Yes, then El Paso."

"Boston."

"Tripoli."

"Santiago," she whispered, and her breath hitched when she saw the faint lines finally cross in front of her. Tears spilled down her face and she felt his hand on her shoulder as he took the shaking pencil from her grasp.

"Very well done, Beatrice! There's my clever girl."
"Found it, Daddy. Can we go for ice cream now?"

He held her as she cried, her tears soaking the front of his shirt. "So close," Giovanni murmured as he stroked her hair. "Brasilia. He's in Brasilia."

Brasilia, Brazil

"Why would he come here?" she asked over the steady hum of the engine.

"In a way, it's very much like Houston," Giovanni said as he steered the old car through the wide streets of the Brazilian capitol. Though it was built in the 1960s as the modern ideal of contemporary city planning, Beatrice thought the capitol and fourth largest city in Brazil seemed empty.

"What do you mean, it's like Houston?"

He turned right at the small road leading to the resort where Isabel and Gustavo's contacts had informed them a quiet vampire going by the name "Emil Gonzales" owned a cottage on the shore of Lake Paranoá.

"If you are trying to remain anonymous, you go to a city like Brasilia. With the popularity and proximity of Rio de Janeiro and Sao Paulo, the immortal population here is very low and tends to mind its own business."

"So not very much politics?"

"Practically none. It's like a ghost town," he said quietly, his eyes scanning the low, red painted cottages with dark roofs. "There," he said, "the one on the end."

She gripped her seat as he parked along the curb, almost unwilling to step out of the car, afraid of what she might find. Giovanni hadn't had any sign of her father for the last two years. He'd dropped off the radar when he finished giving the clues to his location. If they had been together two years before, she thought, she might have seen it sooner.

As if reading her thoughts, she heard him say, "If we've lost him because of my own stubbornness—"

"Can we save that for another time, please?" she murmured as she eyed the small house surrounded by low palms. The cottage was part of a larger resort, though some of the apartments and cottages were privately owned. The gardens surrounding it were well tended, but because it was part of the hotel property, there was no way of knowing who took care of them.

She took a deep breath and reached across the car to squeeze Giovanni's hand. "I'm fine; let's go see if anyone's home."

He pulled her toward him and laid a gentle kiss on her lips before giving her a small smile. His eyes were shuttered, and his shoulders were fixed. She knew he thought they would find nothing.

They walked toward the low cottage tucked into a quiet corner at the edge of the lake. Streams ran through the grounds, under small footbridges, and trickled over rocks through the lush gardens.

"Definitely a water vampire," he muttered, taking her hand as they crossed a small bridge. "And a smart one."

"Why do you say that?"

"He's surrounded himself with his element. The lake, the streams. For him, this is an excellent defensive position."

"Oh."

They drew closer to the small house and she heard him drawing deep, testing breaths.

"Sense anything?"

His nose twitched. "I smell guava. Coffee. No vampires."

She could feel the clench in her chest, but she continued to walk toward the house. They stopped in front of the green door, and Giovanni shot her a sad look as he took a fist and punched, splintering the frame near the lock and pushing it open.

Beatrice stepped into the dim cottage, immediately hit by the musty scent that clung to the room. She reached to flip on the lights but Giovanni's hand stopped her.

"Not a good idea. Better not to draw attention to ourselves, even if it is a quiet location."

"Okay." She pulled out her mobile phone and turned on the small flashlight.

"I'm afraid no vampire has been here for many months, Beatrice."

She sighed. "I was getting that feeling."

They both walked around the small living area, and she noticed the lack of dust on the surfaces, and the quiet hum of the refrigerator and air conditioner.

"Appliances running."

Giovanni sniffed again. "I do smell a human. Older. He smells sick. Cancer maybe."

"A caretaker?"

"Possibly. If he planned on leaving, it's something he might have arranged." He lingered in front of the wall of bookcases that lined one side of the room. "And these books are not molded. In this climate, they would be unless the air conditioner was usually on."

"So why the musty smell?"

"Just the perils of a closed house by the lake, I imagine." He was already lost studying the texts in front of him.

Beatrice roamed through the small house. There was nothing

in the modern kitchen, not even any canned food. A drip coffeemaker sat on the otherwise empty counter, and nothing was in the refrigerator. There were no indications of life anywhere.

She pushed open the door to the bedroom and was surprised to find traces of the man she remembered. A pair of shoes sat at the end of the bed where he would kick them off. A pile of books lay on the bedside table, and there was a note propped on top of it. Heavy curtains were pinned around the large French doors, and one window was covered with carefully cut plywood.

Picking up the note on the bedside table, she noticed it was written in Portuguese; the signature read, 'Maria.' She tucked it in the pocket of her jeans and went to the small desk on the other side of the room.

Under a sheet of glass were several pictures of her and her grandparents, along with blank spaces where some had been removed. There was a finger painting she remembered had been tucked into a childhood scrapbook, along with a poem she had written when she was ten, signed by a juvenile hand.

Beatrice sniffed and rubbed at the tears on her cheeks. She pulled open the single drawer and began to look through it. There were receipts and scraps of paper; most of the notes had been written in Portuguese. Spare change rattled around the bottom of the drawer. Occasionally, she would find something that looked more personal. A single cufflink. A disposable lighter. A rosary twisted into knots.

She heard Giovanni approach and relaxed a little as his arms encircled her waist. She turned and buried her face in his chest, breathing in the comforting smell of wood smoke and whiskey.

"He's not here, tesoro."

"I know," she whispered.

He tilted her face up and she was struck by the anguish in his expression.

"I was wrong to stay away from you for so long." His voice was quiet. "I didn't know. And I hurt you. This is my fault."

"We don't know if we would have found him even if we had been together." She ran her hand up his chest and into the hair at the nape of his neck. "We don't know. He may have left before we could get here years ago. There's no way of knowing."

"I think you need to see a few things on the bookcase."

She sighed and hugged him closer. "Just give me a minute."

They stood holding each other for a few more minutes in the empty bedroom. She heard the trickle of a stream running outside the terrace doors. Eventually, she took Giovanni's hand and walked back out to the living room and the wall of books.

"Here." He pointed toward a corner of the room. "These are textbooks for the study of old Arabic and old Persian. It appears he taught himself how to read both."

"Why?"

"Alchemy. Remember what Tywyll said? The manuscript was about alchemy. Much early medieval alchemic work was done in the Middle East, so if he wanted to learn more, he might have started there."

She paged through the books, looking at her father's familiar scrawl in the margins of each volume. Most of it, she couldn't understand.

"Aristotle," Giovanni murmured, dragging his finger along the spines. "Zosimos, Mary... did your father read classical Greek?"

"A little," she muttered, paging through a dense history of the burned library of Alexandria in Egypt.

"He appeared to be well-versed in Greco-Roman roots of alchemy and was studying the work done in the Middle East. Khalid ibn Yazid. A lot of Geber."

"Who?"

"Ah... he was known during my time as Geber, but he was a Persian, possibly Arab, medieval alchemist. Jabir ibn Hayyan was his Arabic name. It also appears he was looking into Bön, Spagyric—"

"What?" she asked with a frown. "I haven't even heard of those."

"Bön is an ancient Asian belief system. I'm only familiar with it through Tenzin. Spagyric refers to a subset of alchemy, plant alchemy. Again, Tenzin studied it at one point." Giovanni stepped back and shook his head as he surveyed the wall of books. "What were you up to, Stephen?"

She looked through the section in front of her. "I'm also seeing stuff on Newton and Boyle. I know Newton, who's Boyle?"

"Early modern chemistry." He walked slowly, his head cocked to the side as he moved down the wall.

"So chemistry, languages, philosophy, religion... what wasn't he studying?"

He said, "Alchemy is a very twisted subject. It blurs lines between science and superstition. Chemistry and magic." He heaved a sigh, and she could see the air stir in the light of her small flashlight.

"Gio?"

"Sì, tesoro?" he asked, absently bending down to the far corner where something appeared to have caught his eye.

"Why don't we—"

"Beatrice, look at this."

She walked over and knelt down next to him. "What?"

Giovanni pulled out a small book. It was a black and white composition book, like the ones she remembered using in high school. It had no label, only the number "1" written on the front cover in black marker. She pulled it from his hands with trembling fingers, knowing somehow that this book was different from the others.

Beatrice sat on the floor, cross-legged in the corner as Giovanni knelt next to her. She opened it to the first page.

"'August 20, 1996,'" she read in a shaky voice. "'Dear Mariposa, I had to say goodbye to you tonight—'" She choked on the sob that tore from her throat and before she could blink, Giovanni had picked her up and was rocking her in his arms on the floor of the lonely cottage.

Beatrice wept, deep, gut-wrenching sobs that tore at her heart and shook her small frame. Giovanni held her as she emptied her sorrow, fear, and frustration into his chest. He didn't try to calm her, only stroked her back as she let six years of anger and grief pour out into the still night air.

"Why isn't he here?" she finally choked out. "Why?"

"I don't know."

"Is he dead? Is he hiding again?" She shook her head and clutched at his neck. "I want my father! I want all this to be worth it, somehow. Carl and the other bodyguards, and—and the blond girl in Greece. And all the people he killed. And Ioan and Jean's granddaughter and who knows how many other people who had nothing to do with this," she practically yelled. "Why is this happening to me? To us?"

"I don't know."

"Why?" She raised her tear-stricken face to him, but he could do nothing but cup her cheek and wipe at the tears that fell fast and hot. "I'm past sad. I'm pissed-off now! I want this to end so I can get on with my life—with *our* life. Is this ever going to end?"

"Yes," he pressed his cheek to hers. "This is going to end. I told you six years ago that I would find your father and I will, Beatrice. We will find him."

She sniffed, and he reached down to hand her a handkerchief from his pocket.

"Why do you always carry handkerchiefs? You never need them."

He didn't say anything, but she could feel him press the cloth to her cheeks as she lay her head on his shoulder and allowed him to hold her up.

"Beatrice, don't read the notebooks here," he murmured. "There are too many of them. Take them back to Houston. I know your grandmother would want to see them, too."

She clutched the notebook to her chest and nodded. "Okay."

"We should go. I don't think there's anything more."

"Will you remember all the books? Should we make a list?"

"I'll remember."

"Okay," she said before she paused. "Let's go then. There's nothing here."

She sat with her back against a chair as Giovanni pulled out the stacks of composition books. She didn't stop to count them as she dried the last of her tears and piled them by the door along with the few personal items she'd found in the bedroom and small bath.

"Beatrice, look at this."

She glanced over to see Giovanni standing over the same blue atlas that they'd used to play the string game sitting out on the small cafe table near the kitchen.

"Where was that?"

"Behind the notebooks. Tucked against the wall."

She looked at his raised eyebrow and then back to the book.

"There's something in there."

"I believe you're right."

Beatrice walked over to the table and started paging through the atlas in front of her. She grew progressively more frustrated with each map she turned, only to find it devoid of any clue to Stephen's whereabouts. Finally, she felt Giovanni's hand still her own.

"Let me. I have an idea."

"Fine," she muttered, ready to leave the small, empty cottage and go home. He opened to the large map at the center and pointed to Greece.

"He has already studied the roots of alchemy." His finger slid east. "And he told Tywyll the manuscript he took from Lorenzo was Persian."

He looked at her, locking eyes for a moment before she heard his finger move across the page again. This time, it slid farther east, through the heart of the Middle East, past northern India, and over to the far edge of China.

"He had books about Asian alchemic traditions and study, and another that related to Bön. I know of one vampire who is revered for his knowledge of both."

"One vampire? You think my father would have looked for him? Who? Where?"

He frowned and flipped to the page showing a larger map of the Northern Chinese coast and pointed to a small gulf east of Beijing.

She leaned down to look closer and her mouth fell open when she saw a lone pinprick in the center of the Bohai Sea.

"What is that?" she whispered.

He stared at her for a moment before he looked back to the atlas Stephen had left for them to find. "That, tesoro, is Mount Penglai. That is the residence of the Eight Immortals."

"Who?"

He sighed and closed the atlas. "Tenzin is going to kill me."

Twenty-Three

Houston, Texas

"Caspar, do you take Isadora to be your lawfully wedded wife? Do you promise to love, honor, cherish and protect her, forsaking all others as long as you both shall live?"

"I do."

Giovanni felt his heart give a quiet thump as Caspar and Isadora exchanged the vows they had chosen for their ceremony. As it turned out, it was Stephen's presence the two had been waiting for, but when Beatrice and he had returned from Brasilia and given them the news that Stephen remained out of reach, Isadora had nodded in understanding and called her friend Marta's husband to perform the simple ceremony.

Judge Voorhies stood in the beautifully lit gardens of the house in River Oaks, standing under the gazebo with the bride and groom as a few of their closest friends watched the early evening ceremony.

Caspar wore his best charcoal grey suit, and Isadora looked stunning in a deep green dress that set off her beautiful eyes and silver-white hair. He glanced to his side to see Beatrice watching them both with a smile. She squeezed his hand, and he smiled before drawing her closer and kissing her temple. His eyes returned to the bride and groom in the garden. To say he was pleased for his old friend would be an understatement.

After a few more heartfelt words, Isadora and Caspar turned to the group with a smile.

"Caspar and Isadora chose a short reading from the Song of Songs, chapter four. 'You have stolen my heart, my darling, my bride; you have stolen my heart with one glance of your eyes, with one jewel of your necklace... "

Giovanni leaned down, whispering the same sweet words into Beatrice's ear in soft Italian.

"I still don't speak Italian," she whispered.

He only smiled. "You will."

"'How delightful is your love, my darling, my bride, how much more pleasing is your love than wine,'" the judge continued. "And I think we all know, as much as Caspar loves wine, what a truly bold statement that is."

Giovanni smiled as their friends laughed around them and Isadora and Caspar met each other with a sweet kiss. The judge pronounced them husband and wife. Giovanni and Beatrice smiled, Ben gave a little whoop, and the group clapped before going inside to share a meal.

Ben raced in circles, almost knocking Beatrice over in his enthusiasm. The boy had been ecstatic to see them both when they returned from South America, though he'd tried to play it off nonchalantly. He was bouncing with excitement and chattering nonstop about getting back home. Giovanni realized it was going to be a rather complicated discussion.

He was almost sure that Stephen had gone to China. The more he and Beatrice studied the journals the vampire had left behind, the more he became convinced that Stephen had sought the help of one far more ancient. The knowledge was both a comfort and a concern.

He was also growing more certain that Lorenzo had somehow discovered Stephen's plan. All indications from Jean Desmarais and his contacts seemed to indicate that the vampire was heading to the Far East. He was brought back to the present by Beatrice's arm around his waist.

"Hold on to those deep thoughts, love. Not for tonight, okay?"

He looked down at the woman beside him. Beatrice had pulled herself up from the disappointment that ambushed her in Brazil and dove into research, trying to recreate her father's library in the hopes that the books Stephen had chosen to study would give her insight into the manuscript Lorenzo was so keen to recover.

"What?" she asked with a frown.

"I love you very much, Beatrice. I'm very fortunate to have you."

She blushed and bumped his arm with her shoulder.

"Yeah, you are. I love you, too." She paused for a moment, then pulled him down for a quick kiss. "You're getting sentimental in your old age, Gio."

He smiled and bent down to kiss the top of her head.

"Must be the weddings."

"So—" She grinned as they walked toward the house. "—how are you feeling? Your oldest is finally married off. Soon Ben will be dating... "

He clutched his chest dramatically. "I shudder to think."

"You're going to be an empty-nester soon."

He said, "They grow up so fast."

"They do," she said with solemn nod.

He could feel her laughing at him for a moment before they both started chuckling.

"Is Carwyn going to be pissed off they didn't wait for him?"

He shrugged. "I don't think so. He's fairly busy at the moment."

"Back in Ireland?"

He nodded. "Deirdre is... coping. But he needs to be there right now."

They walked in silence, strolling hand in hand through the gardens lit with tiny lights. Giovanni could see the gathering of friends through the French doors, spilling out across the patio. The scent of honeysuckle and roses hung in the air.

His eyes found Ben as the boy gave Isadora a hug and a sweet smile. Caspar leaned over them both to place a kiss on his new wife's cheek. More than ever, Giovanni felt the weight of responsibility to keep them all safe. He wouldn't be able to remain in Houston for long. He felt Beatrice squeeze his waist, and his heart thumped again. At least, he would no longer travel alone.

"'You have stolen my heart, my darling, my bride,'" he whispered again as he pulled her closer.

Beatrice was also watching the group inside. Ben darted through the adults, who were all laughing and enjoying the plentiful wine that Caspar poured for the well-wishers.

"How are we going to keep them all safe?" she asked in a small voice.

"We'll figure something out."

She looked up at him, steely determination in her eyes. "We have to."

He found her reading later that night, half asleep in the library as she studied one of Stephen's journals in front of the cold fireplace. Their company had left hours before, but the house still hummed with quiet activity. Caspar and Isadora were in the kitchen, finishing the wine and enjoying their time together after a busy day. Ben had finally collapsed on the couch in the den, and Giovanni had carried him to his room before making a call to Carwyn on the phone in the study.

"Beatrice," he whispered, picking her up and setting her on his lap. "Why don't you go to bed?"

She looked at the clock over the mantle. "But it's only one a.m."

He smiled, amused by her convenient habit of keeping vampire hours. "It's been a long day. You should get some rest."

"Is Ben in bed?"

"Mmhmm." He ran his lips along her temple.

She paused, and he could feel her head nodding against his chest. "Maybe I will."

"Or just stay here. I could probably find a way to distract you."

He felt her shoulders shake with quiet laughter. "I'm sure you could. How is Carwyn?"

"Doing well. He says hello, and he won't hold it against Isadora and Caspar for too long that they got married without him."

"I'm sure they're relieved."

"He also said that we had better not pull something like that."

She raised an eyebrow. Giovanni just shrugged, and she snuggled back into his chest.

"Have we heard from Tenzin yet?"

"Not yet."

"How about... what's his name?"

"That could take some time. Zhang Guo and his court operate on their own timetable."

"He's older than Tenzin?"

He chuckled. "Oh yes."

"Wow."

"I don't want to go to China until we know more. It's not in our best interests to arrive without some sort of introduction."

"But we will go."

"Yes, I think we must."

"What are we going to do about Ben?"

He sighed and shifted on the couch. "I don't know. I don't like leaving him, but the safest place for him to be is away from us. Lorenzo has already discovered him; I don't like the idea of leaving Caspar and Isadora here alone with him when we know he's a target. Then there's Dez and Kirby in L.A. I think we should speak to your Grandfather Alvarez and—"

She pulled him down and stopped the rambling list with a kiss. Slowly shifting on his lap, she continued kissing him until he forgot about the worries swirling in his mind and all he could think of was her soft skin, sweet mouth, and the feel of her hips under his hands. She ran her fingers through his hair and along the back of his neck, searching for his heated skin as her hands slipped under his collar.

"Tomorrow," she said. "We'll worry about it tomorrow."

"Beatrice," he groaned. "Careful, tesoro. I'm getting... hot. The fire—"

He broke off with a groan and his eyes rolled back as Beatrice's teeth found his ear and bit the lobe between her teeth.

"Gio," she whispered. "I need... "

"What do you need?"

He pulled her closer as she murmured in his ear and rocked against him.

"You guys are so gross."

They both froze when they heard Ben at the door.

"Benjamin, why aren't you in bed?"

"Are you guys going to be doing that stuff all the time now? 'Cause I really don't need to see that."

"Benjamin," they said in unison. Beatrice moved to crawl off Giovanni's lap, but he held her in place, shifting and clearing his throat with a meaningful glance.

"I couldn't sleep," Ben whined before stretching into one of the armchairs. "I think I drank too much Coke at the party."

"Remind me to forbid that beverage when we get home," he muttered.

Beatrice curled up against his chest again, and he tried to distract himself as he played with the ends of her hair.

"Are we going home soon? I miss L.A."

"You miss your basketball hoop," Giovanni said.

"And the neighborhood girls," Beatrice added.

"Well," Ben thought for a moment. "Yeah. I miss those. But I missed you guys, too."

Giovanni smiled at the sleepy boy stretched out in the chair next to them. Ben had a happy, contented look on his face, and he immediately began nodding off again.

"I think he missed his Uncle Gio," Beatrice whispered.

He smiled and kissed her forehead. "I missed him, too."

They sat for a few more minutes, enjoying the quiet.

"Benjamin?" he asked. "Are you asleep?"

"No, what's up?" The boy sat up in his chair.

"We should talk."

Ben's face fell a little before being replaced by a determined expression. "Because you're going to leave again?"

Giovanni frowned and felt Beatrice squeeze his arm.

"It's okay," Ben said. "I get it. I know Lorenzo's still out there. And you haven't found B's dad yet."

Beatrice said, "We don't want to leave you again."

"But you have to."

The boy met his eyes and Giovanni was both relieved and saddened by the understanding he saw there. If he could, Giovanni would wipe away the sad memories that colored the young man's childhood, but he knew it wouldn't be fair. Just as his own childhood had shaped him, so would Ben's. He only hoped he and Beatrice could make life a little easier in the end.

"So," Ben sighed and seemed to rally himself. "What are we gonna do? Am I gonna stay with Caspar and Isadora here? If we do that, can I get a basketball hoop before you go?"

He smiled at the boy and nodded. "Yes, Benjamin. I will make sure you have a basketball hoop."

"Who's getting a basketball hoop?" Caspar asked as he entered the library.

"Ben is. That way, when he stays here while we are traveling, he will not be deprived of his greatest love. The girls, however, he'll have to see to himself," he said as Ben did a small victory wiggle in the chair.

"Ben's staying here?" Isadora came in behind Caspar. "But when will you leave for Asia, Beatrice?"

"We don't know, Grandma. We'll stay as long as we can, but we want to make sure you and Caspar and Ben are safe in case we need to leave quickly."

"We're still waiting for word from Tenzin. She should be able to smooth channels for us," Giovanni said quietly. "As for security—"

"Caspar," Isadora said. She gave him a look before linking her hand with her new husband's. Caspar smiled down at her and nodded before he turned to Giovanni and Beatrice.

"Isadora and I have been talking about this. As much as we love this house, we feel like we need to move to Los Angeles with the rest of the family."

Giovanni blinked when Caspar said, "family." He looked from Ben's sleepy face to Isadora's warm smile. His eyes paused on Caspar for a long moment before he looked back to Beatrice, who was watching him with loving eyes. His arm tightened around her, and he felt his heart thump twice. Giovanni suddenly realized it was exactly what they were. For the first time in over five hundred years, he had a family.

A fierce wave of protectiveness swept over him, and Beatrice ran her hand over his jaw, soothing him as the heat rose to the surface.

"Yes," he said hoarsely, "the family should stay together."

"And if everyone's in L.A., Matt can keep an eye on things if we have to leave," Beatrice said quietly.

"Don't forget Ernesto," Giovanni added. "I'm sure he would be as pleased to meet your grandmother as he was to meet you, tesoro."

"Are you kidding?" she snorted. "Grandma's way more charming than me. Ernesto will love her."

Caspar only nodded. "So, that's settled then. Who wants a drink?"

Isadora smiled and began a rapid-fire conversation with Beatrice in Spanish about the Alvarez clan while Caspar moved to the sideboard to pour drinks.

"So everyone's moving to L.A. after all?" Ben piped up. "Sweet!"

A strange peace settled over him as he began to plan, strategizing to ensure the well-being of the four people who had become, quite unexpectedly, more important than anything else in the world.

He and Beatrice would go to China in search of her father and the manuscript, but Lorenzo was still a threat. Luckily, with the help of his contacts in Los Angeles, he would be able to ensure the best protection for Caspar, Isadora and Benjamin.

Beatrice would go with him, adding her keen intellect to his own as they worked toward solving the puzzle of Stephen De Novo, the missing manuscript, and what his son was trying to accomplish by taking them both.

Giovanni heard the phone in the back of the library start to ring. He frowned at Caspar, who went to answer it.

"Hello? Tenzin, my dear!" Caspar paused as Beatrice's eyes swung toward his. They both rose from the couch and walked to the phone.

"They're right here... yes, here you are."

Giovanni picked up the phone, holding it away from his ear so Tenzin's voice did not deafen him.

"Gio!" He heard her clearly. "Is B there?"

"Yes, did you get our e-mail?"

"E-mail? I never check that stuff."

Giovanni frowned at Beatrice, who only shrugged.

"Gio?"

"Still here, bird girl." Everyone was looking toward the back of the room as he spoke.

"Can you tell me why I'm getting a summons from my sire to meet him at Mount Penglai?"

Giovanni's heart sank. It was happening much faster than he'd anticipated. He looked at Caspar and Isadora, then at Ben's wide eyes from across the room. Finally, he looked to Beatrice, who reached out to grasp his hand.

He took a deep breath. "We'll meet you there."

EPILOGUE

FROM THE JOURNALS OF STEPHEN DE NOVO

Houston, Texas
August 20, 1996

Dear Mariposa,

I had to say goodbye to you tonight. It was the hardest thing I've ever had to do. Harder than controlling the bloodlust that still ambushes me from time to time. Harder than escaping the madman who killed me. Harder than ignoring my mother's pleas to stay.

I doubt you'll ever read this, but I feel stupid writing "Dear Diary" when I'm an immortal bloodsucking predator, so I'll address it to you. On the off chance you do read this, then you know what I've become.

I thought I could be part of your life, at least for a little while, but the first time you saw me, I was reminded of what a monster I am now. I tried to erase the memory from you and try again, but it was no use. Hopefully, you remember me the way I was.

I want you to remember the good things.

I am going away now. Whatever happens to me, I just hope I haven't made you a target. That's the other reason I'm leaving. I couldn't stand if you got pulled into this. I want you to have a good life. I want you to grow up strong and smart. I know Grandma and Grandpa will do their best. They're amazing. I want you to find someone to love, who loves you back. I want you to live a full life and have a big family, with lots of people who love you and challenge you and bring you as much joy as you brought me just by being your dad.

I may live a thousand years. Hopefully, I'll do something good with that time. Whatever purpose God has in all this, I hope I find it. But no matter what else I do in the endless time that's been given to me, you will always be my greatest accomplishment.

I love you so much,

Dad

Dublin, Ireland
March 1998

Dear Beatrice,

I finally met a vampire tonight who wasn't out to get me. Funny, right? I'm sure I've met others, but this was the first one I found that gave me hope I might not have to be a lowly, manipulative bastard who only uses humans for the rest of my existence.

I was doing some research at Trinity last night, and on the way back to my hotel, I sensed another vampire around me. I tensed up. You never know who you can trust.

But when I finally saw him from a distance, he just smiled. He was a doctor, and he was running a free medical clinic in the lobby of an old office building. It was just him with a bunch of poor humans, so I felt like I could relax. I don't know why, but he saw me through the glass and motioned me over to ask if I could help.

See, when I touch people now, I can get a sense of their general health. That, and their smell makes me able to tell if they're sick. I guess he just wanted some company... and some help. The line of people was out the door and it was almost eleven o'clock.

He didn't ask much about me. Just if I was American and if I was visiting anyone in town. I think he could tell from talking to me that I was trying to lay low, so he didn't pry. He asked if I needed any help. He was so nice, I was tempted to spill the whole crazy story, but something held me back. I didn't want to get him involved. Knowing that there was someone good out there, that maybe I could eventually do something useful with this life was enough. It made me grateful to have met him.

After the clinic, he asked if he could pay me for my time. It was nice to say no and just feel good about myself for the first time in years. All the humans that I've fed from since I was turned, I finally felt like I gave something back without taking.

He gave me his card and told me to call him if I ever needed any help. I hope I won't have to use it, but I took it, just in case.

Love, Dad

Gravesend, England
January 20, 2000

Dear Beatrice,

I found a friend today.

Sounds silly, right? Like I'm the new kid at school. But in the last seven years, I've discovered how rare it is to find a friend you can trust. Do you have those kind of people around you? Do you have good friends? I hope so. You're nineteen now. Maybe you have a boyfriend. You better be going to college. I wonder what you'll study. Probably not Dante.

Do you still love Greek myths? Maybe you'll study literature. Or archeology. I'm sure you'd be good at anything, you were always so smart. I bet you're beautiful, too. The last time I saw you, you had that gawky, uncomfortable look that kids have when they're teenagers, but you were only fifteen. I bet you're beautiful now. You always looked like Mom, and she's so lovely.

This new friend of mine is teaching me how to hide better. He's old. Older than you can even imagine. I'm not sure they even measured time when he was human. He's also incredibly powerful. He can control water like me, but much better. He's a good friend, and I feel like I might finally have time to study this book and not spend all my time running around trying to hide.

Love, Dad

Brasilia, Brazil
October 2001

Dear Beatrice,

I'm writing to you from my home. After eight years of

running, I finally feel like I've found a new home. It's quiet here. No one pays attention to me. With all the tourists around, I can feed without bothering anyone, and no one even remembers me.

I feel strange talking to you about feeding, even though I know you'll probably never read this. I tried feeding from animals, but after a while, it got to be too much work. I have to feed a lot more often and drink a lot more blood than if I just take a quick sip from a human.

Forgive any unfortunate juice box comparisons.

I don't look down on people like most vampires do, but it's the easiest way for me to survive. If it makes you feel better, I always pay them. They don't remember where the money came from, but hopefully they just think they forgot about it in their pocket.

It's not all bad. I'm learning so much faster now. I wish I knew a neurobiologist who could study it. It's like my brain can absorb information and my memory—which was always good— is amazing now. I've become fluent in Portuguese, French, Ancient Greek, Old Arabic, Old Persian, Mandarin, and my Latin and Italian are much better, too. My recall and processing are faster; it's easier to make connections. I'm simply smarter than I was as a human. Honestly, I can see why some vampires, after hundreds of years, do feel superior to them.

I'm much stronger. I've been told that if I was in better physical condition when I was turned it would be even better, but my sire was old, so that helped. But he also made a lot of 'children,' which depletes their strength. So unless I find a much stronger vampire who is willing to exchange blood with me, which is unlikely, I'll always be weaker than him.

I think I'm starting to understand this book. I still can't figure out why he wants it, though.

Love, Dad

Brasilia, Brazil
August 2004

Dear Beatrice,

I received a letter from a contact in Rome today.

How can you ever forgive me?

This is my fault.

Please forgive me.

If I didn't need to keep this book safe, I would walk into the sun on his sick little island right now, just to make him leave you alone.

Maybe he's dead. I hope like hell he's dead.

This vampire that petitioned for you in Rome... he's frightening, Beatrice. I don't know why he wants you, but he's Lorenzo's sire, and the stories I've heard make my blood curdle.

A fire vampire?

What does he want from you?

They all want something.

Forgive me!

I can only hope what I've heard is wrong. My contact said di Spada was 'uncharacteristically impassioned' in his claim, that he offered a lot in exchange for you. At least this makes me hopeful his intentions toward you are good. It is hard to imagine, from what I have heard, but I can hope.

Forgive me.

Dad

Athens, Greece
December, 2004

You're in L.A.

You're in grad school.

You're safe.

From what I hear, you're really safe.

I'm not sure what Giovanni Vecchio is to you, but whatever he is, he's protecting you more than any human I've ever heard of.

Maybe he can be trusted. He's powerful enough.

I don't know if I can trust him.

But I think I can trust you.

Iraklion, Crete
February 2005

Dear Beatrice,

Please understand. Please get the message.

Please remember the game.

I want you to find me.

Please remember.

I can't do this alone.

Dad

Shanghai, China
June 2006

Dear Beatrice,

I haven't written in a while. I think I may understand why Lorenzo wants this. But it doesn't make sense. Not really. There's something I'm not seeing. For the first time since I was turned thirteen years ago, I don't feel smart enough to handle this.

I need more information, but I don't know who to trust. Everyone has an agenda.

Remember that.

Everyone has an agenda.

Love, Dad

El Paso, Texas
September 2007

Why does anyone live in El Paso? It's so hot. I don't even sweat anymore, and it still feels hot.

I'm so tempted to go see your grandma. She's so close.

Is she okay? I heard about Grandpa a couple of years ago. I hope she's not lonely. She and Dad... They had that kind of love you always read about, you know?

Is that what you've found with this immortal?

Is it even possible?

You're twenty-five now. I've missed so much of your life. Even the hints I get now, the reports and the notes, they're not enough. I just need to be sure he can be trusted.

I have to be sure.

Dad

Brasilia, Brazil
March 2008

Dear Beatrice,

Okay, game played. Did you follow the clues? Can you find me?

Please find me.

I'll wait for you.

I've found some new avenues for research. I finally understand the basics of this manuscript, but the alchemy is still beyond me. There's just not enough research done on vampire biology. I may contact that doctor in Dublin if I can. Maybe he would be able to make better sense of this.

I just know that there's a piece I'm missing. Something doesn't quite fit. It seems like it should work, but if it does, then why does he want it? The more I learn, the less sense it makes.

Back to my books.

Love, Dad

Brasilia, Brazil
August 2008

Dear Beatrice,

This is the last time I'll write in these journals. I was stupid to depend on a game we played when you were a child. It wasn't fair of me.

I'm leaving Brazil, but in case you ever find this place, I'll leave my journals here. Where I am going, it's best not to bring them anyway.

There is an elder I need to see. I don't trust him personally, but I think I can trust him with the manuscript. I think, from what I've learned, he may be my best chance to keep the book safe from Lorenzo, and to help me make sense of all this.

I'm leaving tomorrow. August 8, 2008.

I'm going West to the East. You know me; I like to be in my element.

Find me, Mariposa.

Love, Dad

END OF VOLUME TWO

ABOUT THE AUTHOR

ELIZABETH HUNTER is a ten-time USA Today bestselling author of romance, contemporary fantasy, and paranormal mystery. Based in Central California and Addis Ababa, she travels extensively to write fantasy fiction exploring world mythologies, history, and the universal bonds of love, friendship, and family.

She has published over forty works of fiction and sold over two million books world-wide. She is the author of the Elemental Mysteries, the Irin Chronicles, the Cambio Springs Mysteries, and other works of fiction.

Also by Elizabeth Hunter

The Elemental Mysteries

A Hidden Fire

This Same Earth

The Force of Wind

A Fall of Water

The Stars Afire

The Elemental World

Building From Ashes

Waterlocked

Blood and Sand

The Bronze Blade

The Scarlet Deep

A Very Proper Monster

A Stone-Kissed Sea

Valley of the Shadow

The Elemental Legacy

Shadows and Gold

Imitation and Alchemy

Omens and Artifacts

Obsidian's Edge (anthology)

Midnight Labyrinth

Blood Apprentice

Vista de Lirio

Double Vision

Mirror Obscure

Trouble Play

The Cambio Springs Series

Long Ride Home

Shifting Dreams

Five Mornings

Desert Bound

Waking Hearts

Linx & Bogie Mysteries

A Ghost in the Glamour

A Bogie in the Boat

Contemporary Romance

The Genius and the Muse

7th and Main

Ink

Hooked

Grit

Sweet